Jack Sheffield was born in 1945 and grew up in the tough environment of Gipton Estate in north-east Leeds. His first job was 'pitch boy', carrying buckets of boiling bitumen up a ladder to repair roofs. In the sixties he trained to be a teacher at St John's College, York, and spent his summer holidays as a Corona Pop Man in West Yorkshire.

In the early seventies, he was a teacher in Keighley in West Yorkshire during which time he earned a reputation as a hard-tackling wing-forward for Wharfedale RUFC.

In the late seventies and eighties, he was a head-teacher of two schools in North Yorkshire before gaining his Masters Degree at York University and becoming Senior Lecturer in Primary Education at Bretton Hall near Wakefield. It was at this time he began to record his many amusing stories of village life.

Jack lives in Yorkshire and *Teacher, Teacher!* is his first novel. The second book about Ragley School, *Mister Teacher*, will be published early next year.

www.**booksattransworld**.co.uk

TEACHER, TEACHER!

The Alternative School Logbook, 1977–1978

Jack Sheffield

CORGI BOOKS

TEACHER, TEACHER!
A CORGI BOOK : 9780552155281

Originally published in Great Britain by Central Publishing Services

PRINTING HISTORY
Central Publishing Services edition published 2004
Corgi edition published 2007

1 3 5 7 9 10 8 6 4 2

Set in 11/14pt Palatino by
Kestrel Data, Exeter, Devon.

Corgi Books are published by Transworld Publishers,
61–63 Uxbridge Road, London W5 5SA,
a division of The Random House Group Ltd,

Printed and bound in Great Britain by Clays Ltd, St Ives PLC

In memory of my mother, Margaret, who
bought me a book and taught me to read
and to whom I have kept my promise.

Contents

Acknowledgements

This novel marks the end of a long journey and many people helped along the way.

I should like to thank Caroline Stockdale, Librarian at the York Central Library, for assisting my research; also, David Boot, Sue and Helen Maddison for their sharp analysis and for verifying my factual accuracy!

In particular, I am grateful to my agent, Philip Patterson of Marjacq Scripts, for his determination, good humour and his appreciation of all things Yorkshire, but mainly for believing in my work. Sincere thanks go to my editor Linda Evans and all at Transworld for their support and hard work.

Finally, I am indebted to my friends and family who encouraged me to make my dream a reality.

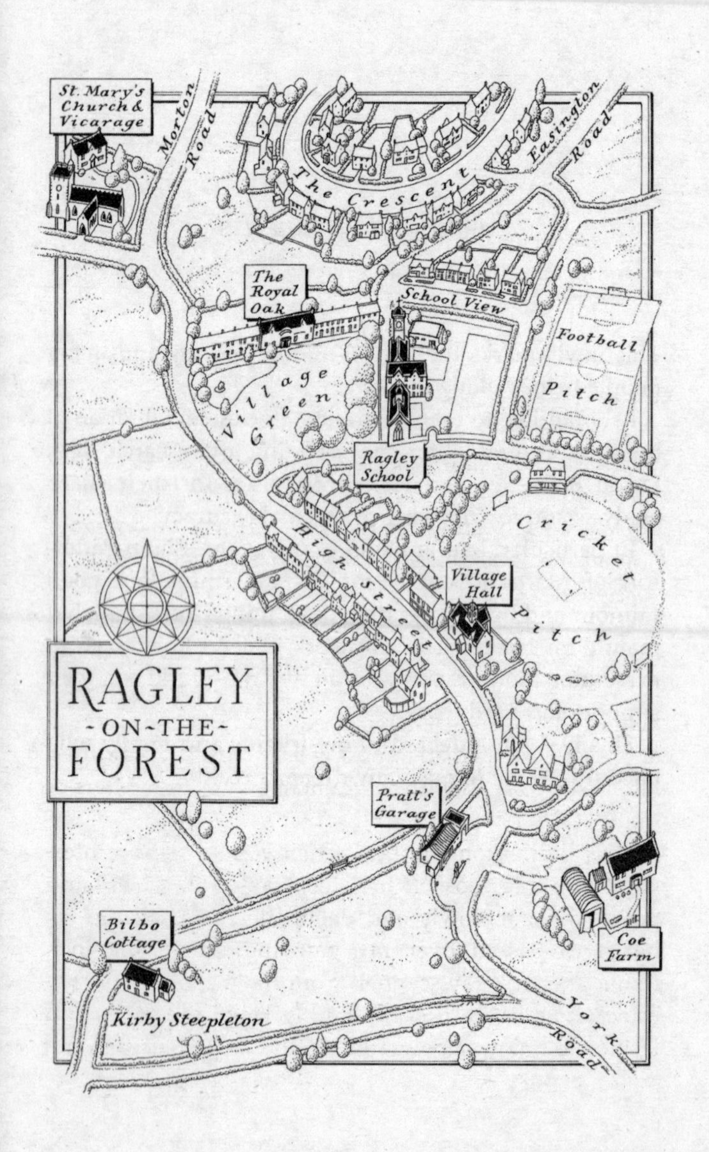
St. Mary's Church & Vicarage
Morton Road
The Crescent
Easington Road
The Royal Oak
School View
Football Pitch
Village Green
Ragley School
Cricket Pitch
High Street
Village Hall
RAGLEY -ON-THE- FOREST
Pratt's Garage
Coe Farm
Bilbo Cottage
Kirby Steepleton
York Road

Prologue

Headmaster required for Ragley-on-the-Forest C. of E. Primary School, near York, from September, 1977, following the retirement of Mr J. Pruett. Application forms from County Hall, Northallerton. Closing date 21 February 1977.

Extract from The Times Educational Supplement

Behind a huge oval table the four horsemen of the apocalypse flanked an imposing lady with purple-rinsed hair and a glare that turned human beings into pillars of salt.

Miss Barrington-Huntley, Chairwoman of the interviewing panel, took off her steel-framed spectacles and polished them slowly and deliberately. As she did so, her eyes passed over my gangling six-feet-one-inch frame like an X-ray scanner, from the top of my unruly brown hair, down past my Buddy Holly spectacles and fashionable flower power tie, to the neat creases in my flared polyester trousers and the toecaps of my polished shoes.

My heart was beating fast. This was the moment I had been waiting for.

'Mr Sheffield,' she said, 'after careful consideration we have decided to offer you the very challenging post of headmaster of Ragley School. First, I must ask you formally, do you accept?'

A nearby church clock suddenly began to chime the hour and a pencil-thin, somewhat distracted man in a clerical collar leaned forward and clasped his long, tapering fingers as if he was about to pray.

'For whom the bell tolls,' said the Revd Joseph Evans, the Chairman of Governors, smiling for the first time and enjoying his little joke. Alongside him, Stan Coe, the Vice-Chairman, glowered at me as if I was to blame for the tight collar that throttled his bull-like neck.

'It tolls for thee,' chuckled Richard Gomersall, the Senior Primary Adviser.

Bernard Pickard, the Assistant Chief Education Officer, never flickered from his note-making and Stan Coe looked bemused, as though everyone had started speaking in Japanese.

'Gentlemen, if you please,' said Miss Barrington-Huntley, restoring the sense of decorum.

I knew my life was about to change with my next two words.

I took a deep breath and said simply, 'I accept.'

So it was that on a bright sunny morning in the summer of 1977, at the age of thirty-one, I left my tiny, bachelor flat in the village of Bradley, near Skipton, filled up my emerald-green Morris Minor Traveller with petrol and drove on the A59 over Blubberhouses and through Harrogate towards the beautiful, historic city of York. The A19 led me out to the north of the city and soon I began to meander through a cluster of pretty villages that nestled on the vast flatland near the foot of the Hambleton hills.

The retiring headmaster, John Pruett, had invited me to meet him during the summer holidays so that he could show me around and pass on the school keys. It was with a feeling of excitement and expectation that I drove slowly into Ragley village and along the High Street, past the General Stores, Piercy's Butcher's Shop, the Village Pharmacy, Pratt's Hardware Emporium, Nora's Coffee Shop, Diane's Hair Salon and a tiny Post Office with a red telephone box outside. Ahead of me was the village green and I stopped the car and surveyed the scene. A large white-fronted public house, The Royal Oak, nestled in the centre of a row of terraced cottages at the far side of the grassy triangle and off to my right, behind an avenue of horse chestnut trees, was Ragley School. In that instant I knew I could be happy here.

The school was an elegant, traditional Victorian building of weathered reddish-brown bricks. It looked tall and solid, with steeply sloping roofs of dark grey tiles and an incongruous bell tower. A waist-high wall of Yorkshire stone, with iron railings mounted on the top, bordered the playground and cobbled driveway and the sun reflected brightly from the high arched window in the gable end.

I walked under the tall Victorian archway on which the date 1878 was chiselled deep into the buff-coloured lintel and into the dark, cramped entrance hall. The only thing that caught my eye in an otherwise featureless corridor was the small brass plate on the dark wood office door. It simply read 'John T. Pruett, headmaster'.

I tapped on the door and a bespectacled man with a gentle, careworn face opened it.

'Good morning,' I said, 'I'm Jack Sheffield.'

He smiled and beckoned me in.

'Hello, Mr Sheffield, welcome to Ragley,' he said. 'I'm John Pruett.'

I followed him into a small L-shaped office with two desks, lots of bookshelves and walls that were lined with black-and-white photographs.

When he sat down in his creaking leather chair behind the cluttered desk it was as if the last piece of a three-dimensional jigsaw had been neatly slotted into place. Mr Pruett fitted perfectly into what looked like his own personal antique shop. I moved a dusty box of Cuisinaire counting rods, a Schonell Reading Test card covered in sticky-backed plastic and a pile of dog-eared exercise books from the visitor's chair and sat down.

He looked up at me and absent-mindedly flattened a few wisps of thin grey hair across his creased forehead.

'Well, I wish you luck,' he said. 'It's a lovely school and I've been very happy here.'

He pushed back his chair and walked over to the white porcelain sink, where he proceeded to fill a battered kettle.

'Coffee?' he asked.

'White, no sugar, thanks,' I replied. It was time to find out more.

'Er, Mr Pruett, how long have you been here?'

He selected two new Silver Jubilee mugs from the set of six on the shelf above the sink and gazed wistfully at the collection of photographs that filled the room.

'Thirty years,' he said quietly. 'I came to Yorkshire after the war and took a short training course at the College in York.'

He opened the fridge under the Formica worktop, selected a small, one-third-of-a-pint school milk bottle, shook it to mix in the head of cream and peeled off the foil top.

'There weren't as many children then,' he continued, 'but the village has grown in recent years. New families have bought many of the old farmhouses for renovation and the council estate is bigger. The old villagers call the new folk "outsiders".'

He glanced back at me, his lined face alight with a twinkling mischievous smile.

'It takes a long time to be accepted here.'

He paused for a moment to let this sink in before he passed me the steaming mug of coffee.

'You'll be needing these,' he said, and pointed to a pile of thick, leather-bound school logbooks. 'The whole history of the school is here,' he said, 'almost a hundred years. Now it's your turn. As headmaster, you have to keep an accurate account of everything that happens. Well, just the official stuff, of course. Keep it simple. Whatever you do, don't say what really happens because no one will believe you.'

* * *

On 1 September 1977, I opened the school logbook and began to write. It didn't tell the whole story. That was kept in my 'alternative school logbook'. And this is it!

Chapter One

The F-word

80 children on roll. Fluorescent lights repaired in hall.

Miss Barrington-Huntley, Chief Education Officer, has informed the HT that she will be visiting school this term to check on progress.

Extract from the Ragley School Logbook:
Friday 10 September 1977

'I've got a complaint, Mr Sheffield.'

'Yes?'

'This school is teaching my children to swear!'

Mrs Winifred Brown's huge bulk filled the doorway of the tiny school office. I sighed and retreated. It was Friday lunchtime and hopes of a school dinner suddenly receded.

'Please come and sit down, Mrs Brown.'

I was nearing the end of my first week as headmaster of Ragley Primary School in North Yorkshire and my education in dealing with angry parents was just beginning.

Mrs Brown manoeuvred heavily into the reception chair and blew her nose like a snorting rhino. A 'Good Luck in your New Job' card fluttered prophetically from the top of the grey metal filing cabinet.

'Now, what exactly is the problem, Mrs Brown?'

'Well, it's like this, Mr Sheffield. My Dominic comes 'ome last night an' large as life it just comes out.'

'What comes . . . er, came out, Mrs Brown?'

'Y'know, the f-word.'

'The f-word!'

'Yes, 'e just comes out with it. 'e leaned over to 'is grandma an' nice as ninepence 'e just shouts in 'er ear, PASS THE EFFIN' SAUCE PLEASE, GRANDMA. 'e 'as to shout 'cause she's deaf as a post.'

I bit my bottom lip in a determined attempt to regain my composure.

'Oh dear, and what happened then?'

'Well, 'is dad clips 'im with a swift back'ander an' 'e asks him what was it 'e just said. So our Dominic says that 'e only asked 'is grandma for the effin' sauce so 'e gets another what-for round the ear. But this is the best of it. It turns out 'e 'eard some boys practisin' it in your toilets. Practisin' it, I ask you. Me an' Eddie think it's disgustin', an' we want you to do somethin' about it, 'cause we don't want no effin' in our 'ouse.'

Mrs Brown was becoming very red in the face so I decided to use the diplomatic approach.

'I'll do my best, Mrs Brown, and I'll certainly have a word with the children concerned.'

'I 'ope you do, Mr Sheffield. I just 'opes you do.'

With that, she raised her large bulk, somehow freeing herself of the tight-fitting chair. As she turned to go she glared back at me. 'An' I'll be back for our Dominic at one o'clock. 'e's goin' to a proper dentist, not your school one!'

She stormed out, leaving the door swinging on its hinges and a patterned heel-print on my 'Good Luck' card.

I followed in her wake to the front door of the school. I needed fresh air and I stood in the steady drizzle on the old stone steps. The scampering feet of generations of children had worn them down since the school was built almost one hundred years before. Rain was falling on the small playground and the school field beyond. Dark clouds scudded across the vast plain of York towards the Hambleton hills in the far distance. Beyond the high wrought-iron railings, a large flag of St George fluttered proudly on the tall flagpole in the middle of the village green as a reminder of the summer's Silver Jubilee celebrations.

For this was 1977. Virginia Wade had won Wimbledon and Red Rum had been cheered to a third Grand National victory. In York, people queued outside the cinema to watch *Star Wars*, whilst children enjoyed the new craze and played on skateboards. Best of all, Geoffrey Boycott had scored his one hundredth hundred in the Test match against Australia on the hallowed turf of Headingley. Yorkshire folk were content and all was well in their world.

The huge bell in the bell tower suddenly boomed out,

reminding the whole village it was twelve o'clock and time for school dinner. I brushed the raindrops from my shoulders, took a deep breath and walked briskly back into school. My first headship was proving much tougher than I had expected.

When I arrived in the school hall, grace had been recited and eighty tubular steel chairs were being scraped in unison on the worn wooden floor. We settled round our Formica-topped, octagonal tables, knees locked together in tense expectancy. With boring predictability the shin-crunching kicking of small feet rapped against my legs as the three six-year-olds sitting opposite sought ways to release their pent-up energy. It has never ceased to amaze me how infant children can remain absolutely immobile and demure from the waist up whilst beneath table-top level their lower limbs are a seething frenzy of destructive activity.

I struggled to find some modicum of comfort for my lanky frame on the hard, plastic-topped chair, designed for the average nine-year-old pygmy. With my knees almost on a level with my chin I prepared to serve the food from the scalding metal tureens placed in front of me by Mrs Critchley, the orange-coated dinner lady.

I was a past expert at dividing any shape of container into eight equal portions of food and now only crusty lemon meringue pie and limpet-like toad in the hole remained anything of a challenge. In seconds, the boys and girls around me attacked the first course, each using their knife and fork like a sword and trident. I stared at my child-sized portion. What it lacked in quantity was countered by its appetizing quality and I prepared to enjoy every mouthful.

'Teacher, teacher, will you cut my thingy, please?' asked four-year-old Hazel Smith, trying to trap her elusive fritter with the blunt side of her local-authority knife. This accomplished, I returned my attention to the rapidly cooling fritter on my plate. The first mouth-watering piece was on the end of my fork when ten-year-old Anita Cuthbertson tugged my sleeve, causing the piece of fritter to grease my left ear and stain my lapel on its way back to the plate.

'Mr Sheffield,' shouted Anita, 'the toilet's blocked and the floor's all runny and Mark said it was Sharon.'

I winced at the thought.

'Could you tell one of the dinner ladies please, Anita?' I asked.

Somehow the fritter looked a little less appealing.

Meanwhile, nine-year-old Billy McNeill had already devoured his meal and was now staring longingly at my fritter. However, I was usually able to steel myself against this kind of emotional blackmail. I had forsaken too many sausages and beef burgers that way. Billy's eyes were only inches from my meal and the two green candles that ran from his nose in parallel unison threatened to drip onto my plate.

Next to Billy, Jimmy Poole's face was going a pale green colour.

'I fweel thwick in my tummy, Mr Theffield,' said Jimmy.

It was obvious the contents of his stomach were about to be disgorged onto the table top and close neighbours at any moment. I beckoned to Mrs Critchley to escort Jimmy to safety. Unfortunately, he didn't quite make the private sanctuary of the boys' toilet and was violently sick in the place traditionally selected by all sickly children, namely right in the doorway of the main corridor leading from the hall. Every child would therefore have to pass this intriguing 'forbidden zone' and pass judgement on the sloppy mess that would soon be covered with sawdust prior to its eventual removal by Ruby the Caretaker. The retching sounds continued unabated, as the door could not now be closed to stifle the noise.

I stared unenthusiastically at my stone-cold fritter.

'I'm ever so sorry to bother you, Mr Sheffield.' It was Mrs Mapplebeck the Cook. She looked concerned. 'It's Mr Pickard from the office on the phone and he says it's important. I'll warm up your fritter if you like.'

I sighed. 'Thanks, Shirley, I'll come now.'

Mr Pickard, the Very Important Person at the Office, sounded agitated at being kept waiting. 'Er, very quickly, Mr Sheffield, Miss Barrington-Huntley, Chair of the Education Committee, will be visiting you some time this term. She always likes to see how our newly appointed headteachers are settling in. Try to make a good impression. Thank you.'

'Very well, Mr Pickard,' I replied. 'I'll look forward to meeting—'

But the line was already dead.

I imagined him strolling down to the County Hall dining room or eating out in some elegant pub, relaxing over his asparagus soup, with a swirl of cream emphasizing its richness. I could see him breaking open a fresh, crusty roll, enjoying soft music and sipping a glass of Beaujolais. The serrated edge of his knife would slice cleanly through his roast beef and he would choose fresh broccoli in preference to cauliflower. Fleetingly, I envisaged him enjoying a delicate, lemon cheesecake, drinking fresh ground coffee and nibbling a chocolate-coated mint. I stared for a few moments at the empty receiver, uncertain whether to swear or smile.

At that moment, Anne Grainger, the deputy head-mistress, popped her head round the door.

'Jack, if it stops raining, I thought I'd send the children out to play for a few minutes. Is that OK with you?'

Anne, a slim, attractive brunette in her mid-forties, could always be relied upon to make the right decisions. She possessed two of the greatest attributes of an effective deputy: realism and a sense of humour. I nodded in agreement.

'Good idea, Anne, they need some fresh air. In the meantime, I must ring Ruby to get her to clean up the unmentionable mess in the hall.'

She grinned and headed outside to check on the rain-soaked playground.

Before I could dial, a tapping on the open door attracted my attention. There stood Jimmy Poole, now completely recovered from his violent sickness. His bright, black-button eyes peered from under a mop of ginger curls.

'Hello, Mithter Theffield,' he said.

Jimmy would obviously go far. He just needed to lose some of his childlike innocence but as he was only five and a half years old this could take some time. He was a survivor and sought out friends in unlikely places. Jimmy had quickly decided that he could make his mark as an informer and had no qualms about dropping his closest allies in at the deep end. It was just that he went about it with such charming naivety.

'Hello, Jimmy, are you better now?'

He stared at me, presumably trying to gauge my mood.

'Do you want a fruit gum, Mithter Theffield?'

The little squashed pastille he pulled from the pocket of his scruffy shorts could conceivably have once been a green fruit gum but occasional sucking and miscellaneous dust had left it looking like a furry owl pellet.

'Thank you, Jimmy, I'll save it for later.'

I placed it with reverent care alongside the brass paperweight on my desk.

The opening gambit now dispensed with, Jimmy plunged in bravely.

'Thum boyth an' girlth were naughty in thchool dinner today, Mithter Theffield.'

'Oh yes, what were they doing?' I asked.

'Well . . . you know when Mithith Grainger thaid handth together eyeth clothed?'

'Yes?'

'Well, Mithter Theffield, thum of them kept their eyeth open.'

'And how did you know, Jimmy?'

'I thaw them, Mithter Theffield.'

I ruffled his tousled hair and returned Jimmy the Informer to the entrance hall where Mrs Critchley was talking to a surly-looking workman. His blue overalls sported the faded words 'Craven Electrical'. He thrust a pink maintenance sheet under my nose.

'Electrics. Fluorescent lights. Where are they?'

I shrugged off his abrupt impolite manner, for this was an important repair job. While I pointed out where to find a suitable ladder, a nagging thought kept recurring that there was something I had forgotten to do.

Mrs Mapplebeck suddenly reappeared, looking anxious.

'Can you spare a couple of minutes, Mr Sheffield? We have a problem in the kitchen.'

My shoulders sank a little lower. It was obviously one of those days. In the kitchen everything appeared normal, apart from the kitchen ladies who were smiling as if they shared some common secret.

'Well, what's the problem, Shirley?' I asked.

'You are, Mr Sheffield.'

'Me!'

The ladies giggled.

'Yes, Mr Sheffield, you're the problem. I make nice meals and you don't sit still long enough to eat them. Come here and sit yourself down for a minute. I'm afraid you've missed your fritters but you're not going to miss your pudding.'

Suddenly a large bowl of gooseberry crumble and custard appeared on the chromium hotplate along with a large mug of tea just the way I like it, black with a slice of lemon.

'Thanks, Shirley, this is marvellous.'

The hot crumble almost scalded my tongue but I enjoyed every mouthful and the tea was delicious. I had just finished when Blue Overalls reappeared.

'You've got to sign my job sheet.'

It was a command rather than a request. He winked at the kitchen ladies and nodded towards me.

'S'all right f'some,' he grumbled. 'Can't be bad, can it?'

I signed quickly and he snatched the grubby piece of paper from under my nose.

'Not only 'ave y'got a nice cushy job but y'get a free dinner f'nowt but looking after a buncher little kids.'

He turned quickly and was gone. In fact, too quickly, for when he reached the doorway from the hall to the corridor I remembered what it was I had forgotten. I should have rung Ruby the Caretaker to ask her to clean up a certain something. Suddenly there was a crash, a yell and a stream of curses. It was Blue Overalls on his backside.

'Aw no! What the 'ell's this? I'm all covered in sticky stuff an' sawdust!'

His curses echoed down the corridor as I quickly sought the sanctuary of my office. I sat down to ring Ruby. Meanwhile, out of the window a throng of children were playing happily, all except one. Bristle-haired Dominic Brown, his clothes splattered in mud, had frozen in mid-stride. He was standing in a muddy puddle and staring in terror at something outside my line of vision.

Inquisitively, I opened the window a couple of notches. Floating clearly on the September breeze from the direction of the car park was Mrs Brown's foghorn voice.

'Come 'ere, y'little sod, an' get off that bloody grass!'

As I eased the window shut Anne came into the office shaking her head in disbelief.

'What a woman and what language! We've got an electrician swearing in the corridor and a parent swearing in the playground. It's a madhouse!'

'It could have been worse, Anne,' I replied.

She looked at me, puzzled, as I dialled Ruby's number once again.

'Jack, what do you mean it could have been worse?' asked Anne.

I placed my hand over the mouthpiece and whispered conspiratorially, 'Be thankful for small mercies, Anne. At least they didn't use the f-word!'

'That would never ever happen at Ragley School,' said Anne proudly and walked off to ring the bell for the afternoon session.

On my way back to my classroom I stopped for a moment in Anne's class. Two small boys were sitting opposite each other at a table covered in plastic building bricks. During my first week I had taken every opportunity to learn the names of children who were not in my class.

'What's your name?' I asked the boy who was putting tiny play people inside the rectangular construction of plastic bricks.

''eathcliffe,' came the blunt reply.

'Heathcliffe?' I repeated in surprise.

'Yeah, 'eathcliffe,' he said and glared at me.

'And what's your name?' I asked his little friend who frowned at me and shook his head.

'This is mi bruvver, Terry,' said Heathcliffe by way of explanation, ''e dunt say nowt.'

'And what are you making?' I asked, trying to stimulate conversation.

''ouse,' said Heathcliffe.

I looked at the four red plastic walls with the group of small dolls imprisoned inside and pointed to the pile of unused plastic windows and doors scattered on the table top.

'If you put windows in, they will be able to see out, won't they?' I said with an encouraging smile.

Heathcliffe shrugged his shoulders and grunted while little Terry shook his head sadly. This was clearly rocket science to him.

Suddenly the bell rang and I said goodbye to the house builders.

It was when I reached the classroom door I distinctly heard Heathcliffe whisper to his little brother, 'Ah told yuh we should've put some f***kin' winders in!'

Chapter Two

The Problem Solver

Roy Davidson, EWO, visited school and checked all attendance registers. He praised Miss Evans' work as School Secretary.

Extract from the Ragley School Logbook:
Monday 26 September 1977

'£12,000 for a small detached cottage?' I exclaimed.

'It's a bargain,' said Vera, the secretary.

'But I'd need a huge mortgage, my flat in Skipton only fetched £7,000,' I said in despair.

'I'll take you to see it at lunchtime,' said Vera confidently. 'You won't regret it.'

Anne collected her dinner register from Vera's desk and whispered in my ear, 'I should listen to Vera if I were you, Jack, she's got a gift for solving problems.'

It was the last week of September and I was living in rented accommodation in York. Since my appointment as headmaster, it had taken me four months to sell my flat and now I was looking for a new home. A local development at Thorpe Willoughby was advertised in the *Yorkshire Evening Press* and included two-bedroom bungalows at £8,450 and I intended to spend the next weekend looking at the site.

It was clear that Vera had other ideas. Her old and very dear friend, Mrs Merryweather, had decided to sell her cottage on the outskirts of Kirkby Steepleton and move to Bridlington to live with her daughter.

'OK, you win, Vera, I'll take a look,' I said.

'It's only three miles away,' she said in a determined manner. 'We'll go at twelve o'clock.'

Vera had proved invaluable in my first few weeks as a headmaster. She knew how to deal with the avalanche of circulars from County Hall, check registers, collect dinner money, keep accounts and answer awkward telephone calls. According to her official job description, Vera was a part-time 'Clerical Assistant' but no one would have dared to call her anything other than 'School Secretary'.

In her mid-fifties, Vera Evans was a tall, slim, elegant woman with neatly permed, silver-grey hair. She was very proud of her job and extremely protective of her own space in the office we shared. Her desk was always tidy and she insisted that Ruby never came near it. When Ruby knocked gently on the door and asked if she could collect the wastepaper from the bin, Vera would leap to the defence of her little empire. She would stand with arms folded in the office doorway, refusing admittance, like a slim ear of corn bravely defying a huge, red, combine harvester. In the school office Vera reigned supreme.

Her appearance was always immaculate. She would arrive at school wearing a conservative blue suit or office-grey two-piece from Marks & Spencer, her favourite shop. Vera was a spinster and lived in the vicarage on the Morton Road with her brother, Joseph, who was both vicar of the parish and Chairman of the School Governors. He, like his sister, had never married and Vera looked after him in a maternal way, making his meals and tidying his library of dusty books.

Vera worked tirelessly each week filling the church with flowers. Whilst this was a labour of love, the real love of her life was her three cats, Treacle, Jess and Maggie. She called them her 'little darlings' and stroked them with her long fingers whenever they demanded her attention. Her favourite was Maggie, a black cat with distinctive white paws, named after Margaret Thatcher, whom Vera regarded as the rising star of the Conservative Party.

'She will be our first woman Prime Minister, just you wait and see,' she used to tell a disbelieving audience in the staff-room.

I soon learned on my arrival at Ragley School that Vera's large, metal filing cabinet was organized upon a completely foolproof system. Once a document disappeared into one of the hundreds of manila folders, only Vera could ever recover it. Fortunately, her memory was remarkable.

I had been baffled by Vera's filing system on my second day at Ragley. Vera was in the staff-room boiling a pan of milk prior to making cups of milky coffee for the teachers. In the post that morning I had received details of an Environmental Studies course at a local teachers' centre. The information was contained on two pieces of paper, one pink and one yellow, and I had searched in vain behind the letter 'E' in the filing cabinet. I looked round the staff-room door as Vera was handing out the coffee.

'Excuse me, Vera,' I asked, 'where's the information that arrived this morning about the Environmental Studies course?'

Vera looked surprised. 'It's filed, Mr Sheffield,' she replied curtly.

'Yes, but where?' I asked.

There was a pause. Anne Grainger looked up and winked.

'Under T,' said Vera sternly, as if she was speaking to someone who was suffering from severe memory lapses.

I took a deep breath and, with trepidation, plunged in.

'But why under T, Vera?' I asked uncomprehendingly.

'For "Trips", of course,' she explained patiently.

Jo and Sally giggled.

Jo Maddison and Sally Pringle were the other two teachers at Ragley School. Jo, fresh from college and in her first, probationary year of teaching, taught the older infant children, the six- and seven-year-olds. She was a diminutive, lively and vivacious twenty-two-year-old with long black hair. Sally, a tall red-haired, freckle-faced thirty-something in a flower power waistcoat and bright tie-dyed skirt, taught the younger junior children, aged eight and nine.

I returned moments later with the pink sheet in my hand.

'I've found this under "Trips", Vera, but where on earth is the yellow sheet?' I pleaded.

'It's under D, Mr Sheffield,' replied Vera stonily, beginning to sound weary of my ineptitude.

Anne Grainger spluttered over her coffee, clearly enjoying the entertainment.

'The letter D, did you say?' I asked in astonishment.

'Yes, of course,' she replied. 'D – for "Days Out"!'

Anne had an apoplectic fit. There was a clatter of crockery. The bell rang and we trundled back to class with me shaking my head in wonderment. Whilst I would need to be a mind reader to understand Vera's filing system, I soon came to appreciate her other skills. For Vera was a problem-solver of another kind and her next case was Ruby the Caretaker.

In complete contrast, Ruby Smith was larger than life. At twenty stones she was big in both size and personality. Shaped like a huge beach ball, she described herself cheerfully as 'well built in all the right places and most of the wrong ones as well'. Ruby's round face was always red and flushed and her bright orange caretaker overall was a massive Extra-Large Double X, the largest size in the school equipment catalogue. Even so, the overall had to be adjusted to provide extra vents under the armpits to allow ease of movement.

Ragley village had been Ruby's home for all of her forty-four years. She regularly boasted that she had never set foot out of Yorkshire. Apart from the annual family bus trip to the seaside, Ruby had never left the village. 'London is full of scarlet women,' she declared, 'and southerners can't make proper fish and chips.'

The thought of going abroad had never crossed her mind.

Ruby always did her shopping at the General Stores in the village High Street and if she ever needed anything from York, her eldest daughter collected it for her. Ruby's six children comprised two sons and four daughters. The eldest, Andy, was twenty-six and in the Army. Racquel was twenty-four and living 'over the brush', as Ruby would say, with a warehouse man in York. The other four children, Duggie, Sharon, Natasha and Hazel, lived with Ruby and her unemployed husband, Ronnie, in their three-bedroom council house at number seven, School View. The youngest, Hazel, was four years old and had just started full-time education in the Reception class.

Each day Ruby would clatter noisily into school carrying a mop and bucket and an assortment of brushes and set about her work. As she swept, scrubbed and dusted she would sing songs from her favourite musicals. Her special favourite was *The Sound of Music*, which she had seen seven times, including once with a reluctant Ronnie, five times on her own and once with the whole family as a birthday treat. After listening to Ruby singing each afternoon as I did my paperwork after school, I was almost as word-perfect as Julie Andrews. Until, one day in the middle of September, the singing had suddenly stopped and Ruby starting writing letters!

I scanned her latest epistle, written in her childlike, shaky printing.

Dear Mr Sheffield, pleese excus our Hazel from school, she hasn't come cos she cudent go and when she's gone she'll come.

As usual, she had apologized when she had delivered her note that morning before school. 'I was good at baking, sewing an' the 'oop race,' said Ruby, 'but sums an' spellin' was allus 'ard.'

Hazel had started school happily but suddenly she appeared to be having half-days off school for the most unusual reasons. Ruby's previous two letters almost defied belief.

Dear Mr Sheffield, pleese excus our Hazel from school as she has Tonso Lighthouse.

Apparently Ruby had looked up 'lighthouse' in the dictionary and was proud of this effort. This was followed by:

Dear Mr Sheffield, pleese excus our Hazel from school as she has dia rear threw a hole in her wellington.

Ruby was beginning to stretch the boundaries of medical science by the time I realized there was a real problem. Hazel seemed to be the picture of health, just like all of Ruby's children, and her absences didn't make sense. I decided to confront Ruby as she locked up the school at six o'clock.

Strangely, she was evasive. I had always found her to

be the most honest and open of people but her round face was flushed when she spoke to me.

'Our 'azel isn't as strong as the others, Mr Sheffield,' she said quickly. 'She 'as a lot of ups 'n downs.'

'It seems a shame, Ruby,' I said. 'She enjoys school so much.'

Ruby seemed to drift into a little world of her own and muttered quietly, 'The first 'n last were an accident but ah love 'em all.'

I said goodnight to Ruby and decided it was a mystery that would have to wait to be solved. Little did I know that a much sharper detective than me was already investigating the problem.

It was when I mentioned little Hazel Smith's absences to Vera that she frowned and said, 'There's more to this than meets the eye, Mr Sheffield.' Then she delved into her large, metal filing cabinet and flicked through the neat, colour-coded labels that only she understood.

The problem of Hazel's absences came to a head when the Education Welfare Officer called into school on his weekly visit. Roy Davidson was a caring man who knew all the problem families in the area and did his best to help them. He went into Vera's office where she presented him as usual with the class attendance registers. After checking the rows of diagonal lines and circles alongside the name of every child, he queried the recent absenteeism of Hazel Smith.

'This is unusual, Jack,' he said, counting the number of neat little circles against Hazel's name. 'I shall have to follow this up, especially as she is absent today.' Vera looked at me and frowned. I caught her stare and she gently shook her head.

'Will you leave it with me until next week, Roy,' I asked. 'I'll have a word with Ruby.'

Roy seemed happy with this arrangement and went off to visit a family of travellers who had just arrived on the outskirts of the village in their mobile caravans. Vera was deep in thought.

'What is it, Vera?' I asked.

Vera smiled knowingly. 'I know what's wrong with little Hazel,' she said.

'What is it?' I asked.

'Nothing,' said Vera, 'nothing at all.'

'Then why is she absent?' I asked.

'It's Ruby,' said Vera slowly. 'She's lonely.'

'Lonely?' I said in surprise.

'Yes, I could see this coming. It must be difficult for her going back to that empty house,' said Vera. 'Don't worry, I know what to do.'

With that, she turned on her heel and began to make some telephone calls.

At twelve o'clock, Vera and I walked into the school car park at the rear of the school. She stared approvingly at my Morris Minor Traveller with its emerald-green body, ash wood frame and gleaming chrome bumper bar.

'You keep it so clean and there's not a spot of rust on it,' said Vera in admiration.

'It's my pride and joy,' I replied with false modesty, buffing up the old yellow and chrome AA badge on the grill with my handkerchief.

We climbed in and drove towards York. After three miles, I began to feel anxious as we reached the outskirts of Kirkby Steepleton. A house purchase was a big decision but I felt reassured as we pulled up outside a pretty cottage with a large, rambling garden full of blackberry and redcurrant bushes. The cheerful sign on the gate said 'Bilbo Cottage' and the bright red front door had a shiny brass knocker in the shape of the head of a roaring lion. A tiny, grey-haired lady answered and clasped Vera's hand in the manner of an old friend.

'Hello, Vera, it's good to see you,' she said as we stepped into the hallway. Then she looked up at me. 'And this must be the new headmaster.'

I smiled and shook hands.

'I'm Millicent Merryweather but everyone calls me Milly,' she said with a smile that lit up the room.

I fell in love with the house immediately and Vera was clearly pleased with my enthusiasm. There were two bedrooms with sloping ceilings, a spacious study full of books and a spotless kitchen with leaded windows. Within fifteen minutes we had agreed the price of £12,000, to include all curtains and carpets and subject to a survey. It seemed appropriate that we shook hands on the deal in the hallway next to the large photograph of Milly's late husband, Roger, resplendent in his major's uniform and military moustache. It appeared that he, too, had given the transaction his blessing.

Before we left, Vera suggested that I had a closer look at the garden while she and Milly chatted in the oak-beamed lounge. The garden was a haven for wild birds and the holly bushes beside the well-kept lawn tugged at my clothes as I wandered to the furthest corner and looked back at the house. I sat on a wrought-iron garden seat and breathed in the fragrance of the pale yellow floribunda roses around me. A faded white plastic label was attached to one of them and on it, in spidery cursive writing, was the single word 'Peace'. At last I felt at home.

As we drove back to Ragley, Vera still had other things on her mind. She was also clutching a large canvas bag that I had not noticed before.

'Just pull into School View please, Mr Sheffield. We've got enough time,' said Vera. Even in off-duty moments, she still insisted on my formal title although she preferred me to call her Vera.

'I want a quick word with Ruby,' she added. 'Just come to the door with me but let me speak to her privately.'

Vera picked up the canvas bag and strode purposefully up the garden path to Ruby's door. I followed a pace behind, taking care not to trip over the old motorcycle parts that littered the overgrown lawn. Ruby looked surprised to see us.

'Oh it's you, Miss Evans, do come in. I'm sorry it's a bit untidy,' said Ruby, looking a little flustered. 'I've just got back from the Co-op with our 'azel, they're selling children's shoes at £1.99.'

'Hello, Ruby. Don't worry, I'm here with some good news for you,' said Vera with a reassuring smile, 'and don't mind Mr Sheffield, he's just giving me a lift.'

I felt like a spare part so I sat on the arm of a threadbare sofa near the fireplace. Hazel ran in from the kitchen clutching a bag of crisps. She looked pleased to see me and thrust the packet under my nose.

'Teacher, teacher, do you want a crisp?' she yelled excitedly.

'Thank you, Hazel,' I said and took one.

For some reason Hazel was always so excited she began every sentence with the words 'Teacher, teacher' when she was addressing a member of staff. Hazel clearly loved life and lived it with breathless enthusiasm. She appeared unconcerned that I was there and had settled on the carpet to watch the television. *Pipkins*, a pre-school glove puppet show featuring Hartley Hare, had just finished on Yorkshire Television so Hazel pressed a button to switch to BBC1. It was 'Closedown' time but Hazel clearly didn't mind as she stared contentedly at the flickering image of the smiling blond-haired girl on the test card.

As Vera and Ruby went into the kitchen and closed the door behind them, I spotted a faded black-and-white photograph on the mantelpiece that showed a slim and youthful Ruby with a cascade of beautiful wavy, chestnut hair down to her waist. She wore a crown and was waving a white-gloved hand to an unseen crowd. Underneath the photograph were the words 'Ragley Village May Queen 1950'. Twenty-seven years, six children and an uncontrollable passion for Rowntrees Lion Bars, Kit Kats and Smarties had gradually ravaged and bloated that youthful frame. Ruby had become a very big lady.

Minutes later, Vera emerged from the kitchen followed by a red-faced Ruby who was now clutching the canvas bag and dabbing away a few tears with a tissue.

Vera gave me a knowing look and said, 'Mr Sheffield, you can go on if you like. Ruby and I will follow you in a few minutes. We'll bring Hazel for afternoon school and then we've got things to discuss.' She tapped the canvas bag reassuringly and Ruby hugged it as if it was something very precious.

At the end of school I was in my classroom, marking problem solving of a different type. The top maths group had to work out how long it took for a snail that travelled only two centimetres every ten minutes to get to the top of a sunflower that was two metres tall. Whilst I was pleased that most of the children had got it right, I was more pleased that they had asked why the snail wanted to get there in the first place. I had just finished putting red ticks on the last exercise book, which included a lovely drawing by Jenifer Jayne Tait of an exhausted snail, when I heard the first verse of 'Climb Every Mountain' echoing down the corridor.

Ruby sounded in good spirits, and I walked out to meet her.

'Climb every mountain,' sang Ruby.

She looked up and rested on her mop.

'I was pleased to see Hazel back at school this afternoon,' I said.

'She's fine now, thanks, Mr Sheffield,' said Ruby. 'She won't be away no more, thanks to Miss Evans.'

I was curious.

'Miss Evans?'

'Yes, she brought me Mrs Merryweather's cross-stitch

kit in a big sewing bag,' explained Ruby. 'She said that Mrs Merryweather wanted me to 'ave it because she 'ad 'eard I was good at sewing an' she doesn't need it any more. So I'm going to go to Miss Evans' Cross-Stitch Club every Tuesday and Thursday morning at 'alf past ten in the village 'all.'

Ruby looked as though she had just got eight draws on the football pools.

A few days later, at the end of school, Anne and I were in the school office looking at a catalogue of library furniture and Vera was filing the last piece of paper from her desk so that, as always, she left it clean and tidy. A timid knock on the door attracted our attention.

'Come in,' said Vera.

Ruby's red face appeared sheepishly round the door.

'Hello, Ruby,' said Vera cheerfully.

''ello, Miss Evans,' said Ruby. 'Would you like me to empty your bin?'

Anne and I buried our heads in the catalogue.

'Of course, Ruby,' said Vera. 'That's very kind of you.'

Vera picked up the wickerwork basket full of crumpled carbon paper, card off-cuts and torn brown envelopes, and passed it to Ruby.

'And how is Hazel today?' asked Vera.

'She's fine, thank you,' said Ruby as she took the bin into the corridor to empty it into a black plastic bag. Anne and I looked on in amazement as Vera went to collect her coat.

When Ruby came back into the office she replaced the

bin, fumbled in the voluminous pocket at the front of her apron and put a tiny parcel on Vera's desk.

'Goodnight, Miss Evans,' said Ruby.

Vera walked back into the office, buttoning her navy blue overcoat.

'Goodnight, Ruby,' said Vera as she noticed the parcel that had been placed on the clean white blotting pad in the centre of the desk.

Vera undid the thick white string and opened the brown wrapping paper. Inside was a small wooden photo frame from with glass removed. In its place was a piece of card over which was stretched a piece of cotton cloth. On the cloth was a beautiful piece of cross-stitch work. It was a picture of a black cat with distinctive white paws.

Vera looked at it for a long time and then placed it carefully on the desk next to the precious photograph of her cats.

In the distance we could hear Ruby as she resumed her cleaning.

Above the clatter of her galvanized bucket, the sweet sound of *Edelweiss* drifted down the corridor.

Chapter Three

Parents Evening

Parents Evening. 7.00 – 9.00 p.m. 72 of 80 children were represented.

A successful evening. All teachers contributed towards a display of work in the school hall.

Extract from the Ragley School Logbook: Wednesday 12 October 1977

'Nothing can possibly go wrong, Jack,' said Anne as she carefully arranged a display of Plasticine animals in her classroom, 'so go and talk to Vera. You're making me nervous.'

Anne was right. I was agitated. It was half past six on Wednesday 12 October and my first Parents Evening was due to begin at seven o'clock. Parent-teacher interviews were stressful at the best of times and even more so when you were a newly appointed headmaster.

It was reassuring that Jo and Sally appeared so

relaxed. They were chatting with Vera who was sitting behind a desk at the entrance to the main hall. Vera looked as if she was in charge of passport control. Every parent would have to check in with her before they looked at the displays of work in the hall, corridors and classrooms.

Vera was engrossed in the front-page article of the *Yorkshire Evening Press.*

'She'll go far that woman,' she said with a voice full of admiration.

'Who will?' asked Sally as she looked at the typed list of interviews on Vera's clipboard.

'Margaret Thatcher,' said Vera. 'Look at that lovely suit she's wearing. She always looks so smart.'

Sally stared at the front-page photograph. 'Marks & Spencer isn't my style,' she said disdainfully. Sally was wearing a trendy floral blouse with a brightly patterned skirt and a vivid orange waistcoat.

Jo looked up from the adjustments she was making to the stopwatch she used for netball matches, which would enable her to time the five-minute interviews accurately.

'Who's the choirboy with the long hair next to her?' asked Jo.

Vera adjusted her steel-framed spectacles and peered closely at the text.

'It's a sixteen-year-old boy called William Hague,' said Vera. 'It says here he made a speech at the party conference in Blackpool and he received a standing ovation.'

'Looks a bit like one of the Boomtown Rats to me,' said Jo, unimpressed.

Vera was not to be put out of her stride. 'The reporter says he was like a young Winston Churchill.'

'He's got too much hair for that,' said Sally with a hint of sarcasm.

'Wonder what he'll be when he grows up,' mumbled Jo, still fiddling with the stopwatch.

'He's interested in the law,' said Vera, scanning the rest of the piece. 'Pity, we'll never know if he might have made a good politician.'

I looked at my watch.

'Well, I'm going to do a final check of my reports, so good luck, everybody,' I said, trying to sound cheerful.

We walked off to our various classrooms and left Vera grumbling about Prime Minister Jim Callaghan and North Sea oil revenue as the hall clock ticked round to seven.

My throat was dry and I couldn't recall being as nervous since my interview.

I looked around my classroom. I'd done my homework and I was ready.

A list of parent-teacher interviews lay before me and the children's desks were piled high with individual collections of folders and reading books. For the tenth time I rearranged the two tiny reception chairs in an attempt to conjure up an arrangement conducive to informal discussion. Everything was prepared and I told myself there was no need to be nervous but my stomach was churning as I saw the first parents walking up the driveway.

I glanced down at my list and tried to forecast the problem interviews. The child who had given me the most headaches was undoubtedly Claire Malarky and I hoped to see her parents. Sadly, they had not booked an appointment. It was usually the case that the parents you most needed to see never made an appearance.

There were three girls in my class called Claire but there the similarity ended. Blond-haired, cheerful Claire Phillips was popular, hard working and captain of the netball team. Her parents were due in first at seven o'clock so a pleasant start to the evening was assured. Plump, ginger-haired Claire Bradshaw, the landlord's daughter, was cheerful, good at mathematics, very trustworthy and ran the school tuck shop. Brown-haired Claire Malarky was unsociable, moody, careless and arrived each day sullen, listless and inattentive. She was a real problem.

The first two parents arrived a few minutes before the appointed hour. I tried not to appear too eager and gave them the opportunity to stroll around the classroom while I attempted to work out who they might be. They stopped next to one of Claire Phillips's paintings and studied it appreciatively. It suddenly became obvious who they were. The mother had that unmistakable blond hair and lovely smile just like her equally attractive daughter. I rose confidently to meet them.

'Hello, it's Claire's mum and dad, isn't it?' I said cheerfully.

'Yes, that's right, Mr Sheffield. We came early to have a word. We've heard a lot about you, haven't we, Ken?'

She gave me that enchanting smile again and I relaxed

with that pleasant feeling of inner security, knowing this would be the perfect interview to start off the evening.

They sat down with something of a bump on the small chairs and I launched into my first report.

'Well, I'm pleased to tell you that Claire is working really hard and puts enormous effort into her work. When you get home tonight please be sure to tell her how pleased you are and I'm sure she'll respond to your encouragement.' Father looked a little confused but nodded in agreement.

'Well, if you think it'll do any good, Mr Sheffield. I must say, this comes as a bit of a surprise to us. She's had some poor reports in past years.' This puzzled me slightly because I was under the impression that Claire Phillips had been a consistent worker and a very popular girl throughout her school career.

'She's obviously taken to Mr Sheffield's teaching,' added Mother thoughtfully, hands clasped together in an angelic pose. I could see where her daughter's good looks came from.

She turned to her husband and looked at him intently.

'We must get that bedroom organized for her, Ken. We've put it off too long. Let's start this weekend. It'll be a lovely surprise for her and a way of saying well done for all her hard work at school. It might even be a turning point. I'm sure she's got it in her.'

She leaned forward and squeezed her husband's arm encouragingly. Mr Phillips pondered the problem and then nodded slowly.

'You're right, you know. It's been all work for months

and I've given her no attention at all,' he said. 'I'll take a few days off and make a really good job of it.'

I had the inner glow of the successful social worker as I watched this domestic drama unfold. By the time I had added a few suggestions about how to help Claire with her mathematics at home and confirmed the dates of the cycling proficiency practices, two more couples were hovering. However, Mr and Mrs Phillips looked eager to leave anyway.

'Thanks for your time, Mr Sheffield. We'll get home now and tell Claire the good news,' said Mr Phillips as we shook hands.

'This is just the news we needed,' said the buoyant and ever-smiling Mrs Phillips. 'I can't tell you what a weight you've lifted from my shoulders. I've been ever so worried about her. Many thanks, Mr Sheffield.'

They were gone and soon forgotten as I launched myself into my next interview. The next couple had settled down as if they intended to stay all night and I found it difficult to get a word in edgeways. Dad went on at length about his recent hernia and Mother was anxious to know if I possessed a cure for arthritis. As they got up to leave, Dad took my pen and jotted down the address of their friend in the Lake District in case I was ever in that region. I had no time to mention their son's petty kleptomania or the fact that my pen had mysteriously disappeared.

Anita Cuthbertson's father came alone and sat down as if he carried the worries of the world on his shoulders.

'I'm afraid your Anita tends to talk a lot in class,' I said apologetically.

He shook his head in despair.

'You should live with 'er mother, Mr Sheffield,' he said sadly. 'Ah never get a word in edgeways.'

I felt sorry for him as he wandered off.

Suddenly, Mrs Sheila Bradshaw, chic and stunning in a silk blouse that left little to the imagination, bounced in briefly from The Oak with a large flask clutched to her prodigious bosom. She flashed an inviting smile as she stooped and placed the welcome refreshment next to my chair.

'Just a little something t'keep your spirits up, Mr Sheffield. I can't stay 'cause we're packed in both bars. Anyway, thanks for all you've done for our Claire. Bye f'now.'

A few heads turned as she swept out, hips swaying with exaggerated confidence, leaving behind her the lingering scent of Lentheric Musk that was only dissipated when Stan Coe, fresh from his pig farm, squeaked by in his damp wellingtons and glowered at me. He had made it clear he didn't approve of 'outsiders' having positions of influence in the village.

''oneymoon 'll soon be over,' he muttered ungraciously as he passed within earshot.

As the evening wore on I found myself repeating the same little phrases but somehow I remained coherent as the concourse of assorted faces came and went. There were faces that stared at me with stern, hypnotic intensity; faces that smiled apologetically for taking up my time and faces that looked as if they had heard it all before and wondered why they kept attending this annual ritual.

There were fathers who had been forced to squeeze into suits that were too tight for them and fashion-conscious mothers who sported new catalogue outfits under the public glare of the hall lights. I spoke to parents whose professional qualifications far exceeded mine, and others who were barely literate. I also received a letter of apology from Mrs Betty Buttle, delivered by her friend from the council estate, Mrs Middleton, who was on her way to a bingo evening in York. The letter read:

> Dear Sir, please excus me from Open Nite but I have bunions with spastic tendencies and my walking is panefull.
>
> Yours truly, Betty Buttle.

I later learned that Mrs Buttle's unique affliction to her pedal extremities did not deter her from winning £73.50 for a 'full house' at the Bingo Parlour. She announced, at her celebration in The Oak, that this had only been achieved after 'sweatin' on Kelly's Eye Number One and Two Fat Ladies Eighty Eight for a full five minutes'.

A jingle of bells suddenly seemed incongruous and I looked up to see an unlikely sight. A short man dressed as a cowboy approached me and the tiny bells on his spurs jingled as he walked. His bright red shirt was decorated with golden thread, beautifully stitched in the shape of an eagle and his brown leather waistcoat sported a highly polished sheriff's badge. He removed his broad-brimmed cowboy hat and sat down.

'Howdy, ah'm Wayne's dad,' he said.

I quickly gathered my composure and looked down at my list.

'Oh, it's Mr Ramsbottom,' I said. 'I'm pleased to meet you.'

'Call me Deke,' he said. 'Everyone else does.'

'Deke?' I asked.

'Yup,' he said. 'Short for Derek.'

'Oh, OK, er, Deke.'

'Hope you don't mind the cowboy gear,' he said, 'but ah'm on in half an hour.'

'On?' I asked. 'On what?'

'No, on where,' he said. 'Ah'm singing at t'Bluebell.'

'Oh, and what do you sing?' I asked and then wished I hadn't.

'Er, well, y'know, cowboy songs,' he explained.

'Sorry,' I said. 'I suppose that should have been obvious.'

'That's OK, Mr Sheffield,' said Deke. 'Ah just called in to say thank you for helping our Wayne with his reading. He seems to be coming on at last.'

'Thanks, Deke,' I said.

'I wish you'd taught my big lads,' he continued, stroking his stubble chin, 'they're no good at reading.'

'You have other sons?' I asked.

'Yup, Shane and Clint,' said Deke. 'We named 'em all after cowboys.'

'Good idea,' I said, not entirely convincingly.

'Anyway, ah'll 'ave t'go, Mr Sheffield. Ah'm on soon, doing the theme from *Rawhide* wi' me big whip. So ah'll sithee.'

He rose from his chair and shook my hand.

'Goodnight, er, Deke,' I mumbled.

With that, he jingled out into the darkness whistling 'Ghost Riders in the Sky'.

Later I met parents who were sympathetic and others who were blatantly aggressive and pitched abuse as if I was a coconut shy. There was also Mr Miles-Humphreys who had an unfortunate name for one so cruelly blessed.

'Nigel is working really hard,' I said enthusiastically but Mr Miles-Humphreys shook his head.

'He's having problems with his m-m-m—'

'Mathematics?' I suggested.

'N-no, m-m-m—' he tried again.

'Music?' I guessed again.

'N-no, m-m-m-m-m—' His face was going red.

I was running out of subjects.

'M-m-mother!' he spluttered.

Predictably this interview ran late and two or three couples were anxiously glancing up at the clock when, at the third or fourth attempt, he managed to bid me a hesitant goodnight.

Eventually, the last couple took their leave and I turned off the classroom lights, picked up the unopened flask and strolled tired, happy and relieved into the staff-room. Anne, Jo and Sally were already there, discussing the night's events. We shared the contents of the flask, which turned out to be coffee liberally spiced with malt whisky, and then sank into our chairs like contented kittens to enjoy our unexpected nightcap.

Problems and light-hearted stories were exchanged as we finished the coffee cocktail and washed up. Soon

Anne and I were left in school checking windows, doors and lights when I noticed a letter on my desk.

'It's from Mrs Phillips,' Anne explained. 'Her neighbour dropped it in.'

Puzzled, I read the letter.

Dear Mr Sheffield,

I regret that my husband and I will be unable to attend Parents Evening to see Claire's work but he has his evening class and I'm on night shift at the hospital. Thank you for all you have done for Claire, particularly with the netball, we were all very proud about that.

Yours sincerely, Mrs Sue Phillips.

I read the signature again and stared blankly at the neat script.

'Everything all right, Jack?' asked Anne as she finished folding the tea towel. I passed her the letter.

'It's from Mrs Phillips saying she can't come to Parents Evening but I saw her at my first interview.'

Anne shook her head. 'That wasn't Mrs Phillips, Jack,' replied Anne. 'I saw who arrived first and there's certainly no mistaking that blond hair anywhere.'

This made no sense to me.

'Blond hair! Well, who was it then?' I asked.

Anne smiled. 'Joy Malarky, of course.'

'Mrs Malarky!'

My mind whirled with thoughts of blond hair, another Claire and mistaken assumptions.

'Oh no!' I exploded. 'I've just given Claire Phillips's

report to Claire Malarky's mum and dad and they were so pleased they've gone home to make her a new bedroom!'

Anne gave me that familiar infectious grin and jangled the bunch of school keys.

'Come on, Jack. Never mind. Let's see what tomorrow brings,' she said.

My journey home to Kirkby Steepleton was troubled by the thought of what the consequences of my mistake might be.

The next morning Claire Malarky came straight up to me bubbling with enthusiasm. She looked a different girl.

'Thank you, Mr Sheffield, for saying all those nice things to my mam and dad,' she said. 'They were really pleased and I'm going to have the little bedroom to myself instead of sharing it with my big sisters. I'll get some sleep at last.'

I was pleased with her sudden enthusiasm but puzzled by her comments.

'Why do you have difficulty sleeping, Claire?' I asked.

'Because my sisters listen to records till really late every night and I daren't tell. But everything's all right now.'

The truth of my first ever parent-teacher interview as a headmaster never came to light. Anne, with true professional restraint, kept my mistake to herself and only the occasional knowing wink whenever interviews were mentioned reminded me of my blunder. Claire Malarky suddenly changed into an eager, receptive pupil and her work improved at a dramatic rate. For fate had bestowed upon her at exactly the right moment the two things she needed most: encouragement and a good night's sleep.

Ten years later, on an April morning, when a gusting wind tossed the great banks of daffodils around York's ancient walls, I met Claire shopping with her mother. Claire had become an attractive young woman but I barely recognized her for now her hair was a startling blond. She bubbled with enthusiasm about her college course and her plans to become a teacher of domestic science. I noticed just how much like her mother she had become, particularly with her new hair colouring.

'Your hair's lovely, Claire. In fact, you look just like sisters.'

Mrs Malarky laughed.

'Mr Sheffield, you say the nicest things. But don't you know where I get my blond hair from?' she asked.

'One of your parents, or grandparents?' I suggested innocently.

They both giggled like schoolgirls.

'Not quite, Mr Sheffield, actually I get it from Boots the Chemist.'

They walked away arm in arm, blond hair flying in the wind, and I was left to reflect upon the fortuitous mistake that had changed their lives.

Chapter Four

The Carrot Champion

County Hall sent representatives of the new grounds maintenance scheme to inform me of the enforced retirement of Mr George Hardisty, School Groundsman, at the end of the month when he reaches the age of 65. The school governors supported the HT's letter of complaint.

Extract from the Ragley School Logbook:
Wednesday 19 October 1977

It was 19 October and a strange clicking noise floated on the warm breeze of an Indian summer through the open staff-room window. I glanced up from my Harvest Festival notice and immediately sensed trouble.

Two young men wearing smart business suits were measuring the school field. One carried an impressive-looking clipboard and scribbled copious notes while the other pushed a clicking trundle wheel around the edges of the flowerbeds.

Curious, I walked out to meet them.

The one with the clipboard and dark, pinstriped suit walked briskly over to me and proffered a limp, reluctant handshake.

'Simon Elliott, Management Support Group Services,' he announced in a confident clipped tone. 'This is my assistant, Mr Jeremy Feavers.' He gestured towards a gangling young man sporting a fluffy attempt at a first moustache.

'Once we've measured up and completed the data analysis, you'll get a copy of the new work schedule,' he continued confidently. 'You're the headmaster I presume?' He looked at my creased suit with some disdain.

'Yes, I'm Jack Sheffield,' I replied, 'but I don't know anything about a new work schedule. So why are you here?'

He looked sympathetically at me with the aloof boredom of undoubted superiority. 'It's the new system for County Grounds maintenance,' he explained. 'It was described in the last County circular.'

I stared blankly as he pressed on with his well-rehearsed speech. He was now in full flow. 'You'll be one of twenty-seven schools in the Easington area to be maintained by a mobile team of six groundsmen who will visit you once every fortnight. It will be more efficient and it will cost less.'

It was a statement that apparently brooked no argument. I stared uncomprehendingly.

'But what about our school groundsman, Mr Hardisty?' I asked.

Mr Elliott looked increasingly irritated and checked one of the lists attached to his black, executive clipboard.

'Ah yes, no problem at all,' he said. 'He'll be retired next month when he's sixty-five.'

'But Mr Hardisty does an excellent job for us and doesn't want to retire,' I said, shaking my head in disbelief.

Mr Elliott was obviously tiring of this conversation. 'You'll be informed in due course, as will Mr Hardisty. I'll be back with our report next week, Mr . . . er . . .'

He turned on his heel and beckoned to his partner. They walked briskly back to their Miami Blue Ford Capri XL, wound open the windows and sped away in a spurt of loose gravel.

I stared around me at the bright flowerbeds and neatly trimmed hedges. Mr Hardisty's regular care was evident everywhere and now it seemed he was to be discarded like a shabby overcoat. I decided to visit him after school.

George Hardisty was a true 'man of the soil' and he tilled an honest land.

Each morning he did two hours' work as school groundsman and, although only a month from his sixty-fifth birthday, he was straight-backed, lean and incredibly fit. His strength was astonishing for such a slight man and his ruddy, weather-beaten face shone with health. Beneath the battered and frayed flat cap a pair of clear blue eyes twinkled with the joy of simple pleasures.

Five years previously he had come down from his sheep farm on the high, bleak, heather-covered tableland of the North Yorkshire Moors. He left behind the ironstones, grits, shale and limestone of the uplands for the gentle and fertile plain of York. He and his wife Mary had bought a tiny, tumbledown two-roomed cottage with its cluster of outbuildings on the Hambleton Road just outside Ragley village. They had transformed it into a picture-postcard home with the summer colour of bright geraniums and the autumn fire of Virginia creeper, rampant on its whitewashed walls.

But it was the adjoining acre of land that created most interest. The once-neglected wasteland had now been cleared and transformed into the finest fruit and vegetable garden for miles around. Envious local gardeners peered over the neatly trimmed hawthorn hedge to watch the progress of his peas, cabbages and giant onions. But no one ever saw his carrots.

These were very special.

In fact, they were quite extraordinary.

George had devoted his life to perfecting the growth of a strain of veritable monsters. Since his arrival in the area, his carrots had won first prize every year at all the local agricultural shows and his many rivals wanted to know the secret. It was widely acknowledged that George Hardisty was, without doubt, the supreme carrot champion.

Mary Hardisty answered the door. Her heavy arms were lightly sprinkled with flour and there were beads of perspiration on her forehead. A faded blue headscarf covered her grey hair. She grinned in recognition.

'Oh, Mr Sheffield, what a nice surprise, come on in. Ah'm all of a lather. It's a baking session today,' she said, patting her ruddy face and rosy cheeks with her flour-covered fingers.

'Thank you, Mrs Hardisty, but I don't want to trouble you. I was wondering if Mr Hardisty was about. I need to have a word with him,' I explained.

She rubbed her hands on her apron and stepped out on to the small back yard of weathered flagstones. Shielding her eyes from the low October sunlight, she scanned the rough, brick path that wound its way through the outbuildings. She shook her head. 'He'll be in his precious garden, Mr Sheffield. Ah'm not jesting, he sees more of them vegetables than he does of me. He only comes in when he's hungry.'

The smell of delicious home baking drifted through the open doorway. I sniffed appreciatively. 'It certainly smells good, Mrs Hardisty.'

She opened the door wider and beckoned me into the linoleum-covered hallway. Wellington boots covered in fresh mud stood neatly on newspaper just inside the doorway.

'Just hold y'horses, Mr Sheffield, while ah get y'something,' she said as she scurried into the dark kitchen. There was a clattering of heavy oven doors. Moments later she reappeared carrying a huge slab of piping-hot apple pie wrapped in a clean, white tissue. 'Here y'are, just something t'keep y'going while y'finding him,' she said.

'Thank you very much, Mrs Hardisty, that's really kind of you.' I wandered off, stooping under heavily laden fruit trees, contentedly munching on the most scrumptious apple pie I had ever tasted and found Mr Hardisty kneeling down alongside a row of enormous onions. Strangely, he didn't seem surprised to see me.

He pushed back his cap and mopped his brow with the darned cuff of his faded, brown tweed jacket.

'Ow do, Mr Sheffield?' he said.

I crouched down alongside him.

'Hello, Mr Hardisty. I'm sorry to trouble you but we had some official visitors at school today. They told me about a new scheme they're going to introduce for looking after the school grounds.'

He sighed deeply and brushed a few crumbs of soil in an absent-minded way from the smooth skin of the onion by his side.

'Ah know,' he said quietly and then stared back at the ground.

I looked around me, seeking inspiration.

'You have a marvellous garden, Mr Hardisty. Everything's growing so well.'

He suddenly stood up straight and beckoned me to follow him.

'C'mon, Mr Sheffield, ah'll show y'summat special.'

We walked at a brisk pace around the back of some old, redbrick outbuildings and creosoted sheds and George led me through a sturdy wooden gate. He glanced over his shoulder with an impish grin as I struggled to keep up with him.

'We shan't be ower long,' he said. 'It's nowt but a spit 'n' a stride away.'

We followed a mazy, well-worn path to the furthest corner of his bountiful garden until we reached an area totally surrounded by high, chain-linked fencing. Some strange-looking mounds of rich, dark earth stood in line, each surmounted by a large, cylindrical, red tile chimney pot, like a row of wartime air-raid shelters.

He explained at length how he carefully selected the correct carrot seed and planted them inside chimney pots to make sure they grew long and straight. Each day he fed them his own secret mixture of liquid compost stirred in an old metal bucket to a recipe perfected over many years.

He opened the gate and we stepped inside. I felt strangely privileged to be there. This was his secret garden and time seemed to stand still. He knelt down and scooped up a handful of the rich, black, peaty soil and then let the fine tilth crumble through his rough fingers.

'Perfect,' he mumbled to himself.

He offered me a handful of the soil and gently sieved it into my cupped hands. It fell like the precious sands of time and he sighed with reverent admiration.

'It teks years t'get it like that, tha knows,' he said proudly.

'It looks beautiful, Mr Hardisty.'

''Tis that,' he replied. 'Tha finds beauty in strange places.'

It seemed a most profound statement for such a straightforward and honest man. His depth of feeling for this mere handful of earth strangely moved me.

But it was his earth.

It was his creation following many hours of honest toil by a man who had grown old in the bosom of nature and measured time in the changing of seasons.

With extreme care he deftly extracted a giant carrot

from one of the chimney pots. It was huge, perfectly shaped and looked about two feet long.

'Tek it,' he said. 'A present for you.'

He passed it to me like a newborn baby and I cradled it in wonderment.

'Oh, thank you very much, Mr Hardisty, but I wonder . . . could I put it in the Harvest Festival on Friday? It could take pride of place among the produce.'

'Aye, if y'like,' he said and nodded.

I weighed the massive carrot in my hands.

'What is the secret, Mr Hardisty? Just how do you grow them so big?'

He smiled a knowing smile and tapped his nose with a gnarled and blackened forefinger. ''Tis the secret ingredient.'

A sudden creaking of the gate caused us to turn round. There stood Mrs Hardisty rubbing her damp, work-red hands on the hem of her faded flower-print apron.

'So that's where you've been hiding!' she shouted. 'Well, ah'll go t'foot of our stairs! An' what y'doing dragging young Mr Sheffield down 'ere t'look at y'blessed carrots? Come on, both of ye. Ah've got a nice pot of tea brewing in t'kitchen.'

I was soon sitting in a battered but comfy chair drinking tea from a large china cup with a matching willow-patterned saucer. Mrs Hardisty was at my elbow again with more apple pie and a refill from a huge brown teapot.

'An' how's all the little bairns at school, Mr Sheffield? They looked real bonny last time ah saw 'em doing that Maypole dancing last summer.'

'Fine, thank you,' I replied. 'The youngest ones have settled in well.'

Mrs Hardisty sat down on a wooden-framed wicker-work chair and leaned on the old pine table. She traced her finger down the rose pattern on the white tablecloth.

'We never 'ad no children, did we, George?'

Mr Hardisty stared into his milky tea.

'But we 'ad 'undred of babies, didn't we, love? All them little lambs.'

She was caught up in the spell of reflected memories and her eyes were shining.

'D'you know, Mr Sheffield, he'd doze off in a chair at lambing time? He never went t'bed. He were sharp as a sixpence an' bright as a button. An' all the weak little lambs he'd bring inside in front of the fire. But ah still kept that farmhouse spick 'n' span. An' he'd come in at night an' say, what's f'tea, our lass? He allus said that. Day in an' day out it were allus the same. An' ah'd say same every night, dry bread an' pull it! I allus said that. An' 'e would laugh. We used t'laugh a lot in them days.'

She drifted into a silence of private recollections and all was quiet apart from the ticking of the old wall clock and the contented mewing of a tabby cat.

Mr Hardisty looked up at me and felt in the pocket of his rough, old jacket. He pulled out a creased, brown envelope and passed it to me.

'An' now they want t'get rid of me,' he said softly. 'Ah'm too old. I 'ave t'retire they say. I love that job at school an' now ah've got t'go.'

I read the letter that confirmed the termination of Mr Hardisty's contract.

'I'm very sorry, Mr Hardisty. Everyone will be sorry to see you go. I just wish there was something I could do.'

George Hardisty shook his head.

'Nay, Mr Sheffield. It's ower for us. There's nowt y'can do. Any road, ah've enjoyed m'time there an' ah do know you'll mek a good un.'

His eyes looked damp and his wife put her hand on his arm.

'Come on, luv,' she said. 'Cheer up, worse things 'appen at sea.'

Soon my cup was refilled and we sank deep into a conversation that ebbed and flowed like a cleansing tide. For over an hour I forgot the busy pressures of professional life and rediscovered the joy of swapping stories.

Mary Hardisty proved to be a fund of tales and legends about the moors. She told the story of a fantastic mythical giant who dug a huge hole with his bare hands and piled the soil into a rounded hilltop that earned the delightful name of Blakey Topping. She then gave a passable imitation of the fierce giant and made violent digging motions with her large, pink hands. Apparently, the hole resembled a natural amphitheatre and became known as the Hole of Horcum.

'But we called it the Devil's Punchbowl,' she explained, 'an' that frightened me when ah were little.' Her eyes were wide with the memory. 'My mother used t'say that if ah looked in t'mirror a thousand times ah would see t'devil hisself.'

I began to see where many of Mary Hardisty's sayings originated. An old framed photograph on the mantelpiece caught my eye. Mary Hardisty picked it up and pointed to the young couple holding hands and looking very much in love.

'That teks me back, Mr Sheffield,' she said. 'That's me an' George when we were courting. We're outside Thompson's barn up in t'dales. It were t'Christmas dance.'

She thrust the photo in George's lap.

'D'you remember, George? You an' Nathan Barraclough would get two long iron bars an' lift that coke stove out into t'snow an' we women would shake Lux soapflakes all over t'floorboards. Mind you, it made 'em all sneeze but y'could waltz all night like a skater.'

Eventually I took my leave with the enormous carrot and a Yorkshire pudding recipe for Mrs Mapplebeck, the school cook.

Two days later it seemed as if the whole village had crowded into school for the Harvest Festival. The hall floor creaked under the massive weight of trestle tables loaded with garden produce, tinned food and home-baked, plaited bread. Sheaves of barley were propped roughly alongside. The centrepiece, however, was the formidable carrot, standing proudly like an Olympic torch.

The vicar, the Revd Joseph Evans, led the service of thanksgiving. He announced to the congregation that 'all of God's bounty would be distributed in and around the village to the poor and needy'. This clearly upset Ruby's mother, Agnes, who was always happy to accept her annual hamper. She didn't mind being thought of as 'needy' but she certainly objected to being called 'poor' and she made up her mind to tell Joe Evans so in no uncertain terms. She still remembered the antics of the teenage Joseph between the wars when she rode on the crossbar of his grocery boy's bicycle. Her eyes twinkled with secret reminiscences as with a communal 'Amen' eighty children and over a hundred parents and grandparents ended the final prayer.

Slowly the crowds thinned but not before many had paused to stare in wonderment at the giant carrot. I persuaded Mr Hardisty to pose, reluctantly, for a photograph with a throng of willing children alongside the produce. Moments later, a familiar mud-splattered Ford Capri speeded carelessly up the cobbled driveway and Simon Elliott strode confidently towards me into the centre of the school hall.

'Sorry to trouble you, Mr Sheffield,' he said, but his eyes remained glassy and insincere. 'Here's the completed maintenance schedule for your school.'

He thrust a red plastic packet in my hand. Inside I could see a spiral-bound, photocopied booklet entitled 'Grounds Maintenance Schedule'. I glanced up at Mr Hardisty who looked slightly out of character in his baggy, ageing, grey suit.

'Mr Elliott,' I said, 'let me introduce our school groundsman, Mr Hardisty.'

George Hardisty's blue eyes never faltered as he shook the soft hand nervously proffered by the pinstriped visitor.

'Ow do?' said George, simply.

'How do you do?' said Mr Elliott, carefully avoiding eye contact.

Mr Elliott's gaze swept along the Harvest Festival display. His eyes widened on seeing the carrot.

'Gosh, what a monster,' he exclaimed.

'Mr Hardisty grows them,' I explained.

'But surely no one will buy them at this size,' said Mr Elliott, shaking his head in disbelief.

'They're not f'sale,' said Mr Hardisty quietly.

'But how do you grow them so big?' asked Mr Elliott.

Mr Hardisty smiled. ''Tis the secret ingredient,' he said.

'And what's that? What is the secret ingredient?' asked Mr Elliott.

Mr Hardisty's blue eyes looked misty. There was a silence as he sought the right words.

'Ah'll tell you what it is, young man,' he said. 'Fifty years' experience.' He glanced down at the neatly bound plastic-coated folder under my arm. 'Fifty years' experience and y'can't buy that in plastic packets.'

Mr Elliott was dumbstruck.

Mrs Hardisty tugged at her husband's sleeve.

'C'mon, George, time t'go,' she said.

I bade the flushed Mr Elliott a curt goodbye and walked down the school drive with Mr and Mrs Hardisty. We stepped onto the grass verge to allow Mr Elliott to drive past. His rear wheel bumped over the corner of one of the flowerbeds as he cut the corner by the school gates.

'There goes the future,' said Mr Hardisty.

I nodded in silent agreement.

Mr Hardisty's fears soon became a reality. In the next few years many of the flowerbeds were grassed over to allow the giant gang mower to lop the top few inches off the lank grass. Hedges became bedraggled and sprays killed off the wild flowers. The school grounds were never the same again.

Each year at the Ragley and Morton Agricultural Show I saw Mr and Mrs Hardisty. Mrs Hardisty continued to win the home baking competitions but Mr Hardisty never won another trophy for his vegetables. An emergency meeting of the show committee made an important and unprecedented decision. After winning the Best Vegetables Trophy for three consecutive years it was decided to let Mr Hardisty keep the trophy. He was also made the judge for all future competitions and this meant that he was happy and all the local gardeners breathed a sigh of relief.

The only loser was the school. We missed George Hardisty, his green fingers, his humility and his love of nature. We also never discovered his 'secret ingredient'. Perhaps it was just as well.

That way he always remained the carrot champion.

Chapter Five

The Best Dressed Guy Fawkes

Mrs Smith, Caretaker, reported vandalism to the school driveway and windows. This will be discussed at the next Governors' Meeting.

Miss Barrington-Huntley, Chief Education Officer, and Miss Henderson, Temporary Adviser, visited school for a full day inspection.

The school bonfire, organized by the PTA, was a success and raised £142.60.

Extract from the Ragley School Logbook:
Friday 4 November 1977

'A-Rhesus negative,' said Staff Nurse Phillips, checking my Blood Donor's card. 'That's quite rare, Jack.'

I stared into her mischievous blue eyes and tried with all my might not to flinch as she inserted the needle into my arm.

'You're enjoying this, aren't you?' I asked.

Sue Phillips was the mother of Claire Phillips in my class and had a wicked sense of humour. After my mix-up at the Parents Evening, Sue had visited school on a number of occasions. As well as being the School Nurse and working part time at York Hospital, she was also an active member of the Ragley Parent Teacher Association and we had progressed to first-name terms in off-duty moments.

I turned sideways on the narrow bed in the mobile caravan and stared out of the window at Ragley High Street. It was only 7.45 a.m. and I was the first customer offering to give blood before I continued on my journey to school. The village was waking up and Deke Ramsbottom rumbled by on a tractor to collect timber from one of Stan Coe's old sheds for the annual village bonfire.

'Well done, Jack. You've earned a cup of tea and a biscuit.'

I glanced up at the smiling Sue. She pressed a gauze swab onto my arm and then restrained me as I attempted to get up.

'Take your time, Jack. You'll feel giddy for a short while. Stay on the bed for a minute or two.'

She came back with a cup of sweet tea and a digestive biscuit.

'Drink this and then you can get off to school. By the way, I'm on the PTA soup and hot dog stall tonight, so I'll see you later.' Sue hurried off to check on her next customer. I drank the tea, stood up a little shakily, picked up my briefcase from the floor, grabbed my jacket from the bed and left.

It was Friday 4 November and a busy day was in store. Not only did we have to prepare for the annual village bonfire but we also had the infamous Miss Barrington-Huntley, Chair of the Education Department from County Hall, inspecting the school. She was due to arrive at 9.00 a.m., accompanied by Beth Henderson, one of the newly appointed local advisory teachers, who had sounded friendly on the telephone. When I told her I was a little concerned, she had reassured me that Miss Barrington-Huntley's bark was worse than her bite.

As I approached the school gate, a frantic Ruby was waving at me.

'Them little terrors!' she shouted. 'This always 'appens just before Bonfire Night an' look what they've done!'

Whilst most of the village children indulged in harmless fun and wheeled their guys from door to door and begged a few pennies, some of the local teenagers used the cover of darkness to damage property.

'It 'appens every year,' complained Ruby. 'They've thrown eggs at the windows and we've got broken glass on the school driveway.'

The rest of the staff had not yet arrived so I made a quick decision.

'You do the windows, Ruby, and I'll see to the drive.'

I rushed into school, dropped my old brown leather briefcase in the office, hung up my tweed jacket on the hook behind the door and dragged on my paint-splattered blue boiler suit that I kept for messy jobs such as mixing wallpaper paste for artwork. Pausing only to grab a broom and shovel, I hurried back down the drive. I had just finished putting the last of the broken glass into a large black bucket when a pale blue Volkswagen Beetle pulled into the school driveway. It stopped a short distance away and the driver popped her head out of the window and gave me an enchanting smile.

'Excuse me. Where do we park please?'

The question was simple but I was rooted to the spot. Next to her in the passenger seat was a large lady in a black coat with a fur-trimmed collar and a striking silver-grey hat adorned with a peacock feather. With a face like thunder she stared at my shabby appearance as if I was a tramp begging for money.

'Hurry up. It's cold. Tell him we're here to see the headmaster,' boomed Miss Barrington-Huntley.

I pointed hesitantly towards the car park at the rear of the school.

The driver flashed me a grin and drove off.

With a burst of speed that surprised Ruby, I rushed through the side entrance of the school, ran into the office, ripped off the boiler suit, flung it under my desk and put on my jacket. Then I left the office door wide open, sat down behind my desk, straightened my tie and grabbed a County Hall circular from the wire tray. I was searching for my fountain pen in my jacket pocket when footsteps approached. Miss Barrington-Huntley had arrived in the entrance hall and was muttering something about how difficult it was to get a decent caretaker these days.

A slim, attractive woman about five feet six inches tall with long, honey-blond hair and a face that shone with health walked confidently into the office. She glanced down at the boiler suit and smiled.

'Good morning,' I said nervously, 'welcome to Ragley.'

'Hello again, Mr Sheffield,' she said.

The first time we had met was two minutes earlier on the school driveway and my change of costume had not gone unnoticed. She raised her eyebrows as we shook hands. Her handshake was firm.

'I'm Beth Henderson,' she said. 'I've been seconded for a year from my deputy headship in Thirkby to support English and Physical Education in North Yorkshire.'

She looked very young to be in such a post.

The brooding presence behind her stepped forward.

'I'm sure you remember Miss Barrington-Huntley, the Chair of the Education Committee,' continued Beth Henderson confidently. 'I'm sorry if we're a little early. You will recall, we're here to observe the children in each class, talk to the staff and see how the school is progressing.'

The Grim Reaper stared at me curiously as if she was trying to recall if we had met before. 'Good morning, Mr Sheffield,' she said.

'Would you like some coffee?' I asked, eager to get off on the right foot.

Right on cue, Vera arrived and took the visitors' coats. Miss Barrington-Huntley carefully withdrew the long pin that secured the magnificent hat to her purple-rinsed, wavy hair. She stroked the long blue feather carefully and handed the hat to Vera as if it were the crown jewels.

'What a delightful hat,' said Vera appreciatively.

'Brown's in York,' said Miss Barrington-Huntley pompously.

Vera placed it reverently on her desk with obvious admiration and proceeded with the coffee-making duties.

Coffee cups rattled nervously as one by one the staff walked in and were introduced to Miss Barrington-Huntley who remained aloof throughout. Beth Henderson was just the opposite, full of encouragement and enthusiasm.

'We shall begin with the youngest children and look at their work and observe their behaviour,' announced Miss Barrington-Huntley.

Anne Grainger left quickly to make her last-minute preparations.

Praying that the day would go smoothly, I set off for my classroom whilst the two visitors made their way to Anne's class.

Inevitably, the first person they met in the corridor was Ruby, sweating profusely from her window-cleaning exertions.

'You must be the important visitors we've been expecting?' said Ruby bluntly.

She put down her bucket, ready for a good gossip, and wiped the perspiration from her red cheeks with a grubby chamois leather.

Miss Barrington-Huntley looked disparagingly at the vision before her in the double-extra-large orange overall, sniffed and walked on.

Beth Henderson paused and smiled at Ruby. 'I'm sorry we can't talk to you now as we have to go into

Mrs Grainger's class, perhaps we can talk later,' she whispered politely.

As I opened the swing doors to the school hall for our visitors, Ruby's singsong voice rang out. 'An' mek sure y'see all that beautiful artwork in Mrs Pringle's back passage!'

Beth glanced up at me and muttered quietly, 'That should be interesting.'

After registration I led the school assembly. The children gave an ear-shattering performance of 'When a Knight Won His Spurs' and the 'orchestra' featured Sally Pringle's recorder group playing 'Morning Has Broken'. I read the story of 'The Selfish Giant' by Oscar Wilde and, apart from mixing up my introduction to the prayer with 'Eyes together, hands closed', everything seemed to go as it should. Then we all trooped back to our classrooms and carried on with our work. The frightening Miss Barrington-Huntley and the cheerful Miss Henderson followed Anne back into the Reception class.

At morning playtime I was on playground duty whilst around me groups of children skipped, kicked plastic footballs, played tig, recited 'What's the time, Mr Wolf?' and sang 'Ten Green Bottles'. Some leaned on the fence to watch Stan Coe supervising the bonfire building whilst others crowded round Anne's husband, John Grainger, who was sinking a makeshift rocket launcher in the school sand pit in preparation for his famous firework display.

Anne came out with a tray of mugs of milky coffee. She left the tray with John, selected two mugs and walked over to me.

'How did it go?' I asked anxiously, sipping the coffee.

Anne shook her head. 'Let's just say Heathcliffe introduced Miss High and Mighty to some choice language!'

The Earnshaw family had recently arrived from Barnsley in South Yorkshire. Mr Earnshaw had got a driving job for the local chocolate company in York and their two children, Heathcliffe, age five and Terry, age four, had both joined the youngest children in Anne's class. Heathcliffe had spiky blond hair and a way with words that sounded just like his mother. Terry appeared barely out of nappies. He clung to his brother and hadn't uttered a single word. Anne was doing all she could to encourage him to communicate.

'So what happened?' I asked nervously.

'Well, the children on Heathcliffe's table were doing jigsaws and he looked up at Miss Barrington-Whatsit and said, "Hey, missus, sit thee arse down 'ere." I tried to explain that he had just arrived and didn't know any better when little Terry started thumping the table. He was doing a three-piece jigsaw of a tiger. He had got the head and body in place but the curly tail was beyond him. He kept turning it round and trying to hammer it in with his little fist. Heathcliffe looked up at Miss You-Know-What, handed her a two-piece jigsaw of an elephant and said, "Hey up, missus. Try 'im wiv this two-piece of the elephant, cos that tiger's a bugger!"'

I shook my head in disbelief and groaned. This inspection wasn't turning out as I had hoped.

By lunchtime the school was a hive of activity. Beth Henderson walked up to me and nodded towards a group of men carrying trestle tables and another group of mothers who were staggering up the drive with bags of old clothes and parcels of newspaper. They had volunteered to help each class make a Guy Fawkes for the bonfire. Anne had told me that this was a tradition at Ragley and there was always fierce competition amongst the children for their class to make the best-dressed Guy Fawkes.

'You've got wonderful support from the parents, Jack. It's really impressive,' she said.

Beth had addressed me by my first name so I plucked up courage to reciprocate.

'Thanks, Beth, I agree. They can't do enough to help, and tonight is a big night. There's a huge bonfire and firework display and I'm told everyone in the village turns up. You should see what's going on in the kitchen. There's food for an army being prepared.'

We walked down the corridor and glanced in the office. Vera had taken charge of a group of ladies who were sorting through a huge pile of old football socks, scarves, hats, gloves and wellington boots. Ruby had appeared and was eyeing up the clothing.

'They're too good for a guy,' said Ruby, 'an' that old jumper would come in for my Ronnie.'

Vera rolled it up, put it in a plastic bag and passed it to Ruby with a smile. Ruby looked delighted.

The rest of the clothes were scooped up by Vera's willing helpers and dispatched to the various classrooms, where excited children were waiting to make their guys.

'Isn't that your boiler suit, Jack?' whispered Beth.

I decided discretion was the better part of valour and said a silent farewell to my well-worn overalls. In the kitchen, Shirley and the dinner ladies were preparing huge pots of soup and Ruby's eldest daughter, Racquel, was making a tray of toffee apples. Mary Hardisty and her friends from the Women's Institute were filling up metal tureens with gingerbread men and slabs of parkin. Outside on the field, a few of the dads, under the critical stare of Stan Coe, were tying some broken chairs to a wooden palette. This would eventually be placed on top of the completed bonfire to provide seats for the four guys.

In the distance, Deke Ramsbottom's tractor was towing a trailer full of old sofas, broken wardrobes and rotting fencing. He waved his Stetson in the air as if he was herding cattle in Texas. His sons, Shane and Clint, were seated on a battered sofa on the trailer, clinging precariously to the bits of furniture that threatened to fall off at any moment.

Beth looked up at me.

'I might even come along myself,' she said. 'I only live a few miles away near Morton.'

'That would be lovely,' I replied. 'I hope you can make it.'

I meant it.

Whilst I had enjoyed casual relationships in the past, I couldn't recall anyone having such an impact on me as this attractive and dynamic woman. I knew I wanted to see her again but this was neither the time nor the place for such thoughts.

I glanced at my watch. It was time to ring the bell in

the school bell tower that had summoned children to their lessons for almost a hundred years.

'Excuse me, Beth. It's time for afternoon school. No doubt I'll see you later.'

She gave me that enchanting smile again.

'Don't worry, Jack. I'll make sure Miss B-H is gentle with you.'

I walked back to my classroom, certain in the knowledge that a woman like Beth would have a boyfriend or partner who showered her with expensive gifts. It was also very doubtful Beth would be interested in a man with Buddy Holly spectacles and leather patches on the elbows of his jackets.

During the afternoon, the children in my class painted pictures and wrote stories about Guy Fawkes in their topic books and, when they had finished, everyone contributed towards making the guy. With its fat tummy stuffed with paper under a checked shirt, a round cardboard face with bright pink cheeks, cord trousers and wellingtons, it looked very much like our Vice-Chairman of Governors, Stan Coe.

At afternoon playtime I met Miss Barrington-Huntley and Beth Henderson in the school hall. They had watched Jo Maddison's science lesson and were clearly impressed. I hoped that we might get a good report after all.

I breathed a sigh of relief as we walked towards the school office but, as we passed the small toilet block outside Anne Grainger's classroom, I heard a little boy crying. Suddenly there appeared little Terry Earnshaw, tears in his eyes and tiny grey shorts and underpants round his ankles. What nature had endowed was hanging free. Miss Barrington-Huntley stopped as if struck by a thunderbolt. Little Terry stumbled forward as if he was last in the sack race. He stopped in front of Miss Barrington-Huntley, stared up at her, dried his eyes with the cuffs of his frayed jumper and cried in a loud South Yorkshire accent, 'Hey, missus, who wipes arses round 'ere?'

Anne suddenly galloped into view, looking very red in the face. 'Oh, there you are, Terry. Please excuse me, everybody.' She scooped him up like a baby chimpanzee, turned on her heel and rushed him back into the toilet.

I didn't know if Miss Barrington-Huntley was going to laugh or cry. She just stood there transfixed. Beth Henderson, who had learned something of the little boy's background, firmly took her colleague by the arm and smiled bravely at me.

'Well, at least he has said his first sentence, Mr Sheffield,' she said with optimism and then frog-marched Miss Barrington-Huntley into the staff-room.

As I collected my coat and scarf from the office in order to go out on playground duty, I could distinctly hear laughter in the staff-room. In amongst it was a high-pitched laughter I had not heard before. It was Miss Barrington-Huntley.

During the final session before the end of school Miss Barrington-Huntley and Beth Henderson observed my lessons. My class completed some imaginative poems about Bonfire Night and then drew colourful fire-work pictures on black paper using coloured chalks and pastels. At 3.00 p.m. Shane and Clint Ramsbottom wandered into the classroom, grinned at their brother, Wayne, and collected our guy to put on the bonfire. I read another chapter of our class story, *The Wheel on the School* by Meindert Dejong, and we finished the day with a quiet prayer. Finally, twenty-two excited children went out in the gathering gloom to take a final look at the four guys on the bonfire before they set off home.

At four o'clock Miss Barrington-Huntley and Beth Henderson sat down with me in the classroom Book Corner to discuss the day.

'This has been a most eventful day, Mr Sheffield,' said Miss Barrington-Huntley. 'I can honestly say it is a school visit I shall never forget. Whilst some of the children are, how can we say, a little rough round the edges, behaviour is good, lessons are well prepared and there is an excellent ethos within the school. The support of the parents is outstanding. Some of your official paperwork is a little lacking but I have discussed this with Miss Henderson and she or one of my team will come in and support. In the meantime, good luck in your new post and please excuse me as I have to leave promptly for another engagement.'

I obviously looked shell-shocked.

Beth Henderson smiled reassuringly and got up to leave. 'Well done,' she said. 'I'll be in touch.'

With that, they were gone. Beth collected the coats and they hurried to the car and sped away.

Three hours later over two hundred people wandered onto the strip of land owned by Stan Coe, between the school field and the village football pitch. As I walked past the hurricane lamps that were hanging on poles above the school fence, I felt a tap on my shoulder. Under a bright red bobble hat was the smiling face of Beth Henderson.

'You made it,' I exclaimed. 'Come on, this deserves a cup of Ragley's finest chicken soup.'

'The best offer I've had in ages,' said Beth with a smile.

We walked past families holding bright sparklers to the line of trestle tables. A lively group of mothers led by Sue Phillips was serving soup and hot dogs.

'Good evening, ladies, two cups of chicken soup, please,' I asked cheerfully.

Sue Phillips leaned towards me with something in her hand.

'Excuse me, Mr Sheffield. Here's your fountain pen,' she said.

'Oh, thanks, I've been lost without it. Where did you find it?' I asked.

The familiar mischievous grin appeared again.

'You left it on the bed this morning!'

There was a stunned silence.

Then all the ladies burst out laughing.

Beth looked up at me curiously.

'I can explain,' I said lamely.

Suddenly a rocket exploded overhead and patterns of colourful sparks filled the jet-black night sky. Anne Grainger's husband, John, was in charge of the firework display and it was his way of announcing that the huge bonfire was about to be lit.

'I'll be back in a moment, Beth. Please don't go.'

I left her in earnest discussion with Sue Phillips and her fellow conspirators.

It was a Ragley tradition that the headmaster lit the bonfire each year. John Grainger thrust an old broom handle towards me on which a rag soaked in white spirit had been tied to the top with baling twine. I held it at arm's length as he lit it and then I approached the mountain of stacked timbers like an Olympic torch-bearer. To the sound of raucous cheers I thrust the flaming torch into the centre of the dry kindling wood at its base and then retreated quickly. Flames roared and crackled and bright firelight illuminated the scene as I made my way back to join the crowds. Under the flickering lights alongside the soup and hot dog stall, Beth was deep in conversation with Sue Phillips.

I stood alongside them hesitantly.

'Don't look so worried, Jack,' said Beth with a smile, 'giving blood is a really good thing to do.'

I relaxed visibly as she handed me my cup of soup.

'Thank goodness,' I said. 'At least nothing else can go wrong today.'

Beth nodded towards the brightly lit school windows. 'By the way, I need to call into school, Jack. We left in such a rush Miss Barrington-Huntley left her precious hat. I promised I would collect it.'

At that moment, a loud cheer went up from all the children. The flames had lit up the four guys tied with old skipping ropes on to the wooden chairs at the very top of the bonfire. They looked eerie in the bright light. One by one they caught alight. Miss Maddison's class guy was the biggest one. He wore a blue paint-splattered boiler suit that looked familiar. He also wore a distinctive hat. As the large feather that was stuck in it caught alight I looked at Beth in horror. 'Oh no, it can't be!' I said.

Beth just smiled. 'Well, you've got to admit, Jack,' she said, 'it's certainly the best-dressed Guy Fawkes.'

Chapter Six

The Governors' Meeting

A meeting of School Governors was held – 7.00–9.00 p.m.

HT and Chairman of Governors presented reports.

A majority agreement was reached to use money raised this year towards a new library area to be sited in the school hall. Parents to be informed.

The proposal to take top class on a summer camp and hold a Victorian Day to celebrate the centenary of the school was agreed unanimously.

Extract from the Ragley School Logbook:
Monday 28 November 1977

'You need to drink a lot of water to cure a headache,' said the Revd Joseph Evans. 'I heard a doctor say it on my long-wave radio.'

It was five o'clock on the last Friday in November and I was tired. I had meant to start writing the Governors'

Report but I hadn't got round to it and the meeting was on the following Monday evening.

'This Governors' Report would give anyone a headache!' I said in despair.

The Revd Joseph Evans looked at me sympathetically from across the school office. 'There's no reason at all to get a headache simply because of a Governors' Meeting,' he said. 'It's not meant to be stressful.'

'I'll have to come in tomorrow and write it then,' I said.

'It's a pity to give up your weekend, Jack, but you need a clear head for your report,' said Joseph, 'particularly your first one.'

I sifted through the contents of the box file that Joseph had brought in for me of the previous reports written by John Pruett.

'It's much more extensive than I imagined,' I said with a sigh. 'It looks as though I even have to provide an up-to-date list of Ruby's cleaning materials as well as everything in the stock cupboard and library.'

Joseph was keen to do all he could to help, including enlisting the help of his sister who was Clerk to the Governors as well as School Secretary.

'Don't worry, Jack, I've arranged for Vera to type up both the headmaster's report and the Chairman's report over the weekend,' said Joseph. 'Perhaps you could drop it in to her at the vicarage tomorrow on your way home.'

Ruby was her usual bustling, helpful self when I asked for her stock list.

'I'll do it tomorrow afternoon when they're out at

football an' the 'ouse is quiet, Mr Sheffield,' she said. 'Just call by when it suits.'

On Saturday morning, I travelled into York market earlier than usual and did my shopping for the week. It was a bright, clear, late autumn day and the Minster looked magnificent against a cold, blue sky. As usual, I bumped into someone I knew. In amongst the Christmas shoppers and tourists, Mr Miles-Humphreys and his wife were suddenly alongside me as I looked in the shop windows of Goodramgate. I hadn't met his wife before but I knew her by reputation as one of the leading lights of the Ragley Amateur Dramatic Society.

'This is m-my w-w-w—' stuttered Mr Miles-Humphreys.

'He's trying to tell you I'm his wife, Felicity,' said Mrs Miles-Humphreys with a disparaging shake of her wiry, jet-black dyed hair.

Felicity Miles-Humphreys, with expansive theatrical gestures and a loud town crier voice, informed me and most of the shoppers around that she was en route to York Station to be an extra in the film *Agatha* starring Dustin Hoffman and Vanessa Redgrave. She had been booked to wander up and down the platform in period costume for the princely sum of eight pounds. The stuttering Mr Miles-Humphreys tried manfully to bid me goodbye but the forceful Felicity could not wait that long and they disappeared into the crowds.

I looked at my watch. A gentle walk by the river was an inviting prospect but time was pressing so I strolled back to Lord Mayor's Walk where my car was parked. Above me, to my left, a party of tourists hurried along the city walls. Behind them a couple wandered slowly. One of them was Beth Henderson, her distinctive blond hair blowing in the wind. Alongside her, a tall, handsome, fair-haired man smiled down at her. I thought of waving but decided not to and felt a sudden pang of disappointment as I climbed into my car and drove quickly back to Kirkby Steepleton.

After unpacking the groceries I attempted to tidy my tiny kitchen but my mind was elsewhere. I wondered if I had missed my chance with Beth Henderson. After a few minutes, I still seemed to have as many pots and pans in boxes on the floor as when I started so I gave it up as a bad job.

By midday I was back in school. I filled my fountain pen and started writing.

It occurred to me that this was yet another aspect of the job for which I had not been trained, but John Pruett's careful and accurate reports proved an excellent template. By mid afternoon I was hungry so I purchased a packet of crisps from Claire Bradshaw's tuck shop box and made a coffee. As I relaxed with my feet up, I tuned in the staff-room radio and Paul McCartney's 'Mull of Kintyre' droned in the background.

The newsreader cut in to give the latest news on the firemen's strike. He said they wanted a 30 per cent pay rise but Mr Callaghan, the Prime Minister, had confirmed he would not budge beyond 10 per cent. In the meantime, an emergency crew had been called out in their Green Goddess to tackle a blazing Ford Cortina taxi in the middle of York.

When David Soul's recent number-one hit, 'Silver

Lady', came on, the telephone rang and made me jump. It was Anne Grainger.

'Hello, Jack, how's it going? I wondered if you wanted to call in for a bite to eat when you've finished,' she said.

'Thanks, Anne, I'd love to,' I replied.

'Who's that singing on the radio?' said Anne suddenly.

'David Soul.'

'Bye,' she said abruptly and put the phone down.

I glanced at the radio. It was a well-known fact that Anne Grainger went weak at the knees whenever David Soul sang. However, when Jimmy Osmond began singing 'Long-Haired Lover from Liverpool', it seemed a good moment to switch off and carry on with a description of our newly purchased scheme of work entitled the School Mathematics Project.

It was just after six o'clock when I stood in the pitch dark outside number seven School View. The streetlight illuminated bits of machinery in the overgrown front garden so that it looked like a motorcycle graveyard.

Ruby's eldest daughter, Racquel, in a bright purple dressing gown, opened the door.

'Come in, Mr Sheffield, you're expected. Mam's in the front room,' she said as she folded up an ironing board and rushed upstairs. Ruby was staring at the television set in the lounge and dabbing tears from her eyes with the hem of her huge apron.

She looked up at me and shook her head sadly.

'Oh, bloomin' 'eck, Mr Sheffield,' said Ruby, 'ah feel all unnecessary. 'e's jus' been on, mi favourite, an' ah'm all of a fluster.'

She perched her massive behind on the creaking arm of the battered sofa. I glanced at the screen just in time to see Basil Brush shouting 'Boom, Boom', and waving goodbye.

'No, not 'im,' said Ruby, rubbing her red eyes. 'It's Demis Roussos, 'e were a guest on t'*Basil Brush Show*, he sings like an angel an' 'e's such a fine figure of a man. Ah do like a man with a bit of meat on 'im.'

It begged the question why she had married Ronnie who was at best seven stones dripping wet.

'Jus' come into t'kitchen while ah finish our Duggie's tea an' ah'll be right with you,' shouted Ruby as she disappeared into the cluttered kitchen.

'I've just come to collect that stock list, Ruby, and then I'll be on my way,' I said, staring in horror at the state of the kitchen. I suddenly thought that mine didn't look so untidy after all.

'It's there on t'kitchen table,' said Ruby, pointing to a grubby collection of tea-stained papers next to a pile of racing pigeon magazines. As Racquel had placed her recently ironed underwear on top, it caused a fatal moment of hesitation.

'Would you mind checking it for me, Mr Sheffield?' asked Ruby, impervious to the hot fat spitting from the frying pan. 'Ah'm a bit worried about some of m'spelling.'

'OK, Ruby, let's have a look,' I said. I moved a bowl of half-eaten cereal from the chair, picked up a pair of muddy football socks from the table in front of me and began to read. The spelling was difficult at first but once I realized Ruby used her own personal phonetic style the meanings of words began to make sense. At six-thirty I was ready to leave, by which time a heated argument had begun in the lounge. Ruby was trying to referee from the kitchen and fry bacon at the same time.

'But it's 'alf past six an' ah want to watch *Man from Atlantis*,' yelled seventeen-year-old Sharon, shaking her peroxide-blond hair.

'Y'can't just switch to Yorkshire TV in t'middle of *Doctor Who*,' shouted fifteen-year-old Natasha with her hand protecting the control buttons of their teak-effect Marconi 20-inch colour television.

Twenty-two-year-old Duggie, the Ragley Rovers number seven, was stretched out on the sofa in his muddy football kit.

'Ah'm off t'pub, ah'm not watching a big curly-haired pansy wi' webbed feet,' said Duggie.

It was unclear whether Duggie was referring to an alien being in *Doctor Who* or the *Man from Atlantis* but, clearly, he had had enough. He trudged upstairs to the bathroom and began hammering on the door. Unknown to Duggie, Racquel was applying mascara so a long wait was in store.

Meanwhile, little Hazel was sitting on the floor wearing odd socks and eating a sandwich dripping with red sauce.

'Teacher, teacher, ah've got a bacon buttie,' said Hazel proudly.

Ruby nearly tripped over her as she came in from the kitchen.

'Mr Sheffield, why don't you stay an' sit down and 'ave a cup of tea?' said Ruby.

I looked warily at the sofa, now covered in muddy patches.

'I don't want to trouble you, Ruby,' I said, edging towards the hallway. 'I only came to collect the stock list.'

'Natasha, get Mr Sheffield a cup of tea and tell our Duggie 'is tea's ready an' to stop shouting at our Racquel,' yelled Ruby above the din of the television.

Natasha gave me a look like thunder and climbed over the back of the threadbare sofa. The hot, sweet milky tea in a heavy mug the size of a small bucket was not to my liking and had the faint aroma of engine oil but I didn't complain. Ruby's untidy lounge looked as if someone had tipped the leftovers from a jumble sale all over the floor but she was quite at ease as she folded up her daughter's ironing. Feeling like a thief in the night, I carefully poured the contents of the mug into the spider plant on the creaking sideboard.

'That was lovely, Ruby,' I said hastily. 'Thanks for the tea and all your hard work.'

With that, I made a quick exit, drove down School View, turned left to the village green then right past The Royal Oak and on to the Morton Road. Within five minutes I had parked beneath one of the magnificent elm trees in St Mary's churchyard. Owls were hooting as I rang the doorbell of the vicarage.

Joseph Evans, complete with dog collar and striped apron, answered the door. To my surprise he was carrying a wine bottle and a glass.

'Hello, Jack, saw you drive in,' he said cheerfully and beckoned me into the kitchen. He looked furtively at

Vera who was sitting in the lounge engrossed in an article about Prince Charles entitled 'Charles the Charming'.

Joseph beckoned me towards the kitchen.

'Jack, you must try my latest creation,' he said, pouring a glass of wine. 'It's my peapod vintage.'

The murky liquid smelled like paint remover and I took a hesitant sip. It was like being hit in the solar plexus by a fireball.

'Needs a bit of refinement, but it's almost there,' he said, sniffing the glass appreciatively. 'Anyway, Vera doesn't approve of my hobby, so perhaps we had better go and say hello.'

Joseph glanced at the kitchen clock; it was approaching seven o'clock. 'If you don't mind, Jack, make sure you're gone by seven thirty. Sorry if that sounds a bit rude but it's Nicholas Parsons, you see.' He looked around furtively and whispered, 'Don't say I said so, but she's absolutely dotty about him. She sees him as the perfect English gentleman and never ever misses *Sale of the Century* on Saturday night.'

We both walked into the elegant lounge adorned with spectacular flower arrangements, highly polished candlesticks and three plump cats in various states of repose.

Vera put down her magazine and stood up to greet me.

'Come in, Mr Sheffield,' she said and pointed me towards a leather armchair. 'Would you like a cup of tea? I'm sure Joseph has been too busy showing off his dreadful wine to remember to ask you.'

'Thank you, Vera, that would be lovely,' I said, recalling my previous cup of tea at Ruby's, 'and here's my headmaster's report to the Governors ready for typing. Ruby's list is in there as well.'

Vera took the sheaf of papers and glanced at her watch anxiously as she hurried to the kitchen. The sound of clinking bottles could be heard as Vera cleared the kitchen table.

Minutes later she hurried back with a beautifully laid-out tray, including a pot of tea, china cups and saucers, matching sugar bowl and milk jug, silver teaspoons, lace-trimmed napkins and a doily-covered plate filled with home-made biscuits. She placed it on an ornately carved dark-oak coffee table and began to pour the tea.

'It's Earl Grey,' said Vera, glancing at her watch again, 'I hope that's OK.'

'Fine, thank you, Vera,' I said and settled down into the armchair.

She passed me the cup of tea.

'Help yourself to a biscuit while I get a copy of my stock report for you.'

When Vera walked out to the study, Joseph nodded at the grandfather clock in the corner of the room and gave me a meaningful stare.

'Don't worry, Joseph,' I said, 'I'll drink my tea and go.'

Vera reappeared and handed me a stock list neatly typed on vicarage-headed notepaper.

'Thank you, Vera, I do appreciate your support. Now, if you'll excuse me, I promised to call in to see Anne Grainger on the way home.'

Vera looked relieved and walked eagerly into the

lounge for her weekly rendezvous with her perfect gentleman whilst Joseph saw me to the door.

The lights of The Royal Oak were bright as I drove past the village green once more and turned left up the Easington Road to the Crescent, an estate of recently built private houses where Anne lived with her husband John, a local craftsman and woodcarver.

As I drove into the quiet cul-de-sac, their detached stone-fronted house looked warm and inviting. John's beautiful woodcarvings were displayed on the window ledges and, as I walked inside, I admired the photographs of the Yorkshire Dales that filled the walls. John was a member of the Easington Camera Club and had won many prizes for his dramatic landscapes.

Anne had prepared a simple but delicious dish of bubble and squeak topped with Wensleydale cheese and fried tomatoes and we ate contentedly in their quarry-tiled kitchen.

After coffee, Anne washed the dishes while John and I went into his garage and examined his wide range of camera equipment. He put a half-finished carving of a magnificent shire horse to one side and laid out a range of camera lenses of all shapes and sizes.

'You can have this if you like, Jack,' he said. 'It's an old zoom lens that I never use and it will fit your old Pentax.'

I was thrilled to receive such a generous gift. I had bought my camera in 1965 whilst I was training to be a teacher at the college in York and it still worked perfectly.

John glanced at his watch. It was almost nine o'clock.

'I have to go out now, Jack, so you'll have to excuse me,' said John. 'I usually go round to my mother's for an hour while Anne watches *Starsky and Hutch*. She's absolutely daft about David Soul, so I make myself scarce.'

Back in the lounge Anne was settling down in front of the television set for another night with her handsome all-action hero. Once again, Anne's heart-throb, along with his little curly-haired friend, was destined to cause havoc on the streets of New York in a brightly painted car that resembled striped toothpaste, then save two children from a burning building, get tied up and beaten unconscious and still find time to fall in love and solve a crime before the evening news at five minutes to ten.

Long before then I had said goodbye and driven back to Kirkby Steepleton. Demis Roussos, Nicholas Parsons and David Soul were an unlikely trio but it struck me as I drove along that no matter what your shape, size or accent, there was someone out there for you.

As I stumbled into my dark hallway and felt for the light switch, I wondered if there might be someone out there for me. A vision of Beth Henderson flashed across my mind until reality dawned once again.

By the time I was settled in my sparsely furnished lounge it was ten o'clock. I switched on the television and was faced with a similar dilemma. Was it to be *Match of the Day* on BBC1 or Dionne Warwick in a celebrity concert on Yorkshire TV or maybe even clearing the pans from the kitchen floor? It was a tough decision but the football won.

* * *

By Monday evening I was ready. The report was written and Vera had typed it up on a Gestetner carbon sheet and rolled off five copies on the inky drum of the huge duplicating machine. The copies had been left to dry on the window ledge to avoid smudges and just before seven o'clock they were stapled together and placed like tablemats around the office desk.

'I declare this meeting open,' said Joseph, 'and I extend a warm welcome to Jack Sheffield as our new headmaster.'

Everyone smiled and nodded acknowledgement, all except Stan Coe who shook his head and grunted like one of his many pigs.

The fifth member of the governors was introduced to me. He was the County Council representative, Councillor Albert Jenkins, an elderly man in an old three-piece suit complete with watch chain. He had been a local councillor for the past twenty years and had attended the school shortly after the First World War. We shook hands and I felt I had gained a good friend.

'Teks time for outsiders to be accepted here but ah'm sure you'll mek it one day, young man,' said Albert with a smile. It wasn't long before I realized he had a sharp mind.

'Now, what's all this talk from that woman who's Education Secretary about putting the school curriculum under control of central government?' asked Albert.

Stan Coe had never heard of Shirley Williams, the Minister for Education, so I explained that she had reassured the teaching unions that this would never happen.

'Well, if they do,' said Albert prophetically, 'no good'll come of it.'

After I had read my report, Joseph asked if there were any questions.

Stan Coe was frowning.

'Ah don't 'ave much time f'this lib'ry idea,' he mumbled. 'It'll tek village funds away from t'Social Club. There's a limit t'fund raisin', tha knows.'

'Let's put it to the vote,' said Joseph quietly.

Everyone voted for the building of a school library except Stan who gave me a stare of pure venom. He scanned the headmaster's report again, seeking faults.

'What's all this abart staff morals are improving?' blustered Stan, pointing a thick finger at the report.

Vera gave him a withering look.

'If you would read it carefully, Stanley,' she said, 'you would see it says staff *morale* is improving.'

Suitably humbled, Stan Coe looked up at the wall clock and glared at Joseph. 'Are we done then, Vicar? Ah've got a darts match at nine o'clock.'

Joseph asked if there was any other business and closed the meeting.

Stan Coe left hurriedly, Albert Jenkins congratulated me on a good report and Joseph unexpectedly invited everyone back to the vicarage for a nightcap.

Thirty minutes later I found myself sitting with Albert and Joseph and sipping percolated coffee served by Vera in the comfortable lounge of the vicarage. It was good to relax and the tension headache I had experienced during the past few days gradually disappeared. Vera made sure her cats were settled and said goodnight.

'If you will excuse me, gentlemen, I'm going to retire,' she said as she picked up a magazine article that described the Dutch Elm disease that had recently swept through the country and caused Vera much heartache.

As soon as she had left the room, Joseph nodded knowingly at Albert who immediately tiptoed into the kitchen.

'What is it this time, Joseph?' whispered Albert.

'It's a variation on my peapod vintage,' said Joseph quietly as he collected a crate of bottles from behind the cellar door.

'Excellent,' said Albert, putting three glasses on the kitchen table.

Joseph poured three full glasses of the murky pale-yellow liquid from an old wine bottle, from which the label had been removed.

'Just see this as a welcome ceremony,' said Albert with a wink.

In no time at all, Joseph and Albert had emptied a bottle between them whilst I was still sipping my first glass. The molten lava disguised as peapod wine had begun to attack my nervous system and a tiny army was attacking my senses of touch, hearing, smell, taste and sight with small hammers.

It was time to take my leave.

Reluctantly they allowed me to go when I appealed to them that it was not safe to drink and drive and somehow I negotiated the drive home. It was with a sense of amazement that I felt so good the next morning at school. I assumed it was the relief of having completed my Governors' Report.

Vera looked concerned when she came in for her afternoon's work.

'Joseph isn't well,' she said.

'I'm sorry to hear that, Vera,' I said with concern.

'He worked very late with Albert Jenkins last night,' said Vera. 'He's too conscientious for his own good. I think I'll give him a call to check he's all right.'

With that, she telephoned Joseph. She seemed to have to wait a long time before he answered.

It didn't appear that the call helped.

'Stop mumbling, Joseph,' said Vera, 'you simply should not work so hard.'

I had an idea.

'Vera, would you tell Joseph that a doctor said on the radio that if you drink a lot it's the best cure for a headache.'

Vera repeated the message. Then she went white.

'Joseph!' she spluttered and put the telephone down.

'Goodness me,' said Vera, shaking her head in disbelief, 'I just hope my cats didn't hear that.'

Chapter Seven

Old Boilers, Sex and Being Overpaid

The school boiler broke down at 4.00 p.m.

Repair was completed by 10.00 p.m.

81 children on roll.

Extract from the Ragley School Logbook:
Tuesday 20 December 1977

My mother, Margaret, was a tough little Glaswegian with a heart of gold. She shared a flat with her sister, May, in the Headingley district of Leeds and with their grey curly hair, dimpled cheeks and thick spectacles, they looked like two peas in a pod. Each year, since the death of my father in 1972, I had invited them to spend Christmas week with me. After that they both went to join their Scottish clan in Glasgow for a riotous Hogmanay.

It was the last week of term and my mother was her usual chatterbox self when I telephoned her to say I intended to collect them after school.

'Och, it'll be good tay see ye again, son,' she said, shouting down the telephone as if I was deaf. In the background I heard Aunt May utter the dreaded words.

'Tell him he must stay for a wee bite tay eat.'

I reluctantly agreed. Cooking was not their strong suit.

Even so, I had just bought them a Prestige Pressure Cooker from the Co-op as a Christmas present. I thought it was £14.95 well spent but it was wishful thinking.

When I pulled up on the steep cobbled road outside their flat they were standing together and looking out for me, illuminated in the window the way they always were, looking like identical twins and waving like synchronized swimmers.

As I sat in the rocking chair next to the tiny gas fire, I looked at the two, framed black-and-white photographs on the mantelpiece. The first was dated 1943 and showed my father in his petty officer's uniform standing alongside my mother, then a pretty nineteen-year-old munitions worker in a Glasgow factory. The second was of my father in his smart naval uniform with his familiar smile and black wavy Errol Flynn hair.

In 1942, at a Christmas dance in Glasgow, my mother had met John William Sheffield, a Yorkshireman on leave and looking for some warmth and peace after the horrors of war. The previous year he had served on the HMS *Prince of Wales* when, on 24 May 1941, with the ill-fated HMS *Hood*, it had engaged the mighty German battleship *Bismarck*. HMS *Prince of Wales* was damaged but scored three hits on the *Bismarck*.

My father spoke little of the war but I remember one Boxing Day family gathering in 1955. We sat round the coal fire and all the grown-ups were telling stories of the war. My father was encouraged to 'open up' and told the chilling tale of the sinking of HMS *Prince of Wales* on 10 December 1941 by Japanese aircraft. He described how he leaped into the South China Sea as the great battleship sank. His life jacket had a flashing light on it and it was this that saved him after many hours in the water.

He also recalled that Prime Minister Sir Winston Churchill was a passenger on HMS *Prince of Wales* on his journey to Newfoundland for the Atlantic Treaty Conference with the American President Roosevelt. That apart, he spoke little of the war and never claimed his medals.

I was born in St James's Hospital, Leeds, in 1945 on the day the war ended. From that day, all I ever knew was encouragement from my mother. She saw education as the passport to a fulfilling life and encouraged me to work hard at school. My headship almost seemed like a gift to her, a way of saying thank you. If only for her sake, it was an opportunity I was not going to waste.

The smell of burning from the kitchen brought me swiftly back to the present. Margaret had cremated a couple of teacakes and was scraping them vigorously over the sink. Meanwhile, May had put on her blue Glasgow Rangers apron and had reheated some soup that both looked and smelled like emulsion paint.

As always, they both chattered continuously but because my mother was deaf in her left ear and May was deaf in her right ear, conversations did not always follow a logical path.

'Are ye looking forward tay y'Christmas holiday?' shouted May.

'When do you start?' asked Margaret.

'They're in the cupboard,' said May.

'What's in the cupboard?' I asked.

'The jam tarts,' said May.

'What did you say?' asked Margaret.

'The twenty-first of December,' I replied.

'What do you remember?' said Margaret.

'Well, ye put them there this morning,' said May.

And so it went on.

I ate all the supper, for I knew it would upset them if I didn't. Then I packed their cases in my car and drove off to Bilbo Cottage. Margaret and May loved my new home and to my relief set to in the kitchen.

'Och aye, it's like Fred Karno's in here,' said Margaret, opening and closing the cupboard doors.

May looked around at the jumble of pans and recalled my father's lack of organization in a kitchen.

'Y'the perfect epiphany of y'father,' said May, whose vocabulary occasionally stretched the imagination.

I left them to it and prepared my work for the next day at school.

The following morning my mother had prepared some porridge for my breakfast. It had the consistency of quick-drying cement but a cup of tea washed it down and I kissed her on the cheek and reminded her that I had a busy day, with a meeting after school.

'Aboot time y'had a nice wee lassie tay help ye with all this,' said Margaret hopefully as she surveyed the cluttered kitchen. It was a regular theme and I had heard hints like this on many occasions. I didn't see Beth Henderson as the domesticated type but thought it would be fun finding out. With this thought and the porridge to warm me I grabbed my scarf and opened the front door.

'Don't worry about my tea, Mam,' I said as I left the house and stepped out onto the frozen driveway. 'I have a meeting after school to make final preparations for the Christmas Party.'

One thing I quickly learned as a headmaster was that you never really knew what was in store when you walked through the school gates each morning. The last thing I expected after my staff meeting at the end of school was to be lying on my back on the concrete floor of the school boiler house. It was the final straw.

The bitter sleet of a freezing December gusted through the open doorway of the boiler house and stung my raw cheeks.

'I hate boilers!' I cried.

I was chilled to the bone and the old potato sack beneath my shoulders was crusted with ice.

'I hate boilers,' I shouted, 'particularly old boilers!'

Fatigue had stripped away the last vestige of resistance and a rasping cough ripped from my aching throat. Double pneumonia seemed just around the corner. Surely this wasn't part of a headmaster's job, I thought.

'Nearly there, Jack. Just 'old that light steady,' gasped Jim the Boiler Man. 'One more turn an' she'll be as good as new.'

I gripped the frozen metal of the torch a little tighter and peered into the arc of flickering yellow light.

Jim was a little grease monkey of a man and his oil-smeared face broke into a startling white-toothed grin as the last giant nut was locked into place. He sighed with satisfaction and stroked the black oven doors with obvious affection. Jim really loved boilers.

'Well, you can 'ave y'Christmas party after all,' he announced cheerily. 'Tell the kids Father Christmas came early an' fixed it for 'em.'

A fit of coughing left me in convulsions. The torch clattered to the concrete floor and the light finally gave out. I uttered a silent curse. I was all in and I knew it. It was nearly fourteen hours since I'd walked into school that morning but it felt like half a lifetime. I was also blackened, sweaty and filthy. No one had mentioned this at my interview. The school's central heating system in the late 1970s didn't appear to have changed much since the 1870s.

Jim had travelled over from Harrogate to answer my emergency call. At the end of the school day the boiler had rumbled to a halt with a bronchitic cough and the temperature had dropped like a stone. The following day was the school Christmas Party and without heat we should have to close the school. Prompt action was required to avoid the prospect of a lot of very unhappy children. Jim had come to the rescue but had required an assistant.

'Thanks, Jim,' I said, 'you're a lifesaver. Come into the staff-room and I'll brew some tea.'

Jim stroked his stubbly chin. 'I'd rather 'ave a bevvy

in The Oak. C'mon, Jack, we've earned one.'

As the boiler hummed back into life, Jim loaded up his van and I locked the school doors. A few flakes of snow began to fall as we drove out in convoy through the wrought-iron gates and around the village green to the car park outside the welcoming orange lights of The Oak. I was tired, hungry and thirsty and I trudged in behind Jim with the heavy-booted gait of a blacksmith's apprentice. Squeezing between two burly, red-faced farmers I thrust some money towards Don, the big, raw-boned barman.

'Two pints of Chestnut, please, Don, and two meat pies,' I shouted over the hubbub of conversation.

Don the landlord towered over me from the other side of the bar. It was a matter of conjecture whether his huge biceps had developed because of his prowess as an amateur wrestler or merely by pulling countless pints.

'Been cleaning chimneys, Mr Sheffield?' asked Don as he placed the frothing glasses of rich, dark mild beer on the bar. I looked at my reflection in the mirror behind the milk stout and bottled shandy. Jim and I looked as if we were about to audition for *The Black and White Minstrels*.

'Almost, Don,' I replied, 'just a bit of boiler trouble.'

'I know what you mean.' He grinned and winked at his wife, Sheila, who pressed her ample frame towards him and dug an elbow in his ribs.

She caught my eye and whispered something that was lost in the chatter around the bar. I leaned towards her expecting some pearl of wisdom or the latest gossip.

She smelled like a perfume factory as her lacquered hair brushed against my face.

'I wonder if I can have a word with you about sex, Mr Sheffield?' she asked.

'Pardon?'

'Sex, Mr Sheffield, y'know, birds 'n bees an' all that.'

Surely I was imagining this.

'Yes, but I don't quite follow . . .' I mumbled.

I looked towards her husband's bulging form that was fortunately out of earshot.

'When are you going t'give some lessons on it?' she persisted. ''Cause if you don't ah'll have t'do it m'self.'

My brain refused to function. I was too tired to work this one out. She was speaking, I was hearing but I couldn't understand a word.

'What exactly is it you want, Mrs Bradshaw?' I asked.

Two beer mats were irretrievably pinned beneath her green lurex sweater as she pressed her astonishing cleavage even further over the bar and looked at me imploringly. I could feel myself beginning to sweat.

'Our Claire's been asking questions, y'know about babies 'n things an' growing up 'n suchlike. Don's a great useless lump 'n I'm not sure 'ow t'start. So, I was wondering if you were going to teach 'em at school.'

Relief washed over me. 'Oh, I see, er yes, we do have a series of talks by the school nurse coming up early next year. You'll be invited to attend.'

Sheila looked pleased.

'Thank you, Mr Sheffield, it's always worried me 'as sex.'

Looking at her voluptuous proportions I found that hard to believe. But it was another problem solved in a day of problems and I was happy.

The warmth of the taproom had softened the hard edge of my fatigue and the mild beer coursed through my veins like a sleeping draught. Jim was deep in conversation with the two farmers about his favourite subject, boilers. So I merely sank into the luxury of personal reflection and stared mistily at the swimming kaleidoscope of coloured bottles. I was only a day away from completing my first term as headmaster of Ragley Primary School.

So much had happened . . . so many experiences.

Memories flooded back as my glass was refilled.

A sharp tug on my coat sleeve brought me back to earth. I looked up into the crimson face of Stan Coe, one of the two farmers propping up the bar. He eyed me blearily.

'I wus jus' telling Tom 'ere about you teachers being overpaid. You only work a twenty-hour week an' we 'ave to pay 'igh rates t'keep you in comfort,' he bellowed.

This was a familiar argument and one I had heard many times. The only problem with Mr Coe was that he was deadly serious. He also weighed about sixteen stones and had just downed his fifth pint.

'We probably do a lot of work you're not aware of, Mr Coe,' I replied as tactfully as possible.

'Like supping at quart' to eleven,' he countered triumphantly.

'An' another thing, this 'ere library y'want t'build is a

waste of time an' money. When I was at school we 'ad no need of such fancy things,' he continued.

'Times change, Mr Coe,' I said softly.

'Aye, ah've noticed,' he answered gruffly. 'You want to teach 'em some manners at that there school o' yours. Kids today are all bloody ignorant.'

Don's cry of 'Time, gentlemen please' gave me an excuse for a quick exit and a cessation of hostilities with the determined Mr Coe.

Heavy flakes of snow were beginning to settle as Jim and I trudged outside. The village was being transformed. The pantile roofs were etched with wavy, white snow patterns and stood out sharp and clean against a heavy, grey sky that promised more snow.

I paused momentarily to stare at the ominous skyscape. The vast skies over the plain of York were always a joy, the crimson nights of summer, the purple sunsets of autumn and the awesome, black expanse on a winter's night. It was good to dwell in my private and peaceful oasis and contemplate the sheer massive splendour of the snowy panorama.

The slamming of Jim's van door shattered the silence. I shouted goodnight to him and three carefully negotiated miles later I arrived back in Kirkby Steepleton village outside my home. The fast-falling snow muffled the slamming of the garage door and a mini-snowdrift had already covered the empty milk bottles on the doorstep as I stumbled inside. The house was still and quiet and there was no sign of Margaret and May. I tiptoed upstairs and had just reached the landing when my mother appeared. With her grey hair, hot water bottle and Wee Willie Winkie nightgown she looked like a Scottish version of Marley's Ghost.

'Och, it's late, Jack. Are ye alreet?' she asked.

'Hello, Mam, don't worry. There were a few problems at school,' I replied and gave her a hug.

'What sort of problems?' she asked. 'Wee ones ah hope.'

I reflected on the events since the end of the school day.

'Old boilers, sex and being overpaid,' I replied a little gruffly and made a quick exit into my room. The bedroom was freezing and arctic draughts whistled through the small window I had left open that morning. My hands and feet had lost all feeling as I slipped into bed. Within seconds my eyes were closing and sleep took over my tired brain. Suddenly, a shrill Scottish voice penetrated the stillness. 'Jack, Jack!'

I sat up quickly.

'Yes, Mam, what is it?' I shouted back.

'But you're not overpaid!' came the reply.

Soon there was silence apart from the sound of the wind blowing snowflakes against the window. I smiled, snuggled under the sheets and reflected that a headmaster's greatest asset is an understanding mother.

Chapter Eight

The Best Christmas Present in the World

All children attended the Christmas Party in spite of a very heavy snowfall. The delay in receiving records from previous schools was discussed with the Education Office.

Extract from the Ragley School Logbook:
Wednesday 21 December 1977

The alarm was ringing.

It penetrated the layers of sleep like a dentist's drill. My attempts to stop it without having to open my eyes had failed. There was nothing else for it. I would have to face the new day.

The windows were covered with a frozen tracery of feather-like, curve-stitching patterns and I peered through them at the white world beyond. The snow was still falling and not a sound of traffic could be heard. That could only mean that Deke Ramsbottom's council snowplough had not reached Kirkby Steepleton and we were cut off. A long walk was in store and it was the day of the Christmas Party!

My worst fears were realized when I went downstairs. A deep drift of snow curved gracefully up to the front door and any attempt to open the heavy wooden garage door was out of question. In any case, my Morris Minor Traveller would not have managed these severe conditions.

I pulled on my thickest socks, laced up my walking boots, grabbed a shovel and cleared a pathway from the front door of the cottage to the gate. Margaret and May were in the kitchen and had prepared a large bowl of hot porridge for me. It was laced with golden syrup and I finished it quickly. Ten minutes later, wrapped in my duffel coat, college scarf and gloves, I set off.

'Good luck, Jack,' yelled my mother from the doorway, 'ring me when y'get t'school.'

Just out of Kirkby Steepleton I reached virgin snow and felt the old childhood thrill of making the first footprints. It always seemed incredible that one night of snow could transform everyday scenery into such weird, alien shapes. A white desert stretched out in front of me and the back road to Ragley village was just a scooped channel in the snowscape ahead. Hedgerows had become mini-cliffs and only the spiky crowns of cow parsley stabbed through the smooth crust of snow.

The reflected light hurt my eyes and I pulled my woolly hat further down to reduce the glare. By the time I reached the Ragley road, I realized a hard slog was ahead. The snow was already over knee-deep and I had almost three miles to go. I tightened my college scarf around my head, hunched my shoulders and pressed forward through the snow.

After two miles I was a walking snowman and a dull, incessant rumbling in my ears was becoming gradually more disconcerting. I finally paused to draw breath. Loosening my thick scarf I was suddenly aware of a monstrous roaring noise immediately behind me. It sounded like an avalanche! I spun round to see an enormous snowplough only yards away and slicing towards me like the prow of a ship. With self-preservation the spur, I leaped sideways into the snow-bank that filled the ditch to my right. The snow-plough crunched to a halt alongside.

'Nah then, ah've been following thee since Roseberry 'ill.'

It was Deke Ramsbottom, ruddy face wreathed in smiles and collarless shirt flapping open at the neck in spite of the biting wind and gusting snow.

I was too breathless to reply.

'C'mon, Mr 'eadteacher, jump up else tha'll be ower late f'school,' he shouted.

Deke was clearly highly amused and my neat dive into the snow-filled ditch was obviously forming the basis for another of his famous stories. I could see him now in the taproom of The Oak describing my plight. I jumped up into the cab and finally arrived at school in grand style just before nine o'clock. A crowd of waving children filing into school greeted us like conquering heroes and I clambered down like a returning astronaut.

Anne Grainger was busy on the telephone in the office.

'Yes, we are open, Mrs Dudley-Palmer. The boiler has been repaired and the party is still on,' she explained.

Anne had compiled a long list on her spiral-bound notebook and was coping with a difficult morning in her usual unflappable style. She possessed the remarkable gift of patience, an asset to anyone involved in caring for young children.

'Jack!' shouted Anne in surprise, replacing the receiver. 'How on earth did you manage to get here?'

I shook the droplets of snow from my scarf.

'Would you believe a snowplough, Anne?'

She grinned and revealed that infectious sense of humour that bubbled just beneath the surface of her sober, schoolma'am appearance. I looked over her shoulder at the list of names.

'What's the situation, Anne?'

Anne glanced down at her notes.

'Seventy-two have arrived and six are on their way. Theresa Buttle and Elisabeth Amelia Dudley-Palmer are expected to be here by party time and one is unaccounted for. That's Debbie Bryant, the new girl who arrived last week. They're not on the phone. That adds up to eighty-one.'

I pondered for a moment. A picture of a nervous little eight-year-old girl with a bruise on the back of her skinny little arm flashed across my mind.

'Thanks, Anne. I'll try to find out about Debbie. I don't want her to miss the party if I can help it. What about the rest of the staff?'

'Well, living in the village, everyone made it. Sally's taking assembly and Jo's checking the jellies.'

The strains of 'Morning Has Broken' filtered through from the school hall and the slam of a fridge door in the kitchen confirmed this arrangement.

'Thanks, Anne, well done. Any other messages?'

'Only another priceless letter from Mrs Buttle.'

Mrs Buttle was our favourite letter writer. The strange assortment of ailments and allergies that affected her many children was a constant source of amazement. But it was her original writing style, totally devoid of grammatical accuracy and correct spelling that made her letters collector's items. I looked at the crumpled piece of paper, obviously torn from a child's exercise book. It read simply, in a scrawled infant script:

> Dear Sir. Plese excus Theresa from scool. She hasent come cos she is in pane under the doctor.
>
> Yours truly,
> Betty Buttle

'Shall I add it to the collection?' asked Anne.

'Yes please,' I replied, 'and can you give me Debbie Bryant's address? I'll call round during lunch break and see if she's coming.'

I put Anne's scribbled note in my pocket and walked into assembly just as prayers had been completed.

Once again I revelled in the happy, family atmosphere that existed in our school assemblies. Our school was small enough for everyone to know everyone else and ten-year-olds sat alongside rising five-year-olds. If anyone had a special piece of news everyone listened respectfully and made appropriate observations. The children were so excited at the prospect of our party afternoon and the deep snow yet to be explored on the school field.

Little Tony Ackroyd was defiantly pursuing a point.

'But you can build a left-handed igloo. I saw it on TV.'

'Well, perhaps we can try to build one during morning playtime,' I suggested.

'I heard shouting last night,' exclaimed Anita, her hand waving in the air for attention.

'Where was that?' I asked.

'Next door,' said Anita. 'That's Debbie Bryant's house.'

Concerned, I probed further. 'Have you seen Debbie this morning, Anita?'

'No, Mr Sheffield, the house was all closed and the curtains were shut when I came to school.'

I hardly heard Sarah Louise Tait telling everyone about how she taught her rabbit, Nibbles, to high jump, or the children filing back into their classrooms. I thought back to my brief encounter with Debbie and her father.

Mr Bryant had arrived a short while ago and moved into rented accommodation on the edge of Ragley. He looked a sorry figure with a pale, sallow complexion and the creased brow of a worried man. His wife was unable to come into school as she was a sales representative for Avon cosmetics and was out at work. He was unemployed but was hopeful of finding a job as a wagon driver in York. The little girl, Debbie, was quiet throughout our brief interview and clung to her father's jacket sleeve. Yesterday, she had arrived with a large purplish bruise on her arm and not a particularly convincing explanation of how it happened. In spite of persistent telephone calls from Vera, her school records had not yet arrived from her previous education authority. I made a mental note to discuss the matter further with Roy Davidson, our Education Welfare Officer, when he made his weekly visit to school.

Lunchtime couldn't come quickly enough for me. Midst the mounting excitement and party preparations, my thoughts were elsewhere. I couldn't get Debbie off my mind. I decided to miss lunch, leave Anne in charge, and visit Debbie's home in order to satisfy my curiosity. I had to know if anything had happened to the girl and if I should have acted more positively to her bruised arm.

As I crunched my way down the school drive, deep in thought, a large shiny Mercedes purred into the gateway. It was Mrs Dudley-Palmer, by far the richest lady in the neighbourhood. Sadly, she went to great pains to make sure that everyone was aware of it. She was sending her daughter, Elisabeth Amelia, to our state school until, at the age of eight, she was old enough to attend a local private school. Mrs Dudley-Palmer obviously felt she was doing us a great favour by sending her daughter to our humble seat of learning.

She beckoned me over to the car window as Elisabeth Amelia Dudley-Palmer scuttled over to school in her expensive fur boots.

'Ah, Mr Sheffield, I decided to bring my Elisabeth to your party as I have important business this afternoon. I'm going to buy her a horse at the Thirkby sale for a Christmas present. It's a secret, of course, though she knows I'm buying her something. I wanted to get her the best possible present and this will be it. As I shall not be back until around five, I assume she will be allowed to stay at school until I pick her up?'

I tried not to let my irritation show.

'I suppose so, Mrs Dudley-Palmer. The staff will be clearing up after the party so someone will keep an eye on her.'

'Also, as a special favour,' she paused to let this sink in, 'could you please ensure that Elisabeth wins one of the games? She gets so unhappy when she loses.'

'I'm afraid not, Mrs Dudley-Palmer,' I said firmly. 'In any case, there are no special prizes for games and we have simple gifts for all the children at the end.'

'Oh, how unfortunate, Mr Sheffield.' She obviously disapproved of my methods. 'Good afternoon.'

The conversation was terminated abruptly and the electrically operated window narrowly missed my nose as it slid smoothly shut. As the car eased its way into the road, I realized that Mrs Dudley-Palmer was going my way.

The Bryants' house looked deserted as I approached but when I knocked I heard a shuffle of feet from within. The door opened and there stood Mr Bryant, unshaven and deathly pale, and wearing a threadbare dressing gown. His eyes were red-rimmed and watery and the hand that held the door trembled slightly. He did not recognize me.

'Are you the Welfare?' he asked weakly.

'No, Mr Bryant, I'm Jack Sheffield from the village school. I was wondering if Debbie was coming to the Christmas party.'

Recognition slowly dawned on his haggard face.

'You'd better come in,' he said.

I stepped inside the gloomy kitchen. Unwashed crockery filled the sink and empty beer cans were scattered on the Formica table.

Mr Bryant sat down and put his head in his hands.

'Where's Debbie, Mr Bryant? Is she at home?' I asked.

'No,' he mumbled, staring blankly at the table and running his bony fingers through the greying streaks in his hair.

'She's with her mother. They left this morning.'

I looked at him, weighing the situation.

'I heard there was some shouting last night.'

He looked as if he was about to cry. 'That was me,' he said.

There was a long pause as we both tried to find the right words.

I sat down beside him.

'Do you want to talk?' I asked quietly.

For the next twenty minutes, Stephen Bryant opened his heart. Simply the act of sharing his anguish seemed to ease the pain reflected in his eyes. The tension that stretched taut the muscles in his neck appeared to slacken and he relaxed with the release of confidences. He had fought a recurring struggle with the pressures of unemployment. Moving into this derelict property had told on him. He said he felt a sense of shame that he could not support his wife and daughter. His wife was working long hours to supplement their meagre income.

Their problems had reached crisis point the evening before last when Debbie had fallen on the broken stairwell, causing her to cry and his wife to shout at him in frustration. A fierce argument followed. The next morning his wife had left for work still deeply upset and Debbie had left quietly for school nursing a bruised arm. He had spent the morning full of remorse and had finally resorted to drinking what alcohol was left in the house. Another night of arguments with his wife had followed, which had only been brought to a halt when they heard Debbie crying. Husband and wife had not spoken since.

'Just look at this place,' he said, as if noticing the untidy state of the house for the first time. 'No trimmings, no presents, not even a tree.'

He looked me in the eyes for the first time.

'Thanks for listening,' he said with a new determination. 'Don't worry; I'll be all right. I'd better start clearing up before they come back.'

I stood up and buttoned my duffel coat.

'I'll call back after school if you like.'

He opened the door to let me out.

'Thanks,' he said and then looked thoughtful. 'I'll manage. I just hope I haven't lost them.'

Back in school, a smart woman in her mid-thirties was waiting for me in the entrance hall. Debbie Bryant, in a printed cotton party dress, was holding her hand and staring in wonderment at the colourful Christmas tree.

'Isn't it lovely, Mummy?' said Debbie.

'Yes, darling, it's just like you said it was,' said Mrs Bryant.

'Debbie made lots of decorations for it,' I joined in.

Mrs Bryant smiled at me. Her red eyes revealed recent tears.

'Hello, Mr Sheffield. I'm Barbara Bryant, Debbie's mother. I'm sorry she's late for school. We've had some difficulties and she was a bit upset. I thought she better stay with me this morning but she was so keen to come to the party. I couldn't disappoint her, so I took her to York to get a party dress. I hope you don't mind.'

I understood why and I also knew it would have been difficult for her to afford.

'No, I don't mind at all,' I said, weighing up the moment. 'I wondered if we might have a brief word in the office before you go, Mrs Bryant?' I asked.

I bent down and smiled at Debbie. 'And I bet Debbie would like to join her class in the party preparations.'

Debbie almost jumped for joy. Then she gave her mother a hug and ran off to her classroom.

Mrs Bryant, like her husband, welcomed the opportunity to talk. She told me of her problems and I related my lunchtime conversation with her husband.

'He needs to get his confidence back,' she said.

There was a long silence.

'He needs you, Mrs Bryant,' I said simply.

She sighed and nodded.

'I know,' she whispered almost to herself, 'I know.'

The sounds of children entering the hall for the party games filtered through the door.

With a new determination, she stood up.

'I know you're a very busy man, Mr Sheffield, and I thank you for your time.'

'Are you going home?' I asked.

She smiled gently. 'Yes, I am. I'm going home.'

For the next two hours I was in the midst of dancing, cheering and balloon-bursting children while a posse of mums prepared a superb party tea. When the last of the jelly and ice cream had disappeared we finished up singing Christmas carols in the hall. Mothers arrived and tired children slowly dispersed, each clutching a Christmas card, a balloon on a string and a paper bag of small gifts from the staff.

It was when I saw Debbie Bryant staring once again at the Christmas tree that the idea struck me. As her mother helped her into her coat the coloured lights reflected in the little girl's shining eyes.

Ten minutes later I carried a mountain of crockery into the kitchen. Anne, Jo and Shirley were putting on aprons.

'Anne, we've no plans for the Christmas tree, have we?' I asked.

'No, Jack, but it needs to come down soon before school is cleared for Ruby's Christmas cleaning. Why do you ask?'

'I thought I'd take it round to the Bryants' house. They need some Christmas spirit at the moment.'

Elisabeth Amelia Dudley-Palmer proved most adept at helping me remove the lights and baubles and these were put safely in a box. Then she went happily to scrape jelly off plates in the kitchen, a chore she was never permitted to enjoy at home.

With the box under one arm and the tree dragging behind, I walked through the darkness to the Bryants' house. Christmas lights illuminated the windows of all the houses except Debbie's home, where chinks of light could just be seen behind the closed curtains.

Mrs Bryant opened the door.

'Come in, Mr Sheffield, what a nice surprise.'

The strain had gone from her face and I stepped into the sparse but tidy kitchen. The smell of cooking was rich and appetizing. Mr Bryant came in holding Debbie's hand. He was clean-shaven and looked greatly recovered. 'We had to clear out the school entrance and it seemed a pity to throw out such a lovely tree,' I explained and stepped to one side so that the tree was visible in the doorway.

For a moment I thought he was going to cry but he just picked up Debbie and held her very tight. The little girl spoke for all of them. 'Oh, lovely, can we decorate it tonight please, Daddy?'

Mrs Bryant took the box from me and looked up at her husband.

'Of course, darling, we can all help,' she said, smiling.

I looked at the three of them. They were a family again.

As I left, Mr Bryant stepped out onto the snowy footpath.

'Thanks for coming,' he said, 'and don't worry about us. We'll make out.'

As an afterthought, he smiled and stretched out his hand to shake mine. 'Merry Christmas,' he said.

'Merry Christmas, and good luck,' I replied.

Good luck was indeed to come his way although he did not know it then.

In early January, Mr Bryant got a driving job in York

and the family prospered. They were soon to become one of the most cheerful and popular families in the village.

Back at school, a familiar Mercedes was waiting in the car park. A complacent and portly Mrs Dudley-Palmer was just about to leave after collecting Elisabeth Amelia.

'Ah, Mr Sheffield, you will be pleased to know my business was completed successfully,' she said.

I recalled the expensive Christmas present.

'What have you bought, Mummy?' asked a little voice from the back seat.

With a self-satisfied grin, Mrs Dudley-Palmer replied, loud enough for me to hear, 'You'll see, my dear. It's the very best Christmas present in the world.'

Snow began to fall again and settle on my shoulders as I watched the bright red lights of the Mercedes move slowly down the drive. I shook my head slowly as I reflected on Mrs Dudley-Palmer's final words. She was quite wrong, of course.

Debbie Bryant's Christmas present was worth much, much more.

Her gift was priceless for she knew she had the love of her father and mother.

Chapter Nine

Snow White and the Six Dwarfs

30 children from all classes will be supporting the annual Ragley village pantomime on 31 December.

Extract from the Ragley School Logbook: Thursday 22 December 1977

'Happy's upset,' said Sally Pringle.

She pointed her Wicked Queen's wand at a group of six-year-olds clustered around their mothers.

'Look at Grumpy,' said Anne, 'he's delighted.'

'It's mumps!' said Sally.

'Who's got mumps?' I asked.

'Happy's got a fever and his glands are swollen,' explained Anne, 'and Grumpy's pleased because he knows everybody's lines off by heart and he's going to play both parts.'

It was five o'clock on New Year's Eve and the village hall was a hive of activity. The annual pantomime was only two hours away and another crisis had struck.

'So what you're saying is, we're a dwarf short,' I added lamely. With some relief, I recalled that I had mumps when I was a child.

'I suppose it's too late to get a replacement,' said Sally as she donned her queen's crown, picked up the hem of her flowing black cape and set off backstage.

A large lady wearing a flowing kaftan and a bright red headband that held back her alarmingly frizzy hair burst into the conversation.

'Well, they'll just have to keep moving around to confuse the audience,' said Mrs Miles-Humphreys in desperation. As producer of the village pantomime the need for Valium to ease her shredded nerves was increasing with every disaster.

Anne put her arm around Mrs Miles-Humphreys' shoulders and gave her an encouraging hug.

'Don't worry, Felicity,' she said, 'this pantomime will be just as good as all the others.'

Not for the first time I thought Anne would have made a good politician.

'Thank you, my dear. I really don't know what I'd do without your loyal support each year,' said Felicity with a pained expression. Then she hurried off, waving her clipboard in the air at Timothy Pratt, electrician and owner of Pratt's Hardware Emporium. He was on a rickety stepladder, fixing the solitary spotlight to a metal bracket attached to one of the wooden beams.

'More to the left please, Timothy,' shouted Felicity. 'You know, where we had it for *Mother Goose*.'

Timothy Pratt knew exactly where the spotlight had been for every previous pantomime and checked the neat ruled lines that he had drawn each year on the supporting beam.

Tidy Tim, as he was known in the village, was always very precise. Not a single countersunk screw was ever out of place in his shop window and the spouts of his galvanized watering cans were always exactly in line, just like the formation dancers in his favourite television programme, *Come Dancing*.

Tidy Tim had recently paid thirty-five pence to become a member of the Airfix Modellers Club, and when he received the unwelcome call from Mrs Miles-Humphreys he had almost completed his Crusader Mark III Tank to a scale of one to thirty-two.

He nodded morosely and shifted the ancient spotlight precisely two inches to the left. Then he screwed the butterfly nut tightly so the spotlight was fixed exactly at right angles to the beam. Tidy Tim liked right angles. Unfortunately, his sense of humour was even less than that of his elder brother Victor who owned the garage at the bottom of the High Street. Each year he was asked to 'do the lights' and each year he grumbled but eventually turned up on the day to do his bit. He was here because his younger sister, Nora Pratt, was once again the leading lady. 'She's the Pratt with talent,' he boasted regularly to his customers.

Anne picked up a bag of different coloured hats and tunics, along with a handful of white beards.

'So, what were the other pantomimes like?' I whispered in her ear.

'Don't ask, Jack,' said Anne firmly and marched off to help the noisy group of children in her class who were destined to be the slightly diminished band of dwarfs.

John Grainger had explained to me that it was a tradition in Ragley to have a family pantomime in the village hall on New Year's Eve that included children of all ages. It always started at seven o'clock and was followed by a village party that included an old-fashioned singsong around the piano plus a late-night disco.

I had volunteered to arrive early and help erect the scenery. Peter Miles-Humphreys had spent the last month in his garden shed constructing a backdrop to the dwarfs' house. He was now on his hands and knees screwing on the hinged flaps to enable it to stand up. His two sons, ten-year-old Nigel, who was in my class, and seventeen-year-old Rupert, who was studying A-level Drama and Art, were holding the various pieces of plywood in place. Rupert was getting upset.

'My tights are getting laddered, Dad,' he shouted in annoyance.

Rupert had a star part. In fact, he had had a star part every year since his mother became artistic director of the Ragley Amateur Dramatic Society. On this occasion, he was the prince.

'H-Hang on, j-just one m-more s-s-s—' stuttered Mr Miles-Humphreys.

'Screw, Dad,' said Nigel, who was an expert at finishing his father's sentences, usually correctly.

The final screw inserted, Mr Miles-Humphreys stood up to admire his handiwork and Rupert dashed backstage like a frightened stick insect to repair the damage to his bright green tights and to apply some more Leichner 5 and 9 make-up to hide his teenage acne.

I helped father and son to carry the new piece of scenery backstage. Mr Miles-Humphreys pointed to a convenient storage place against the back wall behind the curtains.

'Let's l-l-leave it h-h—' he stuttered.

'Here,' said Nigel confidently.

Mr Miles-Humphreys covered his masterpiece with the curtain.

'We d-don't w-want anyone t-to f-f-f—'

'Forget it,' I added helpfully.

He shook his head and looked imploringly at his son.

'Fall over,' said Nigel with authority.

Mr Miles-Humphreys nodded and forced a smile. This was clearly a stressful time for him. Once again he shook visibly as his wife screeched more instructions from the stage.

'Timothy, Timothy!' she yelled. 'Perhaps you and Mr Sheffield could arrange the seating?'

Two hundred plastic chairs were stacked in an alcove at the back of the hall. I collected a few and began to arrange them in rows. Meanwhile Tidy Tim had taken a stick of chalk and a metal retractable tape measure from the pocket of his brown overall and began to mark an accurate line of white crosses on the floor exactly three feet apart. He frowned in my direction and shook his head, clearly not pleased.

'We need to get the end seats on either side of the central aisle in perfect alignment first, Mr Sheffield,' said Tidy Tim in his monotone voice.

I agreed and hastily rearranged the front row. After a while I gave up as Tidy Tim followed me around making minute adjustments to every single chair. It was clear to me that his talents were wasted in the twentieth century. King Khufu of Egypt would have made him chief architect of the Great Pyramids of Giza and provided an army of assistants who, unlike me, would not have sloped off to Nora's Coffee Shop in the middle of a job.

Tidy Tim looked relieved when I told him I intended to take a break and I left him crouched on his haunches, studying the exact sightline of each row of chairs.

Backstage, I looked for Anne to see if she wanted to join me. She was standing alongside Felicity Miles-Humphreys and both of them were busy applying the finishing touches to Snow White's opening costume.

Nora Pratt put on her hand-stitched Alpine leather corset, looked at her reflection in the full-length mirror and imagined she saw someone who resembled a slim, youthful Julie Andrews standing on an Austrian mountaintop. Felicity Miles-Humphreys looked at the same reflection and saw a fat forty-year-old with too much make-up and hips the size of a forklift truck. She shook her head sadly but knew this was Nora's big night and decided flattery was the best form of deception.

'You look a picture, darling,' said Felicity. 'And the pretty little waistcoat provides the finishing touch.'

Nora had been on the founding committee of the Ragley Amateur Dramatic Society. In consequence, every year she voted herself to be leading lady. Nora had been particularly proud of her Goldilocks, Sleeping Beauty and Cinderella, but she believed this part was easily the best. Fifteen years earlier Nora had hoped that her performances would provide a stepping-stone to the York Amateur Dramatic Society but her inability to sing in key and her short, portly figure had resulted in many failed auditions. In spite of being a non-speaking extra in one episode of *Crossroads*, it was soon obvious that speaking parts would always prove elusive. The vital shortcoming that stunted Nora's theatrical ambitions was her complete inability to pronounce the letter 'R'.

Nora looked anxiously at Felicity.

'Where's Wupert?' asked Nora.

'He's rehearsing in the gents, darling,' said Felicity.

'Tell him to come wight away,' demanded Nora. 'That opening dance woutine is wubbish.'

Anne gave me a wide-eyed stare. It was my cue to depart and I decided to walk across the High Street to Ragley's most popular meeting place.

Nora's Coffee Shop still lived in the sixties with its draughtboard tiled floor and bright red plastic tables, but even though its decor was stuck in a time warp, if you wanted the latest village gossip it was the place to go. The old jukebox in the corner was thumping out a crackly rendition of the Bee Gees singing 'How Deep is Your Love' as I approached the white plastic counter. Curvaceous Dorothy Humpleby, whose ambition was to be a fashion model, served me with a frothy coffee and a thick slab of seed cake. She nodded towards the huge poster behind the counter.

'Are y'going to t'panto, Mr Sheffield?' she asked, fluttering her false eyelashes and selecting a moderately clean teaspoon and fork from the grubby cutlery tray.

I glanced at the blurred photo of Nora Pratt in her Alpine corset and surrounded by a full complement of dwarfs.

'Thank you, Dorothy, yes I am,' I replied. 'I see Nora has the main part.'

'She always 'as, Mr Sheffield,' said Dorothy, fingering her huge earrings with her bright silver-painted false nails. 'She's been singing "Someday My Prince Will Come" since bloody October. Ah'll be glad when it's all over.'

In spite of the poor quality of the food and drink, as usual the place was almost full. I sat down at the nearest table, cleaned my fork on a serviette and began an archaeological exploration of the seed cake that on close inspection appeared well past its best. The bell above the door jingled again and I glanced up. To my surprise, Beth Henderson walked in looking stunning in a light grey overcoat over a white polo neck jumper and a black A-line maxi-length skirt.

I felt the familiar pounding in my chest and was about to wave in acknowledgement when I saw she was not alone. My heart sank when a tall slim blond-haired man in a striped open-necked Van Heusen shirt and a smart charcoal-grey lounge suit held the door open for her. He was the man I had seen walking with her on the city walls. They made a striking couple and looked relaxed together as they placed their order with the gum-chewing Dorothy and found the only remaining table on the far side of the coffee bar. Beth sat with her back to me and was so engrossed in conversation with her handsome companion that she didn't notice me. She had spoken to me once on the telephone since the dramatic cremation of Miss Barrington-Huntley's hat in order to reassure me that I had no need to worry. She had also sent a letter of thanks to the staff plus a few hints on how to improve aspects of our school paper-work. That apart, there had been no contact.

I looked enviously at her stylishly dressed partner and then glanced down at my crumpled duffel coat and sighed. I certainly would have no chance with Beth if I dressed like a protester on a Ban the Bomb march.

At ten minutes to seven they left ahead of me, crossed the road and walked down towards the bottom of the High Street to the village hall. Crowds were gathering outside the entrance and thrusting their fifty-pence admission tickets at Mr Miles-Humphreys who was attempting to tear the tickets in half whilst directing people to their seats.

'On the r-r-r—' said Mr Miles-Humphreys.

'Right,' said Nigel, standing alongside.

I found myself three rows behind Beth and her partner who were still deep in animated conversation. Ruby Smith, much to the dismay of the people sitting directly behind her, was on the front row along with all her family, including her husband Ronnie who had made a special effort to look smart in his Leeds United Supporters Club tie as well as the obligatory bobble hat.

Ronnie was manager of Ragley Rovers, the village football team, and he had persuaded the rest of the team to leave the taproom of The Oak and join in the fun. The huge figure of Dave Robinson, the team captain, led the way, followed as always by his tiny cousin, Malcolm

Robinson. 'Big Dave' and 'Little Malcolm' were both local refuse collectors and had been inseparable friends since their schooldays in Ragley, when Big Dave had always protected his little cousin. They took their seats on the back row with pint pots in hand. The rest of the team sounded well lubricated already.

At seven o'clock the three-piece band struck up a rendition of 'Hi-Ho' and the curtains opened. Big Dave was the first to spot the problem with the numerically challenged band of dwarfs.

'There's only six dwarfs,' he shouted.

'Y'reight there, Dave,' agreed Little Malcolm.

'Ah want a refund,' yelled Kojak, the Bald-Headed Ball Wizard.

'Gerrup there, Malcolm, an' mek up t'numbers,' shouted Stevie 'Supersub' Coleclough, raising his pint tankard in the air.

'Ssshhh!' said Vera Evans, looking over her shoulder from the centre row with a face like thunder. Her brother, Joseph, sitting alongside, went slightly pink with embarrassment and with a fixed stare looked straight ahead.

The pantomime limped along with its uncoordinated dance routines and the audience was generous with its applause. They clapped everything and anything, even when Sneezy and Dopey had to go to the toilet in the middle of one of their songs and the complement of dwarfs was reduced to four. They also cheered and booed vociferously, unfortunately not always in the right places. Snow White was booed when she said, 'Shall I eat this bwight wed apple?' and Sally Pringle, who made a brilliant Wicked Queen, was cheered to the rafters by all the school children every time she appeared.

Sadly, when the prince asked the audience if he should kiss the sleeping Snow White to wake her from her slumbers, the football team, with one united voice, yelled, 'No!' and this received the biggest laugh of the night.

Remarkably, the whole audience showed considerable restraint when Nora Pratt, dressed in a huge ball gown big enough for a five-ring circus, sang 'Someday My Pwince Will Come,' slightly off-key. After the finale came the speeches and both Nora and Felicity Miles-Humphreys were presented with a huge bunch of flowers.

Minutes later it was all change as Big Dave and his footballers rearranged the chairs around the edge of the large hall, parents hurried home with young children, John Grainger and Ronnie Smith began to put up trestle tables for a bar and Clint Ramsbottom, sporting sparkly highlights in his Kevin Keegan permed hair, set up his portable disco.

As I walked out into the cold night air I tried to catch a glimpse of Beth Henderson but she had disappeared into the crowds. Suddenly a familiar voice attracted my attention.

'Jack, Jack, hello again.'

It was Beth with her handsome chaperone.

'Hello, Beth, good to see you again,' I said.

The firm handshake was as I remembered it.

'Did you enjoy the pantomime?' I asked with a grin.

'Yes, *Snow White and the Six Dwarfs* has a certain ring to it, don't you think?' said Beth with a chuckle. 'Wouldn't miss it for the world, would we, David?' She looked up at her elegant companion. 'I try to come every year and the party afterwards is even better. Are you coming?'

'Well, I intended to go,' I said, glancing hesitantly at David.

'Oh, where are my manners?' said Beth. 'Let me introduce my friend, David Senior. He's over from his luxury capitalist flat in Leeds. David, this is Jack Sheffield, the local headmaster from Ragley School.'

We shook hands and he gave me a quizzical stare. I sensed he noticed my reaction when I discovered his relationship to Beth.

'Pleased to meet you, Jack, and take no notice of my little socialist girlfriend,' said David with a slightly arrogant air. 'She has a hang-up about me working for Unilever in Leeds and putting in long hours to improve the company profits, without the benefit of lengthy school holidays,' he added with sarcasm.

Beth looked mildly embarrassed and changed the subject quickly.

'Where are you going now?' asked Beth.

'I thought I'd go to The Oak and then come back for the party,' I replied.

'Then join us, unless you have other plans,' said Beth. 'That's all right with you, isn't it, David?'

He gave a tight-lipped smile and a perfunctory nod.

'Thanks,' I said. 'I'd love to tag along.'

It was with mixed emotions that I walked up the High Street. A huge Christmas tree covered in bright lights had been erected in the centre of the village green and Beth laughed like an excited schoolgirl as we walked beside it.

'Don't you just love this time of year?' she shouted over her shoulder.

As I trudged along behind them, David put his arm around her shoulders. He muttered something about 'profits' and Beth pushed him away in mock irritation.

Ahead of us the bright orange lights of The Royal Oak were a welcome sight but my eyes were fixed on the slim figure of Beth, and I knew there was a hint of envy in my heart as the confident David whisked her smoothly through the doorway.

The pub was heaving and even though Don and Sheila had taken on extra staff, there were queues at the bar. This did not deter the tall, imposing figure of David who ordered drinks in a swift and accomplished manner and managed to drink three 'whisky chasers' in the time Beth and I finished a single drink. I noticed that David began to be belligerent when Beth complained that he was getting too loud. Finally, shortly after ten o'clock, David reluctantly got rather shakily to his feet and the three of us walked back to the village hall.

A memorable night was in store. Old Time dancing was in full swing when we walked in and Old Tommy Piercy was playing the piano. His grandson, Young Tommy, stood alongside, turning the pages of the music. Old Tommy was very proud of the upright Victorian piano that his father had donated to the village hall many years ago. On the underside of the piano lid, within an oval of gold leaf, the name of the makers 'Archibald Ramsden (Limited)' was still visible under the proclamation 'By Royal Appointment'.

'This is proper dancing,' he shouted to me as we passed him on our way to find a group of spare seats. Shirley the Cook was serving coffee and mince pies alongside John Grainger who was doing a roaring trade at the makeshift bar. Vera was soon at my side and insisted on teaching me 'The Dashing White Sergeant' and George and Mary Hardisty guided me through 'The Gay Gordons'. Finally, I plucked up courage to ask Beth for a waltz and David reluctantly let go of her hand and resumed his drinking.

Her hair was soft against my face as the lights gradually dimmed and somehow she managed to avoid my size-eleven feet.

'Is everything all right with you, Beth?' I asked hesitantly.

A moment of sadness passed across her face.

'Sorry, Jack, don't worry. Thanks anyway. David promised to curb his drinking excesses but deep down I know it won't happen.'

She gripped my hands tightly and shook her head.

'I've said too much,' said Beth, almost to herself.

'Please let me help,' I asked.

Beth took a deep breath and with a brave smile she said, 'Don't worry, I'll sort things out.' Then she wandered away, deep in thought.

A short interval was announced whilst the disco was set up and I noticed Beth walking quickly to the back of the hall with David lurching behind her. Whilst I was talking with Vera and Joseph, Anne Grainger tapped me on my shoulder looking concerned.

'Jack, I think Beth Henderson has a problem.'

She nodded towards the main doors where Beth was in animated conversation with David who was clearly the worse for wear. Moments later they both left in a hurry.

'Do you think I ought to see if she's all right?' I asked Anne anxiously.

Anne squeezed my arm and smiled.

'Jack, she might even come back. With luck, she's telling that obnoxious man where to go. He's been acting like a pompous oaf all evening.'

A few minutes later, right on cue, Beth reappeared and sat by the piano.

I walked towards her and she gave me a tired smile.

'Sorry, Jack,' said Beth, 'as you've probably guessed, I've just quit as a member of David's appreciation society. I've put him in a taxi and sent him back to Leeds. That's the last time I'll be embarrassed by his behaviour.'

At that moment the lights dimmed again. Clint Ramsbottom's flickering disco lights illuminated the ceiling like demented traffic lights and the base notes of the Rolling Stones' 'Jumping Jack Flash' made the walls shake.

Beth stood up and grabbed my hand.

'I'd like to dance,' she said with sudden enthusiasm. We suddenly found ourselves in the midst of all the twenty- and thirty-somethings who were trying to 'strut their stuff'. At least that's what Clint Ramsbottom told us we were doing over his squeaky microphone. A wild half-hour ensued culminating in the Beatles' 'Twist and Shout', which almost raised the roof.

'Where do you get all your energy from?' I asked breathlessly as we left the dance floor.

'I am a PE specialist don't forget,' said Beth coyly.

We regained our seats as Deke Ramsbottom grabbed the microphone and announced the raffle.

The tickets were drawn by Ada Cade, Ragley's oldest inhabitant at ninety-one years old, with the help of Vera. Each prize-winner had to walk up to the stage to receive his or her prize and everyone received a raucous ovation. Vera won a bottle of wine, Ruby won six free tennis lessons and Beth won one of the booby prizes, a doll with plastic underpants by the name of Ken. The biggest cheer of the night went to Ronnie Smith who won a free hair-do at Diane's Hair Salon.

At five minutes to midnight, John Grainger helped Clint Ramsbottom to tune in his huge ghetto blaster to the sound of Big Ben. Joseph Evans and I stood on either side of Beth, hand in hand, as we linked up with the huge circle of villagers. We sang 'Auld Lang Syne' and then Big Dave and Little Malcolm pulled the strings of a football net and dozens of coloured balloons tumbled down around us.

Big Ben chimed out twelve o'clock and cries of 'Happy New Year' filled the hall. Couples hugged each other, Joseph Evans shook my hand, and Anne Grainger gave me a kiss on the cheek and wished me good luck.

Suddenly I was face to face with Beth.

I felt awkward and held out my right hand to shake hers.

'Happy New Year, Jack,' she said with a smile that lit up the room.

'Happy New Year, Beth,' I shouted above the din, 'and thanks for a lovely evening.'

Then she stretched up on her tiptoes and kissed me softly on the cheek.

As the balloons bounced off my head, I suddenly thought that 1978 had begun in the most perfect way possible.

Chapter Ten

Genghis Khan and the Keep Fit Club

Refuse collections in 1978 will take place on Mondays. Agreement was reached for the refuse vehicle to use the school driveway during lesson time only.

83 children on roll.

Extract from the Ragley School Logbook:
Monday 9 January 1978

'It's Genghis Khan, Mr Sheffield. He's gone missing!'

It was my first telephone call of the Spring Term and I stared at the receiver.

'Has anybody rung you, 'cause it's been two days now?' asked the frantic caller.

It was someone in a call box because I had heard the beeps as they put their money in.

'Who's speaking please?' I asked.

'It's me, Mr Sheffield, Ronnie, Ruby's husband.'

He sounded really distressed.

'Hello, Ronnie,' I said. 'You'd better explain. What's all this about Genghis Khan?'

'Nowt's been going right f'me lately,' mumbled Ronnie, 'an' now this.'

I looked at the pile of paperwork in the wire tray that Vera had told me I must do at lunchtime. I sighed and made a decision.

'Would you like to call in between twelve and one, Ronnie?' I asked.

There was a pause.

'Will our Ruby be there, Mr Sheffield?' asked Ronnie hesitantly.

'Not until one o'clock when she puts the dining tables and chairs away,' I explained.

There was another pause.

'Ah'll come at twelve o'clock, if that's all right,' said Ronnie. 'Thanks a lot, Mr Sheffield.'

'By the way, Ronnie,' I asked quickly, 'who's Genghis Khan?'

But the line was dead.

At a quarter to twelve Big Dave and Little Malcolm's dustbin wagon crunched over the frozen cobbles as it reversed slowly up the drive for the weekly collection of rubbish. Shirley usually gave them a cup of tea as they parked their wagon out of sight by the kitchen door and took their lunch break.

'Bin men are 'ere,' called out Anita Cuthbertson, looking up from her spelling test. Anita didn't miss a thing. Whilst she had problems with her spelling and had just put three fs in 'photography', she could identify different shades of lipstick at forty paces.

At twelve o'clock the bell rang for school dinner and Anita was collecting the exercise books.

'Mr Smith's 'ere,' said Anita.

I glanced out of the window. Scarecrow-thin Ronnie was walking furtively up the drive, looking left and right. His Leeds United bobble hat seemed to be pulled further down his head than usual. I walked quickly to meet him at the school entrance but Ronnie seemed reluctant to come in so I stepped outside to talk to him.

Vera peered out of the office window.

'Don't forget these letters for signing, Mr Sheffield,' she called out sternly.

'I'm just having a quick word with Ronnie, Vera. I won't be long,' I replied defensively.

'Oh, and Mr Dudley-Palmer said he would like to call in later,' said Vera. 'It's a personal matter, he says.'

She gave me a disgruntled look and closed the window. Vera didn't like me to be distracted from important paperwork except when Beth Henderson rang. Then Vera's mood changed, for she clearly approved of this new liaison.

'She's a delightful young woman, Mr Sheffield,' announced Vera during morning break to a captive audience, 'and you really must try to persuade her to join the church choir. She's a leading member of the New Earswick Operatic Society and has the most wonderful voice.'

The other females on the staff were intrigued that I had 'found someone' and were full of interest. Beth and I had been to the cinema and had enjoyed a meal together since the New Year's Eve party, but in a small village it was difficult not to be noticed. A few tongues had begun to wag, not least in my own staff-room.

But that was furthest from my mind as Ronnie and I strolled round to the back of the school, shivering in the January wind.

'So what can I do to help, Ronnie?' I asked.

'Like ah sed, Mr Sheffield, it's Genghis Khan, 'e's gone,' said Ronnie with a haunted expression.

This was becoming too much to bear.

'Who exactly is Genghis Khan?' I asked.

'Now then, Ronnie.' We both jumped. Big Dave's foghorn voice was unmistakable, even through mouthfuls of cheese sandwich.

''ave y'been caught going round back o' bike sheds again?'

Little Malcolm's head popped round the kitchen door.

'Hiya, Ronnie,' he yelled, 'ah'm sorry about your Genghis. 'ave y'found him yet?'

'Shurrup, Malcolm,' hissed Ronnie, looking at the open kitchen door. 'Ah don't want our Ruby to know he's gone. 'e cost me thirty quid did Genghis an' now she's nagging me for a new three-piece suite.'

'Will somebody please tell me, who is Genghis Khan?' I asked.

'Me champion racing pigeon,' said Ronnie. ''e flew off an' never came back to me loft.'

'Oh, I'm sorry about that, Ronnie, but what is it that you want me to do?' I asked.

'Well 'e's tagged is our Genghis an' ah've put school telephone number on 'is leg,' explained Ronnie. 'Ah'd no choice. Our phone's been cut off an' in t'Easington 'n

District Pigeon Club y'can't race 'em if there's no number. Ah never thought 'e'd go astray. If our Ruby finds out ah put t'school number on his leg she'll kill me.'

Ronnie's head sank onto his chest and he scratched the top of his yellow, blue and white bobble hat in anxiety.

'Don't worry, Ronnie, if someone telephones, I'll let you know straight away.'

'Thanks a lot, Mr Sheffield. I appreciate you 'elping us out,' said Ronnie.

'Just one thing, Ronnie, why did you call him Genghis Khan?' I asked.

'Don't tha' know about Genghis Khan, Mr Sheffield?' asked Big Dave.

'Ah thought a schoolteacher would know about Genghis,' said Little Malcolm. 'Wouldn't y'think so, Dave?'

Dave cuffed him playfully round the ear, causing Malcolm to drop his pork pie on the frozen grass.

''e were reight famous were Genghis,' explained Ronnie. ''e were fust wi' a pigeon post an' 'e used it t'send messages to 'is army.'

'It's a good name fur a champion racer, Ronnie,' said Big Dave.

'T'is that,' agreed Little Malcolm, wiping the frosty mud from his pork pie on the sleeve of his donkey jacket.

'I 'ope 'e comes 'ome soon,' said Ronnie. 'Ah've enough on me plate wi' this constitution I 'ave to write.'

I had a sinking feeling as I asked the obvious question.

'What constitution, Ronnie?'

'It's for a keep fit club for t'football team,' said Ronnie. 'From this year, County Council 'ave stopped t'evening classes so we 'ave t'form a private club afore we can use facilities at the big school. Every new club 'as to 'ave an official constitution.'

'Aye,' said Big Dave, 'an' we're meeting in t'Oak tonight at seven o'clock to write it.'

'Aye, we are,' said Little Malcolm. 'We 'ave t'get fit, 'cause we 'aven't won a game yet.'

'We've drawn two,' said Ronnie defensively. As team manager he was proud of his team.

Big Dave put a giant arm round Ronnie's frail shoulders.

'Don't worry, Ronnie. Me an' Malcolm will see to this concertina thing we 'ave t'write. You go look f'Genghis an' ah'll see yuh in t'pub later.'

Ronnie looked up and smiled weakly at his trusty captain.

'Thanks, Dave,' said Ronnie. 'Ah'll see y'later.'

With a slightly more confident demeanour, Ronnie wandered off and I returned to Vera's paperwork.

Beth telephoned to ask if I would like to meet her later that evening at the New Earswick Folk Hall after the operatic society's rehearsals. I agreed a time and you could have heard a pin drop as Anne, Jo, Sally and Vera gave each other knowing and meaningful looks.

At the end of school we had our weekly staff meeting. A busy year lay ahead. We planned the week in May for the School Camp in the Yorkshire Dales and the date of the Summer Fair in June. We also discussed our contribution towards the special celebration in July of the centenary of the school. Anne suggested a Victorian School Day and Jo and Sally were enthusiastic. Sally said she would get a few parents to help her with costumes and Jo said she would invite some of the oldest inhabitants of the village into school for a coffee morning and arrange for the children to interview them.

The meeting rambled on until well after six o'clock and ended with Anne's stock report, which included the fact that the educational suppliers had delivered twelve pairs of slippers to the school and twelve pairs of football boots to the local retirement home.

We had just finished when there was a tap on the door.

I looked outside into the corridor. There was Ruby tidying the entrance hall in preparation for the first session of the year for the village Brownies.

'Excuse me, Mr Sheffield. Mr Dudley-Palmer's just driven up outside,' said Ruby.

Geoffrey Dudley-Palmer was proud of his Datsun Bluebird Mark II, for which he had just paid the extravagant sum of £2,978.00. Whenever he picked up his daughter, Elisabeth Amelia, he loved to show me its state-of-the-art extras, including reclining front seats, tinted glass, a push-button medium-wave radio and, best of all, a boot interior light. With a roar like an angry lion, Mr Dudley-Palmer gave a final rev of the engine and turned off the ignition.

He walked into the entrance hall with a cage under his arm.

'Hello, old chap,' he said. 'I was surprised when the telephone number turned out to be the school's. Your Genghis Khan somehow found his way into my new pigeon loft. I didn't know you raced pigeons but you have an absolute corker here.'

Ruby's eyes were on stalks. She looked from me to Mr Dudley-Palmer and back to Genghis Khan, contentedly fluttering in his cage.

'Ah know that bird,' she said aghast. 'Ah've seen our Ronnie wi' that pigeon. Ah can tell by t'colour. It's the one he's just bought. 'e said 'e got it cheap.'

Mr Dudley-Palmer looked confused.

'I say,' he said, 'would you consider selling it? It would be a fine addition to my stock.'

'It's a bit complicated,' I stuttered.

'I don't want to haggle, old chap, so how about fifty pounds?' said Mr Dudley-Palmer, reaching for his wallet.

A slow smile crossed Ruby's flushed face as she leaned on her broom.

Quickly, she thrust out her plump hand.

'It's a deal,' she said and the five crisp ten-pound notes disappeared magically into the pocket of her apron.

Mr Dudley-Palmer, delighted with his purchase, roared off into the night and Ruby looked suspiciously at me.

'Wait till I see our Ronnie,' she muttered ominously. 'Y'can't trust men.'

I looked at my watch. It was ten minutes to seven and I had a good idea where I might find Ronnie.

The taproom of The Oak was crowded and dense with cigarette smoke. Big Dave the Goalkeeper squeezed his six-feet-four-inch frame onto the bench seat next to the dartboard and surveyed the room. The darts team reluctantly removed their darts and retreated to the bar. No one ever played darts when Big Dave was sitting that close to the board. A hush gradually descended on the room. Little Malcolm the Midfield Maestro perched next to him like King Lear's clown and unrolled a creased school exercise book from the pocket of his council donkey jacket. He licked a thick pencil-stub as he anticipated the first words of wisdom.

'I propose we 'ave a kitty and them's nearest bar gets pints in,' proclaimed Big Dave.

''ere 'ere,' agreed Little Malcolm.

This first motion was greeted with enthusiastic cheers and everyone put a note or coin into the big ashtray proffered by Norman 'Nutter' Neilson, the hard-tackling full-back, whose nickname apparently derived from the regularity with which he would fell opposing forwards by butting them between the eyes.

'I propose we get this conti, er, constitu-er-ation written up afore we start any serious suppin', else secra'ty'll be kaylied afore we've done,' announced Big Dave.

''ere 'ere,' shouted Little Malcolm, already halfway down his first pint.

''ere 'ere,' chorused the congregation as they settled down for the business ahead. Several conversations broke out at once, suggesting how to write a constitution.

'You've got to name the club for a start off,' shouted

Chris 'Kojak' Wojciechowski, the Bald-Headed Ball-Wizard.

'That's right, that's 'ow my wife's Monday Circle started off when they wrote their constitution,' mumbled Stevie 'Supersub' Coleclough, the number twelve who always turned up, even for away games.

Don the Barman looked up from behind the pumps. 'What were you doing at Monday Circle, Stevie, male striptease?'

Stevie coloured slightly. 'Was I hellus like? I was stuck in t'kitchen wi' dog, listening to them bloody giggling an' yakking all night.'

'C'mon, let's get this thing written,' shouted Big Dave. 'It's more like frigging constipation than constitution, all bloody talk 'n no action!'

'Horder, please, let's 'ave horder!' yelled Little Malcolm, eager to show solidarity.

Big Dave rose to his feet, glass of ale in one goal-keeper fist, his eyes searching the oak beams for inspiration. A hush fell on the whole taproom and the silence was just becoming unbearably long when he announced in his best toastmaster voice, 'Number One!'

Little Malcolm jotted this down, licked his pencil then looked up, full of eager anticipation.

Big Dave coughed affectedly. 'This club shall be known as the Ragley Village Men's Keep Fit Club.'

Little Malcolm scribbled furiously as the audience considered this opening declaration.

'Hold on, not so fast. Y'can't say that nowadays,' declared Kojak knowingly.

'How come?' demanded Big Dave, annoyed at the intervention.

'Y'can't say MEN'S club, 'cause of that sex act,' explained Kojak, bald head glistening sweatily.

'Sex act?' asked Big Dave.

'Yes, that 1975 sex incrimination act,' continued Kojak, his status growing by the second.

'Discrimination, y'mean,' corrected Supersub who boasted a Certificate of Secondary Education in English Language. 'It's t'make women think they're equal to us men.'

There was a stunned silence as if everyone had been told the earth really was flat. Clint Ramsbottom, farm labourer and local hippie, shook his Kevin Keegan look-alike hair-do in despair.

'That's really heavy, man,' he said.

Clint's big brother, Shane, who was also proud to be named after one of his mother's favourite American cowboys, put his arm around Clint to console him. Shane, like his brother, was a farm labourer but with more muscles.

'Don't worry, Nancy,' said Shane affectionately. He called his brother 'Nancy' ever since Clint had been to Diane's Hair Salon for his perm. As Shane had fists like coal shovels Clint had not complained.

But it was Big Dave who showed true leadership by recovering first.

'All right, all right, ah know it's 'ard to tek in,' he said. 'Now listen in.'

Once again, all eyes were on the giant goalkeeper.

'Number one,' continued Big Dave. 'This club shall

be known as the Ragley Village Keep Fit Club.'

Little Malcolm firmly crossed out 'Men's'.

'But 'ow y'gonna keep women out?' persisted Kojak. 'They might apply to be members and then 'ow y'gonna put 'em off?'

Big Dave drank deeply, considering the problem. Suddenly he slammed down his empty glass in triumph.

'I know what!' he cried.

Little Malcolm looked up with a start.

'Number One!' shouted Big Dave with a self-satisfied grin. 'This club shall be known as the Ragley Village Keep Fit Club and all members must use the same showers!'

Little Malcolm scribbled again and a loud chorus of cheers welcomed Big Dave's inspired addition. Only Kojak did not look happy. He scratched his bald pate thoughtfully until an idea struck him. 'Ah, but wait on,' he said, 'what about Dorothy Humpleby?'

'Who the 'ell's Dorothy Humpleby?' someone shouted from the back.

'She 'elps out at Nora's coffee bar,' explained the ageing ball-wizard, 'an' she would join just for t'showers.'

'If she joins so will I,' shouted Don the Barman.

'Whashabout your Sheila, I'll shcrub 'er back anytime,' added a drunken voice from the back.

Sheila giggled and made a quick exit to the lounge bar. Big Dave supped on his second pint thoughtfully until, undeterred, he produced yet another ace.

'NUMBER ONE!' A hush settled on the throng.

Big Dave took a deep breath. 'This club shall be known as the Ragley Village Keep Fit Club and all members must use the same showers, AND . . . each member must pass a test of physical fitness.'

''ere 'ere,' cried Little Malcolm.

Big Dave sat down with a self-satisfied grin on his stubbly face.

''old on, 'old on,' persisted Kojak. 'Not so fast. What about that Virginia what gives riding lessons?'

'Thash a funny virgin,' shouted Drunken Voice.

'Y'know,' continued Kojak, disregarding the laughter from the back, 'that Virginia with the big thighs what works at the riding school. She's fitter than anybody 'ere. She runs bloody marathons!'

Suddenly everyone was shouting at once as the inebriated audience recalled local females who were both fit and liberated. It was a moment of crisis for Big Dave and he lumbered shakily to his feet once again. His leadership was at risk and this battle of words with the bald-headed Pole was threatening to go into extra-time. He cleared his throat with exaggerated force for a final onslaught.

'NUMBER ONE!' he roared and thumped his fist on the table. Even the chatter in the lounge bar seemed to cease.

'Number one,' he repeated with slow deliberation. 'This club shall be known as the Ragley Village Keep Fit Club and all members shall use the same showers and each member must pass a test of physical fitness AND . . .'

All eyes were on Big Dave. You could hear a pin drop. Little Malcolm held his breath, pencil poised.

'AND . . . the Chairman's decision shall be final!'

''ERE 'ERE,' cheered Little Malcolm.

Kojak opened his mouth like a baffled goldfish and closed it again when he could find no answer.

''ERE 'ERE!' chorused everyone, including a few interested spectators in the lounge bar.

Unanimous approval broke like a tidal wave over the taproom and Big Dave's chairmanship was confirmed once and for all. More kitty money jingled and fluttered into the ashtray. Don pulled pints with renewed vigour and Big Dave's joy was unconfined. Little Malcolm rolled up his exercise book with a triumphant flourish and put it in his pocket. The drink began to flow once again and no one considered that the constitution might conceivably be extended to a second point. The ordeal was over and it was time to relax.

The taproom door opened and Ronnie walked in, shoulders hunched, and I ordered him a pint of best bitter.

He sat down beside me and looked around nervously like a fugitive on the run.

'No sign o' Genghis,' he said mournfully. 'Ah've been asking round t'other lads wi' pigeon lofts but 'e's not turned up.'

He supped his frothing pint without enthusiasm.

'The lads seem 'appy enough,' he said, taking a little consolation from the raucous group of footballers at the other side of the room.

'Ronnie, I'm not quite sure how to put this but I've got some good news and some bad news,' I said gently.

Ronnie stared at me, a puzzled look in his eyes.

'What's the good news?' he asked.

'Well, the constitution you were worried about has been written and Genghis has been found.'

It was almost sad to see his face so wreathed in smiles.

'Fantastic, Mr Sheffield, fan-blooming-tastic!'

He drank deeply from his pint.

'Oh, an' what's the bad news?'

'Well, it's a message from your Ruby,' I said gently.

Ronnie's eyes were like saucers as he slowly placed his pint pot on the table.

'A message from our Ruby, what message?' he asked, looking like the prisoner in the dock.

I put my arm round his shoulder.

'She says to let you know that Genghis Khan has just bought you a new three-piece suite!'

Ronnie almost ran out of the door.

In years to come, his football team commented that it was the only time in living memory that Ronnie ever left a half-filled glass of Tetley's bitter.

Chapter Eleven

Elvis and the Student Teacher

A Yr 2 student, Miss Erica Twigg, commenced her teaching practice in Mrs Grainger's class.

Mr J. Fairbank from the College visited school.

County Hall requested a copy of the section in our school handbook entitled 'The School Curriculum' following the government's recent 'audit' of the curriculum in primary schools.

Extract from the Ragley School Logbook:
Monday 6 February 1978

It was eight o'clock on a cold February morning and Miss Erica Twigg was waiting for me in the school entrance on the first day of her teaching practice.

I hung up my thick brown duffel coat and old college scarf and smiled down at the tiny figure before me.

'Good morning, Erica, how are you?' I asked.

'Hello, Mr Sheffield, I'm fine thank you,' she said a little nervously.

Miss Twigg certainly lived up to her name. She was a frail twenty-year-old who looked as though a gust of wind would blow her away. Her brown mousy hair was scraped back from her pale face into a tight ponytail. At five feet two inches tall she could easily have been mistaken for one of the eleven-year-olds in Class 4.

'My tutor has asked if you will check my planning,' she said.

The enormous ring binder that she passed to me looked almost too heavy for her to carry. I scanned the carefully printed title on the cover.

It read: *Erica Twigg, Year Two, Second Teaching Practice, Ragley-on-the-Forest Church of England Primary School, Reception Class, Tutor – Mr J. Fairbank, February 1978.*

I walked into the office with her and began to trawl through the huge folder, neatly sectioned with coloured tabs. It had been prepared with the care of the Domesday Book. Page upon page of copious notes described every lesson she had planned. Neat lists of equipment down to the last crayon and sharpened pencil accompanied each activity. It was a folder of which she could feel justly proud.

'Well done, Erica,' I said. 'This is an outstanding effort. You must have worked very hard to achieve this.'

Erica flushed with embarrassment and breathed a sigh of relief.

'I spent most of the Christmas holidays on it,' said Erica. 'I realized how important preparation is on my first teaching practice so I didn't want to leave anything to chance this time.'

Erica had visited Anne's class on three occasions before Christmas and had told us she intended to return to her parents' home in Lincoln to complete her preparations during the holidays. The folder was full of hints and suggestions from her tutor, Mr Fairbank. I smiled as I read his helpful notes in the margin, beautifully written in red ink. Jim Fairbank had been my tutor in York in the mid-sixties and the care and support he gave to his students was second to none.

'You're fortunate having Mr Fairbank as your tutor,' I said.

'Yes,' she replied enthusiastically. 'He's really supportive. The last thing he said to me before I left was that I should never underestimate children because they will always surprise you.'

'That's very true,' I replied and recalled that was the last thing Jim had said to me prior to my teaching practice.

The main project in the folder was entitled 'Ourselves'. It included a visit by the school nurse plus a request for a few babies to be brought into class. The babies were to be measured and weighed, and then their feeding habits were to be investigated. There was a substantial amount of cross-curricular work and first-hand experience. It looked really good and I knew Anne would be impressed.

'Show your work to Anne Grainger and discuss it with her, Erica,' I said. 'She will help to organize the proposed group work. Good luck, work hard and enjoy it,' I added with a reassuring smile.

Later that day, at half past two, the bell went for afternoon break and Anita Cuthbertson was on the look-out as usual.

'There's a man in a suit coming up t'drive, Mr Sheffield,' she said.

The slim, angular man in a sober, grey suit and black shoes with highly polished toecaps was just as I remembered him. He carried the same ancient black leather briefcase and had a coat and scarf over one arm. It was Jim Fairbank, Senior Lecturer in Education from the teacher training college in York.

I hurried to the school entrance hall and shook his hand.

'Welcome to Ragley, Mr Fairbank,' I said, 'good to see you again.'

Apart from a slight greying at the temples he looked just as I remembered him.

'Hello again, Jack. Congratulations on the new job, and please call me Jim,' he said. 'I've just called in to see if Miss Twigg has settled in. She was a little nervous when she returned after Christmas.'

'She's in safe hands with Anne in Reception, Jim,' I said, 'and, thanks to you, she is certainly well prepared.'

A gentle smile flickered across his face for a moment and he nodded in acknowledgement. We walked into the office and sat down. Jim opened his briefcase, took out his notebook, unscrewed the top of his fountain pen with his long, slender, artistic fingers and proceeded to make flowing notes in the most perfect of italic scripts. His careful habits had not diminished over the years. All the time he asked me perceptive questions. Finally, he put the top on his pen and asked in his polite rhetorical manner, 'May I observe her "Story Time" at 3.00 p.m., Jack? It would give me an idea of how well she relates to the children.'

When Jim and I walked into the Reception classroom a few children had remained inside during playtime in order to help Miss Twigg clear up the paint pots and easels. Eager four- and five-year-old children immediately surrounded us. Little Terry Earnshaw, the Barnsley Boy, now speaking at last, grabbed Jim's jacket.

'Are thee 'is grandad?' asked Terry, pointing at one of his little friends.

Jim smiled down at the little boy. 'No, I'm not,' he replied.

'Tha looks like 'is grandad,' said Terry, not to be outdone.

Then he pointed at Miss Twigg. 'Hey, mister, we've got a new teacher.' He walked over to Miss Twigg and grabbed the student's hand. 'Here she is,' said Terry, 'she's called Miss Twit.'

Erica Twigg crouched down beside him. 'No, it's Miss Twigg, not Twit. But that's a good try,' said Erica, looking more relaxed than I had ever seen her. She glanced down at Terry's scuffed shoes.

'Oh, your shoe laces are undone, Terry.'

She tied them in a neat bow.

'And they're all wet as well. I bet you've been playing in puddles,' said Miss Twigg.

Elisabeth Amelia Dudley-Palmer, the eloquent five-year-old, was standing alongside, completely engrossed and sucking her thumb. She watched Miss Twigg as if she was about to split the atom.

'The secret,' said Miss Twigg with a final flourish, 'is to tie a double bow.'

Little Elisabeth looked up puzzled and took her thumb out of her mouth. 'Why is it a secret?' she asked.

But Miss Twigg was already shaking hands with Jim.

At that moment Anne Grainger burst into the classroom, grabbed Terry by the hand and whisked him towards the toilets.

'Excuse me!' said Anne breathlessly. 'I'll explain later.'

Moments later she reappeared.

'Too late!' she said. 'Sorry about that, but one of the children told me that Terry had just wet his pants again.'

'Oh no!' cried Erica as realization dawned. 'That's probably why his shoelaces were wet!'

She looked up at Jim. 'You did say we should expect surprises, Mr Fairbank.'

Jim smiled politely.

'What I mean to say,' she continued, 'is that I've just shaken hands with you!'

They looked at each other, laughed and Anne led them both to the staff washroom.

As I was the only one left in the classroom when the children came back in from playtime, I gathered them all on the bright red off-cut of carpet in the classroom Book Corner. Anne hurried in with Terry, now wearing clean, dry shorts from the 'Spare Clothes for Emergencies' box. Miss Twigg reappeared and picked up the big picture storybook of *The Three Little Pigs*. She settled down on a low stool and in a slow, serious and dramatic voice she began, 'Once upon a time there were three little pigs.'

Jim crept back in and sat at the teacher's desk. He examined Miss Twigg's lesson plan in her folder and glanced up regularly to observe the children staring wide-eyed at the pictures being held up by Miss Twigg as the epic story unfolded. Seeing that all was well, I returned to my class to relate the equally epic story of Captain Scott's last fateful journey across the icy wastes of Antarctica.

Just after 3.45 p.m. the last of the children had set off home and I was in my classroom marking maths books. Jim knocked on the door and walked in. His face was wreathed in smiles.

'How did it go, Jim?' I asked.

'Memorable, truly memorable!' said Jim. 'She certainly got the children involved, particularly little Terry.'

I knew there was more to come. He closed the door to drown out Ruby's rendition of 'Edelweiss' as she swept the corridor outside and he pulled up a chair alongside me.

'It was a good "Story Time", Jack, and Miss Twigg used her voice to good effect. She got to the part where the wolf huffed and puffed and by then the children's eyes were popping out with a mixture of horror and excitement, particularly little Terry. Then she uttered the fateful words, "He huffed and he puffed and he blew the house down." You could have heard a pin drop. There was a long and stunned silence. The children were aghast at the horrible deed. Finally, Terry, shaking his head in disgust, said slowly and clearly, "The bastard!"

'I just didn't know where to look. Poor Miss Twigg handled it very well and agreed with him that he was indeed a very naughty wolf.'

We both laughed.

'He's not been here long, Jim, and he's got an interesting vocabulary,' I said by way of explanation.

Jim showed me his written report on the lesson. He wanted me to see it before he discussed it with Miss Twigg. It was very supportive and praised Miss Twigg's use of voice, effective questioning and good classroom management.

Anne, Jo and Sally were waiting for me in the school office to hear Jim's report on Miss Twigg and they were all delighted to hear the good news, although Anne was concerned to hear little Terry's verdict on the big bad wolf.

The telephone rang and Sally picked up the receiver.

'It's Sue Phillips ringing from the hospital, Jack,' said Sally, handing me the receiver.

Sue sounded in a hurry.

'Jack, I've booked Elvis for one week,' she said breathlessly. 'You can collect him after school tonight if you like.'

'Elvis?' I asked in surprise.

'Yes, Elvis the Pelvis,' said Sue. 'All the student nurses practise on him. Just come down to the Orthopaedic Ward and I can see you there.'

The penny dropped.

'Oh, you mean the skeleton for the student's health

education project. Thanks, Sue, I'll be there about five o'clock.'

'OK, Jack, see you then. Must rush, I'm training a student as well. Bye.'

The line went dead and I replaced the receiver.

'Did I hear you say Elvis?' asked Anne.

Anne had been a big fan of Elvis Presley, even more so since his sad death just a few months before.

'It's the nickname for the skeleton in the nurses' training room at the hospital,' I explained. 'I'm collecting it tonight to support Miss Twigg's project.'

I glanced out of the window. Darkness had fallen and the freezing rain was turning to sleet.

'You had better get home,' I said. 'The weather's getting worse.'

Anne, Sally and Jo collected their coats and scarves when the office door suddenly burst open and the three ladies jumped in alarm. Jo fell backwards against the filing cabinet. In walked our least favourite school governor.

'Early finish, eh?' said Stan Coe, shaking the frozen droplets from his dirty waxed overcoat. He looked down at Miss Maddison and grinned. 'Made y'jump, did ah?' Then he swelled his chest and stood to attention. 'It were National Service made me, tha knows. Discipline an' nerves of steel. An' when you 'ave nerves of steel y'don't frighten easy.'

He marched off to the gents' toilet, whistling loudly.

'Pity the Army didn't teach him to knock on doors,' said Sally, shaking her head in dismay.

'I'd like to see someone frighten him,' muttered Jo

darkly, straightening her dishevelled coat.

'Come on, let's get home,' said Anne, ushering Sally and Jo out of the office like a mother hen, 'and good luck with his lordship, Jack.' She winked at me and closed the door behind her.

'Bulb's gone in there,' grumbled Stan when he emerged from the toilet. 'It's like black 'ole of Calcutta.'

'I'll get it fixed, Mr Coe. Now, what was it you wanted?' I asked abruptly.

'Ah'm coming in t'check on this student tomorrow,' said Mr Coe. 'Ah don't 'old wi' young kids tekkin' classes. If she's no good they can tek 'er back.'

'I don't anticipate any problems so don't trouble yourself,' I replied tactfully. 'Anyway, you must excuse me, Mr Coe, I've an important errand.'

He glanced at his watch, shook his head and wandered out to his Land Rover in the car park.

The lights of York Hospital shone brightly as I parked my car in the car park. The Orthopaedic Ward was clearly signposted and I soon spotted Sue Phillips working with a young student nurse who was pushing the drugs trolley. Sue walked alongside carrying a huge bunch of keys and she waved when she saw me.

As always, she looked immaculate in her light blue Staff Nurse uniform, to which was pinned a spotless white apron starched stiff as a board. Her navy blue belt sported a precious buckle depicting the God of Wind and her silver General Nursing Council badge sparkled under the fluorescent lights. She pushed the trolley to the side of the shiny corridor with the sole of one of her sensible, black lace-up shoes, stooped to pick up a small white book from the bottom shelf of the trolley and handed it to the student.

'Julie, just check Mr Johnson's drugs in the "MIMS" book while I have a word with Mr Sheffield,' she said.

'Hello, Sue,' I said. 'I'm here for the skeleton.'

'It's in the training room at the end of the corridor,' said Sue.

She turned to the student who was checking the drugs lists.

'Julie, would you mind getting Elvis for Mr Sheffield from Room 11?'

Sue glanced up at me as Julie trotted down the corridor.

'Elvis is really popular at the staff party,' she said with a smile. 'By the way, I hope your car's big enough.'

The skeleton appeared at the end of the corridor. It was life-size and hanging from a hook on a tall tubular stand fixed to a wooden base on castors.

'I had no idea it was that big,' I said in surprise.

'Good luck with the project, Jack,' said Sue as she hurried off with the student nurse and the drugs trolley. 'I'll call into school tomorrow to fix up the session with the parents and babies.'

As I pushed Elvis through the corridors of the hospital I received a few startled looks. A man in a wheelchair passed me in a doorway and shouted cheerfully, 'Hey, mister, thy mate looks reight poorly.'

The scene in the darkness of the car park was even more surreal.

The only way I could get Elvis safely into the car was to unhook him from the stand and strap him in the passenger's seat. As I drove slowly out of the car park, startled visitors stared wide-eyed as the head of the skeleton nodded gently to the left and right with the motion of the car. More than once I glanced at him, lit up by the headlights of oncoming cars, as he turned to look at me and nodded in apparent acknowledgement.

Back at the deserted school I was aware of a certain ghoulish quality as I struggled to unlock the school door and carry Elvis like a drunken man into the entrance hall. I was then faced with the dilemma of where to put him. Ruby would receive a rude shock if I left him in the office so it seemed sensible to put him into the gents' toilet overnight. As I was the only male member of staff, it was the least used room in the school.

The next morning, Miss Twigg was waiting for me once again in the entrance hall with a request to check her teaching file before she started work.

We sat in the school office leafing through her notes when Sue Phillips and Jo Maddison came in with some visual aids from the 'My Body' Health Education programme.

'We thought these might help your display, Erica,' said Jo, putting down the large pictures of babies, running athletes and skeletons.

'Oh, that reminds me,' I said, glancing up at Sue, 'I've got a surprise for you, Erica.'

At that moment the office door burst open and Stan Coe walked in as if he owned the building.

'Now then, Mr Sheffield, ah'll be with you in a minute t'see this student o' yours,' said Stan, totally ignoring Miss Twigg. He clearly thought she was one of the children. As usual, he strode through the office without a word to Sue or Jo and walked straight into the gents' toilet, flicked the light switch and walked into the darkness.

'Y'aven't fixed this light then,' he shouted as he pulled the door shut behind him.

Suddenly there was a yell like a wounded buffalo followed by a crash as Stan Coe fell backwards through the doorway with a clatter and Elvis toppled slowly on top of him.

Stan Coe mouthed a silent scream as he stared terrified into the eyeless sockets of the skeleton's grinning skull.

'Who's that?' said Miss Twigg in amazement.

'It's Elvis,' said Sue.

'No, I meant him,' said Erica, pointing to a gibbering and very white-faced Stan Coe.

Jo Maddison grinned from ear to ear as I stumbled forward to lift the skeleton from the terrified farmer. She turned to the wide-eyed Erica Twigg.

'Erica, allow me introduce our Vice Chairman of Governors, Mr Stanley Coe,' said Jo in her best toastmaster voice. Then she added in a stage whisper, 'He's got nerves of steel!'

Chapter Twelve

Dance With Your Eyes

HT visited the Thomas Pemberton Special School in York to coordinate arrangements for a 'pen friend' project – a successful (and enlightening) visit.

Miss Flint in Class 4 – morning session only.

Extract from the Ragley School Logbook: Wednesday 8 March 1978

'My Tracey-Leanne'll catch her death o' cold in her vest,' said the formidable Mrs Brown. 'It's freezing in that 'all o' yours, an' them wall bars are like t'north face of the Aga.'

It was clear that Mrs Winifred Brown did not approve of my Physical Education lessons and, whilst her knowledge of the names of famous mountains was lacking, she had made her point.

'It's a pity, Mrs Brown, because your Tracey is a good gymnast and loves the Movement and Music lessons we have each week,' I explained. 'Why don't you call in and see for yourself? We have a lesson on Wednesday afternoon.'

Mrs Brown seemed surprised by the invitation.

'Aye, mebbe ah will,' she said, 'an' ah'll 'ave a word with our Dominic's teacher at t'same time. 'e were black bright when he came home from football t'other night.'

I had learned it was always wise to let Mrs Brown have the last word so I smiled politely, nodded and walked back into the office.

Vera was waiting for me with a list on her spiral note pad.

'Mrs Phillips called, Mr Sheffield,' said Vera. 'She says you can visit the special school in York at ten thirty on Wednesday morning.'

This was good news. During her last visit to school, Sue Phillips had asked if I would agree to the children in my class becoming pen friends with some of the children at the Thomas Pemberton Special School in York. Sue wanted to strengthen links between our able-bodied children and those children in the special school who were recovering from illness or accident. It sounded a great idea. My visit to meet the headmistress and tour the school was intended to establish a working relationship and make arrangements for the exchange of letters.

Vera was enthusiastic.

'It's a lovely school,' she said. 'My friends at the Women's Institute put on a party tea for them during the Silver Jubilee celebrations.'

'Thanks, Vera,' I said. 'I've not been to a special school before so I'm looking forward to it.'

* * *

On Wednesday morning Miss Flint, the supply teacher, came in to teach my class. I completed registration and confirmed the work that had been planned for the morning. While Valerie Flint's slate-grey eyes rarely showed any emotion, our relationship was now almost cordial. My predecessor had held fast to the rule that female staff should not be permitted to wear trousers during working hours. Before the end of my first day, I had withdrawn this outdated and illegal practice. It proved very popular with all the staff, particularly Miss Flint. Today she was dressed in a tailored safari shirt with a long pointed collar and a brown pin-stripe trouser suit. Her stylish sling-back clogs with their thick heels and soles ensured she was marginally taller than me.

The top of the blackboard was uncharted territory for the five-feet-three-inch frame of the diminutive Miss Maddison. Not so for Miss Flint, who picked up a stick of chalk and in neat italic handwriting wrote 'Wednesday 8 March 1978' in the top-left corner of the board. Then she placed the wooden board ruler down the left edge and drew a vertical line to represent the margin. Under the date she wrote the title 'Spelling Test' and then turned to face the children.

'Number one,' said Miss Flint, 'flour; we use flour to make bread.'

I tiptoed out of the silent classroom and left the children to their ordeal.

Sally Pringle was in the hall with her class. The children had removed their slip-on plimsolls and taken off their socks in preparation for their Movement lesson.

Like every other experienced teacher of young children, Sally had instructed every child to put a single sock in each plimsoll, preferably their own. Years of misplaced socks, gloves, scarves, hats and, especially, wellington boots had conditioned Sally Pringle's decision-making. The rebellious spirit of flower power had gradually been eroded by the discipline required to ensure that a group of tiny human beings went home dressed in the same clothes in which they arrived. This metamorphism of her organized soul was not without cost.

The previous weekend, Sally had accompanied her husband on his works annual dinner. They had bought tickets at £4.75 for a three-course dinner, dance and cabaret, featuring Roy Castle, at the 3Bs Theatre Bar in Bridlington. When Sally had sat down with her husband and all his friends from work, she had taken out her school notebook and asked those who wanted a starter to raise their hand. Fortunately, she refrained from making sure everyone had gone to the toilet before they left for home.

However, Sally's status as the school fashion icon remained undiminished. As I walked through the hall she was sitting on a chair pulling off her trendy, knee-length, horizontal-striped, rainbow-coloured socks with a pocket for every toe. The stripes exactly matched those on her sleeveless tank top. Sally's colourful fashion sense was greatly admired by the children and frowned upon by Vera.

'I won't forget to tape the Music and Movement lesson,' said Sally as I passed by. 'I'll leave it on your desk ready for this afternoon.'

'Thanks, Sally,' I said. 'I'll be back at lunchtime.'

A few minutes later I was on the forecourt of Pratt's Garage on the High Street. Victor Pratt, the owner, lumbered out to serve me with petrol from the single pump. His thick hands and unshaven face, as usual, were smeared with black streaks of grease and oil.

'Ninety pence a gallon,' moaned Victor. 'If it ever gets to a pound ah'll be out of business.'

Petrol prices had just leaped by 20 per cent since the recent tanker drivers work to rule.

'Ah blame t'government,' said Victor.

No one had ever seen Victor smile. Moaning was a way of life for him.

'Thanks, Victor,' I said and handed him a ten-pound note.

Victor returned with a few oil-smeared coins and dropped them in my hand.

'Looks like rain again,' he said with a scowl at the heavy clouds.

I drove towards York, breathed in the strong smell of cocoa as I passed the Rowntrees factory, and marvelled once again at the Minster when it came into view and dominated the medieval skyline. As I crossed Lendal Bridge I glanced down at the river below. Beneath me a team of eight rowers pulled mightily in perfect unison and left fleeting herringbone patterns on the surface of the Ouse with the symmetry of their strokes. The city was waking from winter and soon the pleasure steamers would be chugging back into life.

I followed an ambulance past the railway station and Micklegate Bar and thought of the children I was about to meet. Two miles south of the river, I saw the Thomas Pemberton School sign and I pulled into the car park.

A sprightly woman in a bright blue tracksuit jogged out to meet me.

'Hello,' I shouted, 'I'm Jack Sheffield. Pleased to meet you.'

'Jack, welcome. You're just in time to help out,' she said breathlessly. 'Everyone lends a hand with this lesson, so do you mind coming straight into the hall?'

She trotted towards the entrance doors and beckoned to me to catch up.

'I'm the head, Jill Sanderson, by the way,' she called over her shoulder. 'We'll do introductions later. Hope you don't mind.'

With that, I followed her into a wide corridor that was heaving with activity. Children in wheelchairs jostled playfully for position on the sloping ramp that led into a large school hall. Others on crutches entered by another door, whilst able-bodied adults hurried from every corner of the school as if it was a fire drill. Some of them carried young children; others placed large rubber mats in a big circle around the edge of the hall.

The headmistress plugged in a large radio and quickly tuned it in and turned down the volume control. To my amazement, I realized she was about to use the same Music and Movement programme that I used with my class. A few minutes remained before the start of the broadcast and Jill Sanderson stood in the middle of the hall and smiled at all the children. She radiated confidence and enthusiasm and pointed towards a group of children who had callipers on their legs and crutches under their armpits.

'Now, those of you who can walk,' she said, 'I want you to dance with your legs.'

Then she waved to a group of children in wheelchairs. One little boy, his head cruelly swollen with hydrocephalus owing to an excess of fluid in the brain, smiled up at her.

Jill held her arms in the air and said enthusiastically, 'Those of you who can wave your arms, dance with your arms.'

A few children had been carried in and laid gently on cushioned mats on the polished floor.

Jill crouched down beside them and held the hand of the nearest child.

'And those of you who can move your heads,' she said, 'dance with your heads.'

One small girl had been placed at my feet. A woman stroked her face tenderly and looked up at me.

'My daughter, Annie,' she said quietly. 'This is her favourite lesson.'

Jill came over and knelt on the mat beside mother and daughter. She gently pushed a lock of blond hair from the child's face and whispered, 'Annie, you can dance with your eyes.'

I felt tears beginning to well up. Embarrassed, I turned away for a moment. This was outside my range of experience. These were real children but I had never met their like before. Everyday tasks I took for granted were complex problems for them. Yet none of them complained and I felt humble in their presence. No training course I had ever been on had prepared me for this moment. My throat felt sore and speech was difficult but I didn't fully understand why.

Annie's mother lifted her carefully from the large green rubber mat and held her in her arms. The teacher turned up the volume on the bulky ghetto blaster and a BBC monotone voice introduced the first piece of music. It was Prokofiev's *Peter and the Wolf* and Annie's mother carried her daughter around the room, swaying in rhythm to the music.

Jill Sanderson stood alongside me and explained that Annie had been almost completely paralysed following a fatal road accident in which her father had been killed. Her mother brought her in every day for treatment and friendship.

I watched the children moving slowly around the hall. It was clear they loved the music and they moved their limbs as well as they could in response to the rhythm. For the adults the work was strenuous and soon Annie's mother was red in the face.

'This keeps me fit,' she said as she paused next to me, breathing heavily.

I looked down at Annie. Her eyes were alive and shining.

'Shall I take a turn?' I asked quietly.

She smiled and nodded, clearly grateful.

I was struck by her appearance. She was a beautiful woman. For someone who had suffered so much pain in her life, there was freshness to her skin, vitality in her movement and peace in her eyes.

She looked down at Annie.

'This kind man is going to help you with the next dance, Annie. Is that OK with you?' she asked.

Annie's smile would have melted stones of ice.

For the next fifteen minutes I ran myself to a standstill, swooping high and low with the small girl in my arms. Like a fairground horse on a carousel, I circled the room and her mother waved each time we passed by.

Soon the last bars of music faded and Jill Sanderson switched off the radio.

Exhausted, I returned Annie to the mat on the floor.

Jill bounded over towards me. Her energy was remarkable.

'Well done, Jack,' she said. 'Now you can see why we need so much help for these lessons. I really appreciated you joining in.'

Annie's mother shook my hand and picked up her daughter.

'Thank you so much. Annie doesn't usually have a chance to dance for so long,' she said. 'We could do with your help every week.'

I nodded in acknowledgement. The right words were difficult to find.

'Come on, Jack, let's have a coffee and organize this pen-friend idea,' said Jill. She seemed to understand my awkwardness and led me quickly back to her office.

'Takes a bit of getting used to, doesn't it?' she said when she closed the door. 'But I wouldn't change my job for the world. Success for us can be lifting a spoon or saying a sentence. Every day brings achievement.'

It was clear to me that Jill Sanderson was born for this profession. Her enthusiasm for the job shone through and she was so proud of the work of her school. The guided tour emphasized the positive ethos of a caring community. I met teachers who were keen to tell me of the progress of each child and adult helpers who wanted to write letters on behalf of those children who were unable to hold a pencil. By the time it came for me to leave I had learned a lesson in life and humility.

Back at school, Miss Flint was marking exercise books. One book was open on top of a pile. A wavy red line had been drawn through a sentence in Anita Cuthbertson's Anglo-Saxon project folder that read, 'Anglo-Saxons have rough mating on the floor.' Miss Flint was clearly unimpressed by the sexual preferences of Anglo-Saxons and she had moved on to the spelling test. I glanced at the book she was marking. Kenny Flanaghan's spelling of the word 'testicle' was perfect. Unfortunately, he had been asked to spell 'terrestrial' and Valerie Flint, who did not share my sense of humour, added yet another red cross.

The afternoon passed slowly. The experiences of the morning filled my mind and the time came at last for our final lesson. Sally Pringle had taped the broadcast as promised and, for the second time that day, I heard the introduction to the Music and Movement programme. The contrast was amazing. The children in my class expended huge amounts of energy as they danced, leaped and ran around the hall and soon they were red-faced and panting.

As the lesson neared its conclusion I heard a familiar voice in my ear.

'She's neither use nor ornament.'

It was Mrs Winifred Brown. She thrust a woolly jumper in my hands as she walked through the hall.

'Ah told 'er to tek 'er jumper,' she said, glaring at Tracey-Leanne who had suddenly stopped doing acrobatic cartwheels across the floor.

'Please will you sit down, Mrs Brown?' I asked politely but firmly. 'The lesson is nearly over now but, as you can see, all the children are fine.'

Mrs Brown was not convinced.

'Ah'll go see to our Dominic,' she said bluntly. 'Ah don't want 'im kicking a football around tonight.' She waddled towards Sally Pringle's classroom door.

Soon the children were pulling on shirts and blouses and collecting their rubber-band-powered models of cars and tractors that I had promised they could take home.

I asked Tracey-Leanne to wait for her mother in the school entrance while Ruby swept the floor of my classroom and I did some paperwork in the office. It wasn't long before I heard Mrs Brown's voice in the corridor.

'C'mon Dominic, y'like one o'clock half struck, get a move on,' yelled Mrs Brown. 'An' you, young madam, you do as y'told in future, else you'll get what for.'

I heard the scampering of Tracey-Leanne's feet as she ran down the corridor followed by a slamming of the main door.

I stared out of the window as the last group of children left school. Dominic ran like a hare to catch his friends and Tracey-Leanne skipped along behind her mother like a newborn lamb. As she came within arm's reach, Mrs Brown grabbed her roughly and yanked her by the shoulder.

'Walk properly!' she yelled. 'Stop dancing around an' behave y'self.'

Subdued, Tracey-Leanne walked in step with her mother and they disappeared into the gloom.

From the hall I heard the squeaky castors of the Music Centre as Anne wheeled it across the hall in preparation for her class assembly the next morning. 'Music Centre' was a rather grand name for a wood-veneered, conti-board trolley on which a radio and a record player had been fitted on the top shelf. A hinged lid kept the dust off the vinyl records and on the bottom shelf two bulky speakers were stored.

I knew Anne would be going through her ritual of selecting a long-playing record, sliding it carefully out of its cardboard sleeve and cleaning the grooves on its vinyl surface with an anti-static cloth. Then she would place it carefully onto the circular rubber mat on the turntable, adjust the dial to 33 revolutions per minute and click the start lever with her thumb. With great precision, she would lift the plastic arm across the spinning record and lower it gently until the sharp stylus settled into the black groove at the beginning of the selected track. Anne always made sure the whole operation was completed without ever putting a greasy fingerprint on the precious surface of the record.

To my surprise, Anne had selected *Peter and the Wolf*, and the opening bars filled the silence and echoed in the Victorian rafters. I stood quietly by the window, looking out at the swirling mist that shrouded the school driveway. I imagined a little girl with blond hair skipping down the cobblestones and her mother clapping her hands in delight. The little girl stopped and stared at the bright lights of the school. She waved and smiled, a bright shadow in the grey mist. Then she turned and skipped out of the school gates.

It was Annie. Or rather, it was the Annie that could never be, except in the imagination. This would be a dream that her mother would cling to for the rest of her life.

Until then, when Annie's eyes were open, she would dance with her eyes; when they were closed, like a ballerina, she would dance in her dreams.

Chapter Thirteen

The Football Match

Mr R. Smith requested the use of the school field for the Ragley Rovers football team.

This was granted following discussion with Revd Evans.

Extract from the Ragley School Logbook:
Thursday 26 March 1978

'Tactics,' said Ronnie Smith. 'That's what wins football matches.'

The Ragley Rovers football team looked puzzled but nodded anyway. Ronnie had never let them down before and he took his job of team manager very seriously.

'Y'mean anything above grass 'igh, kick it?' asked Big Dave the Goalkeeper.

'Sort of,' said Ronnie.

Stevie 'Supersub' Coleclough leaned forward with obvious interest. Stevie liked to be noticed and considered himself to be a trendy fashion icon in his multi-coloured tank top, knitted by his colour-blind Auntie Maureen.

'Are y'talking about that Ziggy Freud psychology stuff?' asked Stevie.

Stevie had also been to Sixth Form College and liked everyone to know.

'We studied all that stuff at college,' he added knowingly.

'Well, not exactly, Stevie, but you're on t'right lines,' said Ronnie, not wishing to discourage his enthusiastic number twelve, even though he rarely got his knees dirty.

The previous day, Ruby the Caretaker had approached me on Ronnie's behalf. Ronnie wanted to use the school field so that the team could practise before Saturday's big game against the rival village of Morton. It was raining heavily so, immediately after school had ended for the day, I had unlocked the gates leading to the old school cycle shed to provide shelter for Ronnie to deliver his team talk.

'Why don't we just give 'em a good kicking like we usually do?' asked Norman 'Nutter' Neilson. Nutter liked to keep his football simple.

'Cos that way we always lose,' said Chris 'Kojak' Wojciechowski, the Bald-Headed Ball-Wizard.

Ronnie ignored the interruptions and pulled out of his pocket a creased brown envelope covered in scribbles. He held it up as if he was declaring peace in our time.

'Ah've got a dossier on the Morton team,' he announced proudly. 'Ah've 'ad 'em watched.'

Ronnie was a disciple of the Don Revie School of

Football Management and he had read about the detailed notes the famous Leeds United manager prepared on opposition players.

'Who watched 'em, Ronnie?' asked Clint Ramsbottom, suddenly breaking off from braiding his hair and taking interest.

Ronnie coughed affectedly and mumbled, 'Our Sharon.'

Sharon was one of Ronnie and Ruby's daughters. At seventeen years of age she had begun to take a great interest in football, particularly in Rodney Morgetroyd, the eighteen-year-old Morton centre forward with the golden locks and handsome good looks. Handsome Rodney had knocked on Ronnie's door recently, hoping for a glance of the voluptuous Sharon, but he was quickly sent packing back to Morton on his 150 cc Lambretta with its antennae of chromium rear-view mirrors and a triangular pennant fluttering on a six-foot aerial. Ronnie didn't like anything flashy and was very protective of his daughter.

'Your Sharon?' asked Big Dave, looking puzzled. 'What does she know about football?'

'Don't knock our Sharon,' said Deadly Duggie Smith, the pacy right winger. 'She's not as daft as she looks.'

'Deadly' Duggie was Ronnie's son. He was also the local undertaker's assistant, hence the nickname. It was an irony that the fastest player in the Ragley team spent his working life walking at two miles an hour behind a hearse. 'Go on, Dad,' continued Deadly Duggie. 'What did our Sharon say?'

Ronnie glanced down at the notes on the envelope.

'She says they're nearly all young 'n' fit, all except for Fat Ernie the Goalie.'

Ernie Morgetroyd, Rodney's father, weighed eighteen stones and liked his food. Fat Ernie and Handsome Rodney were the Morton village milkmen.

'So what's these tactics that's gonna 'elp us beat 'em?' asked Big Dave.

'We're gonna play to our strengths,' said Ronnie. 'Weather's perfect for us. Rain's coming down like stair-rods and bottom end is like a paddy field. Morton can't play their fancy football on that mud 'eap. First 'alf, we defend bottom end like them lads at Rorke's Drift. Second 'alf, we 'it em on t'break. Don't fanny about in midfield, 'it it long to our Duggie so 'e can use 'is 'lectric pace.'

Deadly Duggie drew deeply on his Castella cigar and nodded modestly.

I watched the team practice from the staff-room window. It appeared to go well and I was determined to watch the epic encounter on Saturday afternoon.

Dark black clouds were full of foreboding as the day of the match dawned. Beth Henderson had called in unexpectedly at Bilbo Cottage to volunteer to tidy up my kitchen. So it was with a feeling of guilt that I hesitantly suggested going to watch the football match.

Beth grinned and surveyed the disorganized kitchen.

'I think it would be better if you were out of the way, Jack,' she said, trying not to hurt my feelings, 'but it will cost you a slap-up meal in York tonight.'

'It's a deal,' I said and I drove off wondering how a man like me could be lucky enough to have a woman as beautiful as Beth doing his housework.

Wind and rain battered my umbrella as I walked from the school car park across the school field and climbed over the fence to the Ragley Rovers football pitch. I joined the small band of hardy supporters to cheer on the team.

Ronnie, Big Dave and Little Malcolm had spent their lunchtime with a bucket of whitewash battling against the pouring rain and splashing the touchlines in a forlorn attempt to mark out the pitch.

Predictably, Freddie Kershaw, the referee, never even considered calling off the game. It was his view that if he was expected to deliver coal in this weather then these soft lads could kick a ball around. Freddie was also committed to conservation of energy so, with a gale-force wind blowing straight down the muddy slope, Freddie blew his whistle and then positioned himself strategically on the edge of the Ragley penalty area where he could watch all the first-half action. Freddie wasn't wrong. Wave after wave of Morton attacks were repulsed by the brave tackling of the Ragley team and the occasional wrestling hold behind the back of the referee. At half time the Ragley players sucked their quarter slices of orange like fluorescent gum shields whilst Ronnie praised them for keeping the score to 0–0.

'C'mon, lads,' he cried, 'this is our day.'

Big Dave led his team to the top end of the field and smacked his huge right fist into the palm of his left hand and gave his own version of a tactical team talk. 'OK, lads, if y'it anybody, ah want rest o' team to pile in cos ref can't send us all off.'

In the second half, the faster, youthful Morton team

looked dangerous every time they got the ball but all the Ragley players tackled like demons and the minutes slowly ticked by.

After eighty-eight minutes, the score was still 0–0 and Ronnie was looking anxiously at his watch. Almost an hour and a half of bone-crunching tackles, hacks and trips had left both teams looking like competitors in a mud-wrestling competition. Against all predictions, the Ragley team was somehow holding out for an unexpected draw. The biggest crowd of the season, twenty-three brave souls, including old Mr Connelly's guide dog, huddled under umbrellas and cheered on their heroes. A magnificent result was in sight when disaster struck. Morton made one last desperate assault on the Ragley goal. Handsome Rodney, who had been kicked from pillar to post all afternoon by Nutter Neilson, suddenly found the ball at his feet in the Ragley penalty area. He pushed it skilfully past the onrushing Big Dave who grabbed his ankle and pulled him down. It was a definite penalty. The referee blew his whistle and pointed deliberately to a muddy depression in the pitch that had once been a whitewashed penalty spot and was now a circular puddle.

While Big Dave protested his innocence to the referee, the ball rolled behind the goal and Ronnie jogged round and picked it up. Ronnie stared hard at Handsome Rodney as he trotted over to collect the ball. The young striker looked confident. He hadn't missed a penalty all season. As he took the ball from Ronnie's outstretched hands there was a moment's hesitation. It seemed as if Ronnie was unwilling to let go of it.

'C'mon, 'urry up,' the referee shouted through the swirling rain. 'Time's nearly up.'

Ronnie appeared to be whispering something into Handsome Rodney's ear. The young blond Adonis looked thoughtful as he trudged to the penalty spot and carefully wiped the ball dry on his shirt. Then he placed it on a damp divot of mud and stepped back four paces. Time seemed to stand still. Rodney was obviously deciding which side to put the ball. Big Dave the Goalkeeper stood menacingly with arms outstretched. Rodney looked to the heavens, took a deep breath, trotted up to the ball and chipped it gently, straight at Big Dave. The Ragley crowd roared and the Morton players stared, open-mouthed in disbelief, and groaned.

Meanwhile, Freddie Kershaw glanced at his watch and thought of his welcome mug of Bovril in the pavilion. As he did so, Big Dave began the move that would go down in Ragley folklore and dominate the discussions in The Royal Oak for the rest of the season.

Whoever said that everyone is famous for fifteen minutes had not really intended to include ordinary folk like Deadly Duggie Smith, the Ragley village undertaker's assistant. But if they had said fifteen seconds, it would have been different, for Deadly Duggie's time had come. This was his fifteen seconds.

Big Dave, with the strength that launched a thousand dustbins, threw the ball with all his might out to the left touchline. It landed in an explosion of mud and grass at the feet of Clint 'Nancy' Ramsbottom who shook his drenched Kevin Keegan locks and looked around him. To his surprise, he was alone. The Morton defender who had marked him all afternoon had gone up to the edge of the Ragley penalty area in anticipation of Rodney scoring the penalty. So Clint set off like a frightened rabbit and the Morton team began the chase like a pack of hounds.

The referee, blinded momentarily by the pouring rain, began to chug back downfield. He was unaware of the mayhem behind him as Big Dave tripped the Morton players and Nutter Neilson added insult to injury by stepping on them.

At the precise moment that Clint received the ball at his feet from Big Dave's long throw, Deadly Duggie set off on a mazy run that he would remember for the rest of his life.

'Pass it, son,' shouted Deke Ramsbottom from the touchline, the incongruous turkey feathers in the brim of his cowboy hat drooping in the steady downpour.

'Clint, Clint, pass it!' screamed Deadly Duggie as he ran up the right wing and cut in towards the Morton goal.

'Pass it, Nancy!' yelled Shane to his younger brother, as he tore up the centre of the field, tugging back two Morton players by the tails of their shirts.

'Stick it in the box, y'big puff!' commanded Big Dave from the other end of the field.

'Aye, stick it in the box,' gasped Little Malcolm the Midfield Maestro, hands on hips in the centre circle.

Deadly Duggie, with only the Morton centre half to beat, put in a final lung-bursting sprint.

Danny Booth had been the Morton centre half for as long as he could remember, almost since he stopped eating rusks. In recent years he had filled out to the size of a bus shelter and there was no way that Deadly Duggie was going to get past him. So with the finesse of a runaway brick lorry, Danny chopped Deadly Duggie's legs from under him.

The referee, Freddie Kershaw, did not blow his whistle, as he recognized this act of violence as a normal part of the cut and thrust of lower league football. Only grievous bodily harm was penalized and, even then, he only penalized players who were not on his coal round.

At that moment, Clint Ramsbottom curled his left foot round the ball and hit it like a shell into the Morton penalty area.

With his eyes tight shut, Deadly Duggie, now parallel to the ground with arms outstretched and looking like a Spitfire about to crash land, was on a collision course with the muddy leather football as it carved its path like Halley's comet towards him.

The force with which the old-fashioned leather ball hit Deadly Duggie's head left him with the triple X imprint of the laces on his forehead and, for the rest of the weekend, he resembled an escaped convict from a science fiction film.

Almost in slow motion, the ball rebounded from Deadly Duggie's head and arced gently in a perfect parabola over the outstretched hands of Fat Ernie the Morton goalkeeper. Ernie's wife always made sure that he was well fed and Saturday lunchtime before a match was no exception. Ernie's brain sent him an instant message to leap cat-like through the air and tip the ball over the crossbar but his body had long since ceased to be cat-like. As his feet remained firmly stuck in the mud, Fat Ernie regretted the extra helping of Yorkshire pudding followed by jam roly-poly and custard.

At the moment the ball hit the back of the net and nestled in the patch of thistles next to Fat Ernie's wet towel, thermos flask and Tupperware box of sandwiches, the Ragley supporters yelled, 'Goal!' They shouted with such force that Vera Evans, feeding the ducks by the village pond, dropped her bag of sliced brown Hovis. With cheers ringing around the ground, Freddie Kershaw blew for full time and the players shook hands and trooped off for a welcome hot bath.

Burly, rain-drenched Deke Ramsbottom, the Club Chairman, marched over to the jubilant Ronnie and put his arm round his shoulder. 'Listen to that, Ronnie,' he said proudly and passed him his silver-plated hip flask. 'It warms cockles of my 'eart to 'ear supporters shouting like that.'

'Y'right there, Deke,' said Ronnie, taking a swig of Irish malt. 'An' ah'll tell yer summat, if Michael Caine's lads at Rorke's Drift had shouted like that, them Zulus would 'ave dropped t'spears an' buggered off 'ome.'

Deke had not seen the film *Zulu* and didn't know what Ronnie was talking about but he agreed anyway.

'C'mon, Ronnie, let's tek all these 'eroes t'pub,' said Deke. 'It's time t'celebrate.'

In the taproom of The Oak, Sheila was serving pints as fast as Don could pull them. Deadly Duggie's wonder goal had been related countless times and Old Tommy Piercy was racking his brains to recall a finer goal by a

Ragley player in the past fifty years. Deke and Ronnie were in pride of place at the corner table near the dartboard. In spite of the heat of the log fire, Ronnie still wore his favourite 'Billy Bremner' bobble hat, although by now it was at a rakish angle over one eye.

Big Dave was reflecting on his penalty save.

'It were a soft penalty,' said Big Dave.

'It warra soft 'un,' agreed Little Malcolm.

'Your Sharon could've saved it,' said Big Dave, smiling at Ronnie and supping deeply on his fifth pint of Tetley's bitter.

'She could've saved it easy,' said Little Malcolm, matching Big Dave pint for pint.

Kojak wasn't easily convinced.

'Strange 'e didn't blast it like 'e usually does,' he shouted above the din. ''e's never missed one this season.'

'What did y'say to him, Ronnie, when y'gave 'im t'ball?' asked Big Dave. 'Ah saw y'muttering summat jus' afore t'penalty.'

Ronnie pulled out a large dirty handkerchief from his pocket, scattering some old birdseed on the wooden floor. He blew his nose loudly.

'Nowt special,' he mumbled.

At that moment, Handsome Rodney, the voluptuous Sharon clinging to his arm, strolled past the taproom door in the direction of the lounge bar.

Deadly Duggie looked in amazement at his father. 'Hey, Dad! That were our Sharon wi' Goldilocks. Ah thought you'd sent 'im packing t'other night.'

'No, he's not a bad lad,' said Ronnie.

'Y'could 'ave fooled me,' said Deadly Duggie. 'So when did y'say 'e could go out wi' our Sharon?' he added.

'Oh, ah forget,' said Ronnie evasively.

Big Dave leaned over to Ronnie and whispered in his ear.

'It wouldn't 'ave been just afore that penalty, would it, Ronnie?'

Ronnie looked up into the eyes of the giant goal-keeper and winked.

Big Dave dug him in the ribs.

'Y'crafty ol' bugger,' said Big Dave.

A few moments later buxom Sheila and Don the Barman staggered in with two huge trays full of pints of frothing beer. The glasses were passed around and at a signal from Big Dave everyone shut up. Ronnie looked up surprised as Deke suddenly lifted his ample backside from the bench seat he was sharing with Ronnie. Sheila turned down the Abba record on the jukebox and Big Dave cleared his throat in an exaggerated manner.

'Listen in, everybody,' shouted Big Dave. 'Ah'd like to propose a toast. Today's been a big day for Ragley Rovers. It's a while since we've beat them cocky sods from Morton.' This was greeted with cheers and resounding thumps on the tables. 'Everybody 'ere played their 'earts out.' More cheers and table-thumping followed. Big Dave was warming to his speech. 'A special well done to Deadly for 'is wonder goal.' Clint and Shane Ramsbottom grabbed Deadly Duggie's wrists and held them high in triumph. The whole team cheered, raised their fists and punched the air. A few cheers were beginning to ripple through from the lounge bar where

Handsome Rodney, oblivious of the celebrations near by, was telling the voluptuous Sharon that she was the spitting image of Olivia Newton John in *Grease*. Meanwhile, Deadly Duggie bowed to the baying crowd and modestly pointed to the scars of victory on his forehead. Another ovation rattled the pub windows.

Big Dave had saved the best till last.

'An' now ah want everyone t'be upstanding for t'best football coach in Yorkshire.' Everyone shuffled unsteadily to his feet. Pint tankards scraped on the tabletops. 'Ah give you Ronnie Smith.'

The cheers from the lounge bar almost rivalled those in the taproom.

'Speech!' yelled Don the Barman.

'Speech,' shouted everyone at once.

Ronnie stood up, stepped to one side and leaned back against the dartboard. Then he did something no one had seen him do before. He removed his bobble hat. It was rumoured Ronnie not only went to bed in his bobble hat but had been married in it as well. He held it to his chest like a badge of honour and bowed his head slightly. Ronnie was almost completely bald except for a few grey wisps around his ears. It explained the bobble hat a little more.

'Ah'll never forget today,' said Ronnie with watery eyes.

Everyone cheered. It didn't really matter what Ronnie said. By now the team would cheer anything.

'Whilst ah'm real proud of our Duggie's winning goal, it were a real team effort by all eleven, er, twelve players,' said Ronnie, catching the eye of Stevie 'Supersub' Coleclough.

More cheers resounded round the room.

'But most of all, we used t'right tactics. Like ah said afore, tactics win matches.'

Tumultuous cheers raised the roof as Ronnie regained his seat.

Half an hour later, Ronnie was standing in the gents' toilet, forehead leaning against the white tiles. Handsome Rodney suddenly appeared alongside him.

'You OK, Mr Smith?' asked Rodney politely.

Ronnie gazed up blearily at the young blond footballer alongside him, now resplendent in his best flared trousers, John Travolta shirt and Cuban heeled shoes.

'Aye, lad,' said Ronnie, 'all the better f'seeing you miss that penalty.'

'Ah'd do owt f'your Sharon,' said Handsome Rodney wistfully.

'Remember the deal,' said Ronnie sternly. 'Ah want 'er back by midnight.'

'Aye, midnight it is,' said Rodney as he turned and left Ronnie leaning like a flying buttress against the toilet wall.

Eventually, Don the Barman called 'Time, gentlemen please' and Ronnie staggered home with the help of his son, Duggie. Ruby took off his muddy wellingtons and jeans and helped him into bed. She looked concerned.

'Ronnie, our Sharon's gone out wi' that Rodney from Morton,' said Ruby.

'Ah know, don't worry, ah've shpoken tuh Rodney,' mumbled Ronnie.

'But when will she be 'ome?' asked Ruby.

'Midnight, eggshatly midnight,' said Ronnie and fell asleep.

Ruby put on her cotton winceyette nightdress, which her daughters had bought her from Boyes in Ousebridge for £5.50, and listened for the door latch.

On the stroke of midnight she heard the door slam and the sound of her beautiful daughter as she scurried upstairs to her bed.

'Goodnight, Sharon,' said Ruby.

'Goodnight, Mam,' said Sharon.

Ruby looked down affectionately at her sleeping husband and wondered whether she should remove his bobble hat. She was reassured he had known the time Sharon would come home. As Ronnie began to snore, Ruby smiled and gently kissed the top of his woolly hat. She knew that, whilst he loved his football and smelled like a brewery, he had some good points. Ruby lay back, turned off the bedside lamp and thought how lucky she was to have a husband who always put his family first.

Meanwhile, Ronnie dreamed on and thought of more tactics.

Chapter Fourteen

The Boat Girl

84 children on roll. A new starter arrived, Ping from Vietnam, a temporary placement prior to permanent move to Newcastle.

The HT expressed concern to the Education Office regarding the process of the transfer of educational records.

Extract from the Ragley School Logbook:
Monday 3 April 1978

Her name was Ping.

I shall never forget our first meeting. It was Monday 3 April and the season was changing. The grip of winter had passed and the heavy rains of March had gone. Bright yellow forsythia brightened the school driveway and lifted my spirits as I drove into school. The first parents were dropping off their children at the school gate and hurrying to work. Everything looked familiar, a day like any other. Except this day was destined to be different. It was the day I met Ping.

Clutching the hand of her foster parent, she was waiting for me to arrive in the entrance hall. I opened the office door and asked them to go in. The little girl stood like a broken fawn. Her skinny legs were trembling and the biggest oval, brown eyes I had ever seen were holding back the tears. She was ten years old and I had never seen a more frightened child.

Her brown Vietnamese face was framed beneath straight-fringed, jet-black hair. It possessed a serene kind of beauty. But behind the innocence of childhood lay visions of death. I soon learned that her mother had died of disease and malnutrition and her father had drowned during a desperate flight across the South China Sea. He had been an irrigation engineer in the Mekong Delta with proud dreams for an improved rice crop and self-sufficiency for his country. When their tiny craft finally sank, Ping was part of the human flotsam picked up by another vessel.

Her Vietnamese foster parent spoke in clear, precise English. She was clearly a well-educated woman.

'This is Ping,' she said. 'She is a very good girl. Please can she come to your school?'

A telephone call on the previous Friday afternoon from Roy Davidson, our Education Welfare Officer, had warned me to expect a new arrival. He explained that a few Vietnamese refugees had arrived in the area and were expected to secure permanent homes in Newcastle in a few weeks' time. Our job was to provide a little security in the interim. This was commonplace with the children of travellers who occasionally came into Ragley and Morton, parked their caravans on waste ground, stayed a short while and then moved on. However, a child from overseas was something new for all of us.

I didn't know then that in the short time Ping was to be in Ragley School she was destined to become our best ten-year-old reader and a remarkable poet. I smiled and gestured towards the two visitor's chairs.

'Of course,' I said. 'Please sit down.'

Unfortunately, Ping's arrival had swept around the gossip mongers at the school gate. An abrupt knock at the door was unwelcome at that moment. I opened it to be met by the considerable bulk of Mrs Winifred Brown. Vera had gone to work in the staff-room, Anne was choosing the hymns for school hymn practice with Sally on the piano and Jo was preparing her classroom for her first lesson. I stepped out into the corridor and hastily pulled the door closed behind me.

'I'm afraid I'm very busy at this moment, Mrs Brown. If you could just wait until—'

But Mrs Brown was in no mood for waiting.

'I'm 'ere on be'alf of a lot o' parents,' she announced. 'We don't want no Vietnams 'ere, if you please. They'll bring our kids down to their level. So we don't want no Boat People 'ere.'

As a headmaster I had learned to hold my temper on many occasions and at that moment I realized I was at breaking point. This kind of ignorant bigotry had been fuelled by some of the tabloid press and Mrs Brown was more gullible than most. I took a deep breath and told her that I was disappointed to hear her views and that I could not see her until the end of the week.

'We'll see about that,' she shouted as I closed the door in her face.

Ping's foster parent looked anxious at the sound of raised voices.

'Don't worry,' I said, 'everything will be fine. Ping is very welcome here and I'm sure she'll soon make friends.'

The inner office door opened and Vera walked in from the staff-room. She seemed to have summed up the situation very quickly and had heard the confrontation with Mrs Brown. Vera smiled at Ping.

'What a beautiful little girl,' she said. 'Welcome to Ragley. Now, who would like a cup of coffee?'

Ping's foster parent looked surprised but relieved.

'Yes please, you are very kind,' she said politely.

Minutes later, Vera had taken over in her usual inimitable style and had begun to complete a new admissions form.

'Did you say Ping's date of birth is 3 April 1968?' asked Vera.

Ping's foster parent nodded in agreement.

'Mr Sheffield, Ping is ten today,' announced Vera. 'We must do something special for her birthday.'

I looked at Ping and had an idea.

It wasn't difficult to find Ruby. She was singing 'My Favourite Things' as she put away her dustpan and brush at the end of her morning shift.

'Ruby, can you do me a favour, please?' I asked.

Ruby locked her store and looked at me inquisitively, her face flushed after sweeping and dusting the entrance hall.

'What is it, Mr Sheffield?' asked Ruby. 'Y'look proper flummoxed.'

I pressed on, uncertain whether or not Ruby had paid me a compliment.

'I need your help, Ruby,' I said. 'Can you do some baking?'

'That sounds reight up my street,' said Ruby enthusiastically.

I explained to Ruby about the arrival of Ping and that it was her birthday. Ruby knew exactly what was needed.

'Ah'll get all t'ingredients in t'village, Mr Sheffield, an' ah'll 'ave a word wi' Shirley in t'kitchen. She'll let us use a mixing bowl an' t'oven.'

Back in the office, Vera had completed the paperwork and was deep in conversation with Ping's foster mother.

'Don't worry about the dinner money,' said Vera. 'I'll sort that out for you.'

It was time to take Ping to the classroom. School assembly was over and the children in my class had taken out their English exercise books and textbooks in preparation for their first lesson of the day. They had learned to get on with their work when I was delayed with the business of headship. Their eyes were wide with interest when Ping came into the classroom.

'Boys and girls,' I said, 'this is a new girl in our class and I want you to make her welcome. She has come from a far-off country called Vietnam and her name is Ping.'

Fortunately, no one giggled at the strange name so I pressed on.

'Today is a special day for Ping. It's her birthday and she is ten years old. So I would like a volunteer to help Ping make a birthday cake.'

Every hand shot up into the air and I made a careful selection.

'Claire Bradshaw and Kenny Flanaghan,' I said.

'Mr Sheffield, will we all get a slice?' asked Anita Cuthbertson. Anita was emerging as the class shop steward.

'That's up to Ping,' I said with a smile.

Anita fixed Ping with a gritted-teeth smile, the sort she usually reserved for class photograph day. To my surprise, Ping lost some of her shyness and smiled back.

I turned to Ping and her foster parent. 'Now, if it's all right with you, perhaps you would like a tour of the school? Claire and Kenny can show you round.'

The four of them trotted off and it was noticeable that Ping had visibly relaxed. Claire Bradshaw put her arm around her shoulders and said, 'Come on, Ping, I'll show you my tuck shop first, you can help me sell crisps at playtime.'

Twenty minutes later, Ping and her foster parent had finished their guided tour and were standing at the classroom door. Shirley the Cook suddenly arrived.

'Ruby's told me about this cake, Mr Sheffield. She's coming back at one o'clock and I was wondering if all the other children might like to make some iced buns. I can stay on a bit and help if you like. It'll be a bit of a party at the end of school.'

I looked at Ping's foster parent.

'Perhaps you would like to come back to school this afternoon and join in the cake making?' I asked.

'I would love to,' she said with enthusiasm, 'and I should be interested to learn your recipe.'

Shirley beamed as she recognized a kindred spirit. 'I'm sure you know many recipes as well,' she said graciously.

Ping's foster parent bowed modestly, gave Ping a big hug and left quickly.

Ping sat down on the spare chair next to Claire Bradshaw, picked up an English textbook and began to read it quietly.

Soon all the children were writing in their exercise books and I asked Ping to come to my desk. It was an opportunity to get an idea of her ability. There were no records from her previous school and, such was the system, these were unlikely to arrive before the Education Welfare Officer's next visit.

In the top drawer of my desk, on a sheet of white A4 card, covered in sticky-backed plastic, was a reading test we used throughout the school. The Schonell Word Recognition Test comprised one hundred words typed in groups of ten in order of difficulty. It began with the words 'tree, little, milk, egg, book' and progressed to more difficult words. A simple calculation provided the notional reading age of the child when compared to their chronological age. It was a crude tool but in 1978 it was widely used by primary school teachers.

The mispronunciations of particular words were a source of amusement in staff rooms up and down the country. The most common errors were 'scissors', pronounced 'skissors'; 'soloist', pronounced 'socialist'; and 'canary', pronounced 'cannery'.

Ping came and stood beside me and scanned the long list of words. Before I could explain to her what to do, Ping pointed without hesitation at one of the small-print words and said 'antique' in a clear, confident voice.

It became obvious to me very quickly that she was one of the very few children in my class who could read every single word on the card.

'What reading book are you reading at the moment?' I asked.

'*Swallows and Amazons*,' she replied. 'It's a really good story.'

The tears were gone now and her confidence was growing.

I recalled Mrs Brown's derogatory comments outside the office door. Her daughter, Tracey-Leanne, could barely get a third of the way down the reading test and had a reading age well below her chronological age. Ping's was well above.

At morning playtime, Ping went off happily with Claire Bradshaw to sell crisps whilst I found Roy Davidson waiting for me in the school office. Roy had a large folder with him, which helped to fill in some of the details of Ping's life since the fall of Saigon in the summer of 1975. From a United Nations refugee camp in Thailand, Ping had finished up in Hong Kong. It was there her new foster mother had taken responsibility for this little orphan of the war.

At the outset of 1977, Ping and her foster mother had travelled to London where they lived in sheltered housing and Ping attended a local school. It was there her educational records began and her first teacher had written about her 'excellent vocabulary and good writing and number skills'. The few hundred Vietnamese families that had arrived with her were eventually dispersed around the country and each local authority provided temporary or permanent housing. Ping was due to stay with us for three weeks prior to a permanent move to Newcastle with a small number of other Vietnamese families.

'She will be fine with us, Roy,' I said. 'If you get a chance, call back later for a slice of birthday cake.'

Shortly after one o'clock, Shirley the Cook and Ruby the Caretaker were surrounded by groups of children up to their elbows in flour. Vera had collected Ping's foster parent from their council flat and both had donned aprons and were helping children weigh out the ingredients. Claire Bradshaw and Ping appeared to have struck up an inseparable partnership and were taking turns to stir the Victoria sponge mixture in a large metal bowl. I had borrowed a very fetching blue-checked, North Yorkshire County Council apron and joined in. My lack of knowledge was immediately apparent and the children were amused that I had to ask for directions from Shirley and Ruby.

'I thought teachers knew everything,' said Anita Cuthbertson, shaking her head in bewilderment as a myth was ruined for ever.

Ping's cake was iced and Ruby helped her write her name in runny pink icing whilst Shirley added ten candles. Ruby explained to Ping about making a wish and I took a photograph of her as she blew out her candles. I shall never forget the delight on her face. The children enjoyed their iced buns and lemonade and Kenny Flanaghan summed up everyone's feelings as the bell rang for the end of school.

'That were a great afternoon, Mr Sheffield,' he said through a mouthful of crumbs. 'Ah'm reight glad Ping came into our class.'

On Friday morning it was the turn of my class to take morning assembly. Word that Ping was going to read a piece of writing from her English book had spread throughout the village, so a larger group of parents than normal filled the back row in the hall. Stories and poems were read out and, finally, Ping stood up to read her piece of writing. Her foster parent leaned forward in expectation. Vera and Ruby, who did not usually attend morning assembly, had crept in, and the brooding presence of Mrs Winifred Brown was visible in the far corner of the assembly hall.

Ping opened her exercise book and began.

'I like Ragley School. It is a nice place. There are lots of books and I like reading books, especially those with a happy ending. Soon I shall be leaving this village. My new mother says we are going to a big city called Newcastle. She says when we get there we can live in peace.'

Ping's voice was clear and her reading was excellent. The parents at the back of the hall were clearly moved by the direct way in which she expressed herself. I looked across at Vera and Ruby and their eyes glistened with admiration for this little girl. Ping continued in a confident voice.

'I am in Mr Sheffield's class and I have lots of friends, the best is Claire Bradshaw who lets me help her with the school tuck shop. On my first day here I made a birthday cake. I have never seen a birthday cake before. It had candles on it. Mrs Smith and Mrs Mapplebeck helped me to make it. I tried really hard. Mrs Smith said to me, "If a job's worth doing, it's worth doing well," and she is right. She said I could blow out the candles and make a wish. I can't tell you what my wish is because if I do it might not come true. So I have only told my mother and father in my prayers.'

For a moment no one moved. Everyone in the hall was silent. Ruby's eyes were red and she rubbed them with her dumpy knuckles. Vera took off her spectacles and dabbed her eyes gently with a tiny lace handkerchief. Shirley gripped her hands tightly together and bowed her head. Ping turned the page of her exercise book and continued to read.

'When I was a little girl there was a war in my country. Saigon is a big place in Vietnam and that was my home. My mother and father and all my relations had to leave quickly. We sailed in a small boat across the South China

Sea. It was very dangerous and everyone was frightened of pirates. The sea was very big. In the atlas in the library, it says the sea is a quarter of a million square miles but we still found our way. We landed in Thailand. All my family died because they had no food. They gave me some water and I was the only one left. Before she died, my mother was too weak to walk but not too weak to smile. I will always remember her smile. It was like the candles on the cake.'

Ping closed her book and sat down.

At the back of the hall and without warning someone began to clap. It was Sheila Bradshaw, Claire's mother. With the exception of Mrs Brown, the mothers around her joined in and, like a forest fire, it spread around the hall. Children and adults alike began to applaud. It had not happened before and was all the more special because of it.

Roy Davidson, the Education Welfare Officer, had arrived at school during the assembly and was standing at the door of the hall. As the children went back to their classrooms, he came over to me.

'Jack,' he said, and gripped my arm, 'count the successes and enjoy every child.'

I looked at him curiously.

'That's what my boss said to me when I started this job and I've never forgotten it.'

So that's what we did. We enjoyed Ping's contribution to Ragley School and she enriched our lives.

A few weeks later we waved goodbye to her and she continued to send long letters to Claire Bradshaw and in this way we kept in touch with her progress.

Now, many years later, I still get Christmas cards from old pupils of Ragley School. A particular one is always immediately distinguishable by its American stamp. It is from a talented paediatrician who was once a frightened little girl. I will never know if the wish she made when she blew out her candles ever came true, but I like to think that it did.

Each year, when she signs the card, she does not use her married name. She simply signs it 'Ping'.

Chapter Fifteen

The Headteachers' Training Course

HT attended the training course for newly appointed HTs at High Sutton Hall.

School invited to display a selection of artwork and children's writing.

Miss Flint in Class 4 – afternoon session only.

Extract from the Ragley School Logbook:
Friday 14 April 1978

It had been a stressful week. Everyone in school seemed to have a sore throat and the end of term couldn't come soon enough. On top of that, the phone had never stopped ringing. Without Vera's help, teaching my class and answering a hundred and one queries would have been impossible.

It rang again as I was making a lemon and honey drink during afternoon break.

'Hello,' I croaked.

'Hello, Jack, Miss Barrington-Huntley needs a favour.'

It was Beth Henderson ringing from the Education Office. My spirits lifted a little. She sounded her usual animated self.

'It's about this weekend's course for newly appointed headteachers.'

It was Thursday 13 April and I was due to leave after school the following day for a residential conference at High Sutton Hall.

'Hello, Beth, good to hear from you again,' I said, trying to sound cheerful. 'How can I help?'

Beth's name was on the list of delegates for the course and I was hopeful of spending some time with her. For my part, I knew I was completely infatuated with her but she behaved as if we were just good friends. It was clear we enjoyed each other's company but we had not progressed from a meal or an evening at the Theatre Royal in York. When we said goodnight, it was accompanied by a simple kiss on the cheek but never any more than that. I guessed that Beth had been badly hurt by her break-up with David but it never cropped up in conversation and I was unwilling to probe further.

Beth sounded in a hurry.

'Miss Barrington-Huntley wants you to arrive at lunchtime,' she explained. 'I told her about your lovely artwork and children's writing and she would like it for a display in the entrance hall. Is that OK? I know it doesn't give you much time, so I thought I could call in tomorrow to give you a hand and offer a lift to High Sutton. We could travel up together.'

Whilst some of my more worldly colleagues would

have politely declined; as a young, inexperienced headmaster I was flattered by the request to show off the work of my school. Much more than that, it was also an opportunity to talk to Beth again.

'That's fine, Beth,' I said. 'I'll get Miss Flint to cover for me tomorrow afternoon and I'll be ready at the end of morning school.'

'That's marvellous, Jack, I knew you would help. Sorry about the short notice but it's been a bit hectic here. It should be a good weekend. We've got Sylvester Quinn, the Stress Management guru from America, giving the lead lecture on Friday night.'

'That's just what I need at the moment,' I said mournfully. What I really wanted to say was that I was delighted Beth was going as well.

'By the way, Jack, there's a walk around the grounds on Saturday morning. Something to do with "team-bonding", so don't forget your wellies.'

'Thanks for the reminder, Beth, I'll pack them tonight.'

She rang off and I asked Vera to locate the course information from the filing cabinet. I wanted to be well prepared. The headed notepaper looked very grand and included the itinerary for the weekend, a helpful map and some photographs of the magnificent hall and its grounds.

On Friday morning I packed a holdall with some clothes for the weekend and bundled my wellington boots, thick socks, old gardening trousers and a waterproof anorak into a large black dustbin liner. I threw them into the back of my Morris Minor Traveller and set off very early for school.

There was a lot to do. I took down a display of pastel drawings from my classroom and stuck a collection of beautifully illustrated children's poems into an A3 sugar-paper folder. I stapled the pages together using the long-arm stapler and wrote the title 'Poems by children of Ragley School' on the front cover in thick felt pen. Gradually, the pile of work filled the large cardboard boxes in the entrance hall and I stacked them behind the front door next to my holdall and the black plastic bag.

Beth was punctual. She was waiting for me at twelve o'clock in the school office and she and Vera were reading the local newspaper. Vera had just spent seven pence on a *Yorkshire Evening Press* and was thrilled to read the headline, 'Mrs Thatcher says a five per cent swing will win the next election'. Vera was trying to convince Beth that Mrs Thatcher would be the answer to all the country's problems. Beth looked relieved to escape.

'I've just met the little Vietnamese girl,' said Beth. 'She was cleaning out the rabbit hutch with another girl. Isn't she a wonderful speaker, Jack? I've heard a lot about her.'

The telephone rang and Vera beckoned me over.

'Miss Barrington-Huntley for you, Mr Sheffield,' said Vera, holding out the receiver.

I groaned. It was always the case that when you were in a hurry to leave school, someone always telephoned. Beth pointed to the pile of children's work.

'I'll load up, shall I?' she asked.

'Thanks, there's my holdall as well,' I said, grabbing the receiver, 'and a black bag with my wellies.'

Miss Barrington-Huntley sounded stressed.

'Have you organized the display work with Miss Henderson?' she asked.

'Yes, we're loading it now,' I said, looking out of the window. Beth was struggling to put the cardboard boxes into the back of her slightly rusty, pale-blue Volkswagen Beetle. Then she threw the holdall and the black bag in the boot.

Minutes later we were off. It was the first time Beth had driven me in her car and I became aware of the scent of Rive Gauche perfume and her fast, competent driving as we sped along the Ripon road. The stress of school and the irritating sore throat were soon forgotten as we chatted about music, a shared interest in historical buildings and what was going to happen to her when her one-year secondment ended and she returned to her deputy headship. I was almost disappointed when, at five minutes to one, High Sutton suddenly came into view. The hall was spectacular and we slowed down as we crunched over the long, winding gravel driveway. The grassy banks were studded with daffodils and the mature trees stood like giant sentinels in the vast silence of this beautiful place.

High Sutton Hall was one of the finest Georgian mansions in England. Set in 500 acres of magnificent Yorkshire countryside, it was a country house that provided a reminder of the style and grandeur of bygone days. The lake looked spectacular and the walled garden brickwork was covered in honeysuckle and variegated ivy. Now it had become a welcome retreat for teachers, a place to meet, talk and to recharge batteries. Better still, it also had a reputation for good food and excellent hospitality. The course for newly appointed headteachers in North Yorkshire provided a good opportunity to meet colleagues who were experiencing similar problems.

We pulled up outside the front door and unloaded the displays of work. Then we parked the car in a small courtyard next to a sign that read 'Stable Block'. Beth seemed to know her way around.

'This is the accommodation block, Jack. We can come back later when we've checked in.'

As we walked into the huge entrance hall, a very loud bell rang and dozens of delegates in smart suits walked towards the dining room.

'Good timing, Jack,' said Beth. 'You go ahead and have some lunch while I check in with the advisory team. I'm supposed to be helping with the organization.'

The smell of pork chops was too much to resist so I walked in.

There was no one I recognized so I sat at the nearest table and the remaining three seats were soon filled.

'Hello,' I said, trying to break the ice.

The curly-haired man to my left looked at me curiously.

'Have you just started then?' he asked. 'I haven't seen you here before. What school are you at?'

'Ragley, near Easington,' I said. 'I started there last September.'

'So what sort of floors have you got?' asked the lady on my right. Her hair had been dyed lurid orange and I wondered what her staff made of that.

'Floors?' I asked in surprise, thinking I had misheard.

The bald-headed man opposite leaned forward.

'Yeah, y'know, wood block, plastic tiles over concrete,' he said, abruptly.

I looked back to the lady. 'We've got a wood block floor in the hall and old timber floors in the classrooms. Why do you ask?'

'I was wondering what sort of floor polish you used,' said Orange Hair.

'It's in a big tin with some red writing on it, I think,' I explained.

Bald-head was unimpressed.

'Y'don't seem t'know y'stock,' he said, shaking his head.

'What about high windows over six feet,' asked Curly, 'are there many o' them?'

I thought hard. It seemed a technical question but I presumed it must have some significance. Not for the first time, I promised myself that I really would read all the weekly circulars that poured in from County Hall and not leave it entirely to Vera to decide what I should read.

At that moment an elderly man approached our table shaking a soup dish filled with fifty-pence pieces.

'Collection f'Billy,' he said, rattling the plate in expectation.

I put a fifty-pence piece on top of the pile of coins.

Meanwhile a waitress came round and filled everyone's wine glass.

A plump man on the next table suddenly stood up and raised his glass.

'Ah'd like you t'join me in a toast to our friend and

comrade, Billy, caretaker at Blackwater Secondary School for twenty-eight years. Please stand.'

We all lumbered to our feet, raised our glasses and said, 'Billy.'

The toastmaster added his final rallying call.

'Remember, unity is strength. Us caretakers must stick together. Ah'll see you all again next year. Thank you and safe journey home.'

The penny finally dropped.

I had unwittingly attended the final meal of the previous conference. The rest of the meal continued with me trying to avoid direct answers to questions about automatic boilers and the rate of wastage of paper towels.

After the meal I returned to the entrance hall and worked with Beth on the display of work. The caretakers took their leave and Orange Hair gave me a puzzled look as she struggled out with her suitcase. An hour later the first headteachers began to arrive and the hall filled again with people whose first question appeared to be the whereabouts of the bar.

It was almost time for the evening meal by the time we had finished.

'Come on, Jack, we've earned a pre-dinner drink,' said Beth. 'Don't worry about your bags. I asked the porters to put them in your room. You're in Room 14 and you can collect your key from reception.'

It was good to relax over a drink and I began to realize how much I enjoyed Beth's company. The bar was full of headteachers, still in suits and looking forward to a relaxing weekend.

'Look,' said Beth, pointing to the other side of the bar, 'there's tonight's speaker sitting with Miss Barrington-Huntley. It's the stress guy from America, Professor Sylvester Quinn.'

Miss Barrington-Huntley fussed around him like a mother hen. Professor Quinn was almost bald, looked about sixty, and wore what could only be described as a baggy lumberjack shirt. The raised heels of his brown winkle-picker boots compensated for his diminutive frame and he waved his black cheroot cigar in the air as he chatted in animated fashion and sipped his double whisky.

Miss Barrington-Huntley was hanging on every word.

After dinner, Beth and I were amongst the last to walk into the lecture hall. As usual, all the back rows were completely filled. After a hard week in school, a couple of drinks and a good meal, no one wanted to be too visible. The headteachers who had arrived early sat smugly in the knowledge that they could switch off their brains, avoid eye contact with the speaker and be first into the bar at the end of the talk.

There were two remaining seats on the front row and Beth and I sat down. To my right an eager young woman sat with clipboard at the ready, pen poised. She was waiting for words of wisdom that would transform her ramshackle collection of creaking huts in the middle of a boggy field into a centre of excellence. To my left, beyond Beth, sat three men who had affected a glassy-eyed stare that suggested keen interest in the forthcoming lecture. However, I suspected their minds were focused on whether High Sutton Hall had a television set and if there was a good pub and a fish and chip shop within a ten-minute drive.

They soon livened up when an unexpected bonus appeared. Professor Sylvester Quinn had a distinct nervous twitch that manifested itself in a wink of the left eye. Apparently this only seemed to appear when he was under pressure and, because he was under pressure, he was unaware of the problem. Throughout his career and his long travels across the American states, no one had mentioned this to him. As Miss Barrington-Huntley waded through her carefully prepared introduction, she became aware that every time she paused and gestured towards the principal speaker, he winked at her. Miss Barrington-Huntley felt like a young teenager again as she spoke with glowing praise of the American icon.

'As Professor Quinn states in *The Stress-Free School* and *The Storm before the Calm*,' said Miss Barrington-Huntley, quoting from her notes, '"know your stress, know yourself."'

She glanced to her left and Professor Quinn nodded slowly in an all-knowing sort of way as if he had just discovered penicillin. Then he gave her a big wink. Miss Barrington-Huntley's cheeks reddened as she regained her seat and an unenthusiastic smattering of applause greeted the vertically challenged lumberjack.

'Hi, everybody,' said the professor, whilst removing his spectacles so that they hung on a long chain around his neck. 'I'm pleased to meet all you folks in Yorksheer,' he continued in his mid-west drawl, 'especially, mah dear friend, Fiona.'

He turned to Miss Barrington-Huntley and gave her

another big wink. For good measure he gave another big wink to the front row and began to jangle the keys in his pocket. This seemed to be another of the professor's irritating habits.

'So what causes stress and, what's more, what can we do about it?' said Sylvester with another rattle of his keys and a big wink to Miss Clipboard who was writing furiously.

Professor Quinn switched on his overhead projector and the large black image of a dead fly that was stuck to the transparent plate was projected onto the screen. Blissfully unaware that the star of a cheap sci-fi movie appeared to be perched on his bald head, he stood in front of the white screen, rattled his keys, winked at the three men on the front row and asked us to close our eyes.

'Now, think about a stressful experience you have had recently,' he said in a hypnotic voice, 'and ah wan' you to fix it in your mind.'

I peered through half-closed eyelids at the people around me. They appeared to be doing the same.

'Have you done that?' said the rattling, winking American. 'Now, write it down.'

'Can we open our eyes first?' asked a desperate voice from the back row. It was clear he thought this lecture was developing into a waste of good drinking time.

The American professor ignored the interruption and pressed on regardless.

'Ah would like you to find a partner with whom you can share your problems. Choose someone you don't know. Tell them what causes you stress and then they must come up with two solutions. Then vice versa, so to speak. You will feed back to the whole group in ten minutes. Your time starts now.'

A suppressed groan echoed across the room. The three men on my left homed in on Beth and engaged her in conversation.

Meanwhile, Miss Clipboard leaned forward and caught my eye and I recalled why movie stars wear sunglasses.

She looked at me with the intensity of a Belgian detective, read my name label on my lapel and said, 'So, what causes you stress, Jack?'

I pondered for a moment to think of a relevant reply.

'Difficult parents,' I said.

'That's easy,' she said and scribbled on her pad.

'According to Professor Quinn, your two solutions are, number one, deep breathing and number two, avoiding negativity.'

I breathed deeply. But it didn't seem to help. I still thought the lecture was a waste of time.

'Now it's my turn,' she said eagerly.

I sighed and thanked my lucky stars that I hadn't been asked to play Monopoly with her.

'So what gives you stress?' I asked meekly.

'American professors who have no idea what it's like to teach thirty-five children in a cardboard box,' she answered. 'They're so self-opinionated! It makes me furious!'

'Oh!' I said as she walked to the back of the room.

I looked at my blank sheet of paper and then at Beth

alongside me. The three men had surrounded her like bees round a honey pot. All of them wanted to be her partner.

'Sorry,' she said, 'I already have a partner.'

Beth came and sat in the seat vacated by Miss Clipboard.

'Is that what I am, Beth?' I asked quietly. 'Your partner?'

She lowered her eyes and looked as though her thoughts were far away.

'I've been hurt a few times, Jack,' she said, 'and I don't want to spoil what we've got,' she explained and squeezed my hand.

It was the first time she had opened up to me and I wanted to put my arms around her and tell her everything would be fine. Unfortunately, Miss Barrington-Huntley's voice boomed out, 'One minute left, everybody,' and the moment was lost. Beth blinked and sat up in her seat.

I wasn't the only one who had lost his audience. Professor Quinn was now nervously rocking backwards and forwards as the ten minutes drew to its close and all the delegates were sitting with their arms folded, waiting for something to happen. He also made the mistake of selecting Miss Clipboard to begin the feedback. She had moved to the back row and took the opportunity to attack the educational theorists who issued advice from ivory towers.

'Large classes, poor pay and too much government interference,' she said. 'That's what causes stress and I can't see how all this theory is going to help.'

Miss Barrington-Huntley looked horrified, while the rocking, rattling and winking Sylvester had clearly lost the plot.

'I agree!' shouted a male voice from the back row. At least one of them had stayed awake.

'You need to breathe deeply and avoid negativity,' mumbled the professor but with little conviction.

The lecture ended thirty minutes early. Both Professor Quinn and Miss Barrington-Huntley looked as though the Gestapo had just questioned them.

With a brave smile, Miss Barrington-Huntley waved a copy of Professor Quinn's latest stress-bashing masterpiece, *American Stress*.

'Don't forget, Professor Quinn will be signing copies of his new book in the bar.'

He sold three copies.

Apparently Miss Barrington-Huntley had two sisters.

The next morning, after breakfast, a group of cold headteachers huddled in small groups in the courtyard in front of the stable block for the walk around the grounds. Hot coffee and a warm fire were certainly preferable to a forced march disguised as a 'team-bonding' exercise. It was a cold, cloudy morning and everyone was dressed in wellington boots, old trousers and warm coats. That is, everyone except me. I was still dressed in my suit and looked and felt very much out of place.

Beth came up to me looking concerned. I was too cold and stressed to notice the subtle way in which her pink scarf matched her bobble hat and that the cut of her jeans emphasized her shapely figure. I felt my sore throat returning and I began to sneeze.

'What's wrong, Jack? Where're your wellies?' asked Beth in a concerned voice.

I looked at her and my anger softened. It was just that whenever I was with her, life seemed to backfire on me.

'Beth, do you remember putting a black dustbin liner in your car along with my holdall?'

Beth nodded.

'And do you remember two girls had just cleaned out the rabbit hutch?'

Beth nodded again, still looking puzzled.

'Well, I've just looked in my wardrobe and opened the black bag. Guess what was in it?'

Beth's eyes widened.

'Oh no,' she said, 'it wasn't! It couldn't be!'

'Yes, I'm afraid so, rabbit droppings!'

So for the rest of the morning I tiptoed around the edge of streams, avoided cowpats and silently froze to death. Whilst the loan of the pink scarf was welcome, it did little to enhance my rugged outdoor image.

Shortly before lunch, Beth and I walked into the bar. Beth bought the drinks while I huddled in front of the log fire. Slowly warmth began to reach my fingertips and toes. Professor Quinn looked as though he had spent the morning trying to get to the bottom of a bottle of malt whisky.

'Hi there, mah good friend,' he shouted across the bar. 'Had a good morning?'

I must have looked as though I wanted to throttle him.

Beth arrived with the drinks, squeezed my hand and whispered in my ear, 'Remember, Jack, take a deep breath and avoid negativity.'

Chapter Sixteen

The School Camp

22 children from the top class will be attending a five-day camping holiday in Skythorns near Grassington, commencing Monday 22 May. All members of the teaching staff, plus John Grainger, have agreed to accompany the party.

Extract from the Ragley School Logbook: Friday 19 May 1978

'Definitely diesel,' said the spotty-faced garage attendant.

'Are you sure?' I asked.

'Yeah, definitely diesel,' confirmed Spotty Face. 'Ah know me engines, ah do. Y'can tell by t'sound, they tick over different.'

I had driven Victor Pratt's huge wagon into the forecourt of a small garage on the outskirts of Skipton. It was Saturday 20 May, the weekend before the school camp, and the wagon was full of tents, tools, cooking equipment, boxes of food and a giant marquee. The College in York had provided all the equipment and Miss Twigg and three of her student friends had volunteered to give up their Spring Bank Holiday to do the cooking. Anne Grainger's husband, John the Woodcarver, had offered to help me collect all the gear from the College and then transport it to our campsite in the Yorkshire Dales.

We had planned to meet Deke Ramsbottom and his sons, along with a posse of parents, at lunchtime in the little village of Skythorns just outside Grassington. They had volunteered to prepare the campsite prior to the arrival on Monday morning of the twenty-two children in the top class.

It was a beautiful, sunlit Saturday morning and everything had gone well so far.

'What do you think, John?' I asked. 'It didn't occur to me to ask Victor about his wagon and he's a man of few words anyway. I was just grateful for the loan of his vehicle.'

'Sorry, Jack,' said John. 'I've no idea. I don't even know what a diesel engine sounds like.'

I scratched my head. The last time I had driven a wagon was when I was a student and I had delivered Corona pop around the streets of Leeds. The pop wagon was always full of fuel when I took it out. Victor's had been nearly empty.

It was time to make a decision.

'OK,' I said to Spotty Face, 'fill her up.'

I should have known better. On a lonely road, half a mile from Skythorns village, the battered old wagon finally spluttered to a halt. I looked around for help but the quiet road was deserted. In the distance I spotted a five-barred gate set into the limestone wall beyond which a narrow track led to a small cottage. Wood smoke was billowing out of the chimney so I set off to ask for help whilst John stayed with the wagon.

An old farmer was repairing a dry-stone wall and he was clearly an expert. I had learned as a boy that a Pennine wall is constructed from two walls that are bound together by large stones called 'throughs' and topped with capstones.

His black-and-white sheepdog barked a welcome and trotted up to me.

'Heel, boy!' the farmer shouted and the dog obeyed instantly.

'Hello,' I said, 'I'm sorry to bother you but our wagon has broken down. I wondered if I might use your telephone?'

The old farmer smiled.

'Nay, lad. Baint got no telephone 'ere. No use for them fancy things,' he said.

I nodded towards the dry-stone wall.

'That's a good wall,' I said appreciatively.

'Aye, it'll last a 'undred years, will this,' he said, modestly. 'Mi father taught me, tha knows. Ah work end in an' end out. One upon two an' two upon one.'

He stood up, wiped his palms on his rough cord trousers and we shook hands.

He could sense my concern and walked down the track with me back towards the gate. His name was

Samuel and he was one of the hard breed of Yorkshire hill farmers. I explained about the camp for the children.

'Ah well, don't fret, young man. We'll sithee reight.'

An hour later we had transferred all the equipment from the wagon to Samuel's flat-topped trailer and hitched it to his tractor. As we bumped through the gateway into the camping field in Skythorns village, Deke and his sons were leaning on their Land Rover talking to the other parents. They looked up in surprise as we jumped down from the trailer.

'What's 'appened, Jack?' asked Deke. 'Where's Victor's wagon?'

I explained about the diesel.

'Yon garage lad knows nowt,' said Deke. 'It'll be pinking. Y'know, when fuel's not going through proper like. My lads'll drain it an' bring it back. Don't worry, Jack.'

Shane and Clint drove off in the Land Rover while John Grainger took charge of unloading the trailer.

I thanked Samuel for all his help.

'We're having a campfire and a barbecue on Friday night, Samuel. You're welcome to come along and join us.'

'Aye, mebbe ah'll sithee, then,' said Samuel with a smile. 'Ah'm glad y'bairns won't be disappointed.' His dog jumped up on the tractor seat alongside him and together they chugged out of the field with the empty trailer bouncing behind them.

The campsite soon took shape once the marquee was erected. I felt like a travelling circus performer as we pulled on the thick guy ropes and raised the vast roof of canvas. Deke and John hammered wooden pegs into the ground and suddenly the campsite had a focal point. A group of parents carried the folding trestle tables and benches inside and arranged them alongside a set of gas cylinders and a cooking range. A gas-fired water boiler was soon whistling and a welcome tea-break followed.

Four tents for the children were erected near the stream that ran through the corner of the field and two tents for the staff were pitched close by. By late afternoon grease pits had been dug and toilet tents that looked like sentry boxes had been discretely positioned in amongst the clumps of trees. Everything was ready and it was time to relax.

John had agreed to stay in camp over the weekend, leaving me free to drive back to Ragley on Sunday morning in Victor Pratt's wagon and return on Monday morning in the coach carrying the children, the staff and the students.

Before he left, Deke wandered over with a small rucksack. It clinked as he walked. 'Here's a nightcap f'you lads. 'ave a good week an' ah'll sithee on Friday.'

The sun was low in the sky as his Land Rover disappeared down the track and John and I took our bottles of Yorkshire Pale Ale onto the nearby hillside. We leaned back against a tree, drank deeply and looked at the beauty of the dale below us. This indeed was a little piece of heaven.

'I'm reminded of my Scripture lessons, Jack, when I see the earth and sky in such perfect harmony,' said John, stroking his beard thoughtfully with his strong woodcarver's fingers.

It was strange to hear this quiet man wax so lyrical.

I nodded in acknowledgement and watched the fiery orb of the sun slowly sink behind the distant hills. Briefly, the high clouds were crimson and the surface of the stream resembled hammered bronze.

'The Book of Job says, "Speak to the earth and it shall teach thee,"' said John. He grinned in my direction. 'Don't worry, Jack, I won't start talking to the trees. It just came back to me. I think I understand what it means now.'

He stood up, supped the dregs from the bottle and wiped his mouth on the sleeve of his rough Arran sweater. 'Come on, Jack,' he said, 'it's been a long day.'

I slept like a log and next morning, after a brief shower of rain, it dawned bright and clear. When I opened the tent flap, the new day burst in with a rush of scents and sounds. It felt good to be alive.

In the woodland clearing, the misty blue carpets of bluebells had given way to early foxgloves and the pale yellow blossoms of wood sage. Bird's eye primroses and early purple orchids sparkled like jewels on the rain-washed grass and the pure air was filled with the evocative scent of broad-leaved garlic. The baa-ing of lambs and the cry of curlews echoed across the dale.

'This really is God's own country,' shouted John as he carried two mugs of tea from the marquee.

Back in Ragley, early on Monday morning, it was a hive of activity in the schoolyard. Anne Grainger, Jo Maddison and Sally Pringle were in the centre of a throng of parents collecting last-minute medication for a host of potential ailments. At last, twelve girls and ten boys clambered aboard the bus clutching teddy bears, rucksacks and bags of sweets. The staff sat on the front seats, sorting through boxes of clipboards, half the stock of Boots the Chemist and various sizes of sick bags.

The children cheered when Miss Twigg and the other female students boarded the bus. Midst much waving of tear-stained handkerchiefs, the parents scurried along-side the sides of the coach and we were off. Within minutes the children had struck up a rapport with the students and were discussing the chores list. Each student had been nominated to supervise a daily chore and the four groups of children rotated each day. 'The Drips' had to collect water in a milk churn and transport it on a small trailer to the marquee. 'The Lumberjacks' had to collect fallen wood for the Friday-night bonfire. 'The Soapsuds' had to wash up after breakfast and evening meal and 'The Litterbugs' had to pick up every scrap of litter around the site. The coach driver turned on the radio and Boney M belted out their top-ten hit, 'Rivers of Babylon'. Everyone joined in and the miles flew by.

Soon the flat plain of York gave way to the stunning scenery of the Yorkshire Dales with its rugged hills and winding valleys, criss-crossed with dry-stone walls.

John Grainger waved as we all clambered off the coach in Skythorns and walked up the track to the campsite. He had boiled water for a hot drink and Samuel and his wife, Rose, had driven by and delivered a wicker basket of freshly baked scones and two large jars of homemade jam.

Within minutes, the boys had unpacked their sleeping bags and set up a game of cricket in the big open space between the tents. Gradually, the girls joined in and Miss Twigg made up a new set of rules including one-handed catches when the tennis ball rolled off the roof of the marquee.

Claire Malarky, after hitting the ball over the marquee, for 'a six and out' according to Miss Twigg's rules, shouted at the top of her voice, 'This is better than telly, miss.'

Anne walked over to me, sipping the scalding tea. 'It really is worth all the effort, isn't it, Jack?'

I smiled and nodded. 'This is almost too good to be true, Anne. All the children look so relaxed and happy. It's a good start.'

New and spontaneous activities were beginning as children tired of the cricket game. Sally Pringle was sitting under the trees with Claire Phillips and Claire Bradshaw. They were in a little private world of their own, sketching an early purple orchid. Jo Maddison was supervising the students' first attempt at cooking stew and boiled potatoes for thirty-one people. John Grainger was working with Wayne Ramsbottom and Kenny Flanaghan by the stream. They were constructing a makeshift washstand from branches and baling twine.

Soon a pattern developed to our new lives, free of alarm clocks, television sets and parents. Long walks, chores, games, meals and sleep filled our lives. New friendships were formed, especially between boys and girls who barely communicated in the school play-ground. It surprised the boys that Claire Phillips could out-walk any of them and the female students reported that Wayne Ramsbottom knew more about cooking for large numbers than they did.

On Wednesday we booked a local coach to take us to Malham village. From there we walked by the beck that ran down to Janet's Foss. We sat in silence as Sally Pringle told a captivating story about a fairy called Jennet who was supposed to live in this enchanting place.

John Grainger led the way up Gordale Scar, the great chasm carved out in the Ice Age. The children clambered up the rocks like mountain goats into the dry valley of Gordale Beck. By the quiet banks of Malham Tarn, we ate our packed lunches.

'Food tastes better 'ere, miss,' said Claire Bradshaw to Miss Twigg.

'And this spring water tastes like wine,' said Miss Twigg, holding her water bottle aloft.

As we sat eating our ham and cheese sandwiches, Sally, who was proving a fount of knowledge, told all the children about life in the Middle Ages when the monks from Fountains Abbey would come to fish for trout in the Tarn.

Tired but happy, we descended slowly into Malham Beck with the sheer cliffs of Malham Cove providing a stunning backdrop. With red faces from the sun and wind, we sat on the grass outside the Lister's Arms in Malham sipping lemonade until the coach arrived to take us back to camp. That evening, after washing in the stream, we enjoyed a superb meal prepared by the students and slept like logs. I should have known it was too good to last.

A loud voice shattered the peace of my dreams.

'Jack, Jack! There's been a cloudburst!' It was John Grainger. In the dawn light of Thursday morning, I peered out of the tent. Dark clouds filled the sky and sheets of water poured down the hillside and threatened to swamp our campsite. I struggled into my clothes, pulled on an anorak and boots and ran to where John was trying to dig a shallow ditch alongside the first of the six tents.

'We've got to divert this water, Jack, or the tents will be flooded,' he yelled as he dug frantically at the water-logged earth.

At that moment, Samuel arrived on his tractor. The rain bounced off his sou'wester as he pulled up along-side.

'Jack, dust tha want to get the bairns under cover? They can shelter in my barn while we tackle this job,' he shouted.

Samuel knew the weather and had summed up the seriousness of the situation. Fifteen rain-soaked minutes later, Anne, Sally and Jo had gathered the children in the marquee, all dressed in cagoules and wellington boots. Then they marched them all across the field to Samuel's barn, followed quickly by the students who carried carrier bags of loaves, butter, jars of jam, plastic mugs and a bucket of boiled eggs.

With Samuel directing, he, John and I dug a drainage ditch, a spade's depth along the line of the tents towards the stream. After two hours of hard labour, soaked and tired we leaned on our spades.

'That'll do t'job,' said Samuel, barely breathing heavily

after such massive exertion. John and I could hardly stand, never mind reply. We nodded and watched in triumph as the water ran into the ditch and gurgled around the tents and into the stream.

'C'mon, get some dry clothes and we'll get to t'barn,' said Samuel.

John and I changed in Samuel's front room while his wife, Rose, made a huge pot of soup. Soon we were all sitting on dry bales of hay in the barn, enjoying a mug of soup and a hunk of bread. The children were undeterred and had obviously enjoyed the adventure. The students had worked hard making sure everyone had something to eat and Anne, Sally and Jo were checking on those children who needed medicines and tablets. It looked like a refugee camp but everyone was safe and dry.

As the rain eased outside, everyone relaxed in the dark barn and by the flickering light of half a dozen hurricane lamps, the children gathered around Samuel and his sheepdog. They began to ask him questions about his life in this bleak but beautiful part of Yorkshire. He told them a tale of the savage winter of 1940 when fifteen feet of snow covered Spiggot Hill and Tarn Moss. His flock of sheep had huddled together, covered by a crust of snow that froze in the bitter winds. The children cheered when he told them how the Royal Air Force had come to his rescue in the equally severe winter of 1947, dropping fodder from the sky to save his starving sheep.

It was a very sleepy group of children and teachers that walked back to the tents. After a makeshift lunch the drizzle returned and dampened our spirits again.

Chores that were completed at the beginning of the week without a problem began to be overlooked, not least my daily tent inspection. This was to provide a rude awakening for me.

Early on Friday morning the rain had stopped and the sun came out. Anne and I rushed around the children's tents to open them up and let the warm fresh air circulate once again. When I approached Kenny Flanaghan's tent an unpleasant aroma filled the air.

I untied the tent flap and looked inside. Five grubby faces grinned up at me from the jumble of sleeping bags and rucksacks.

'Hello, sir. Are y'coming in? We're 'aving a game o' three-card brag,' said one of the little chimney sweeps.

I squeezed my head and shoulders inside the tent and, with the force of a physical blow, a terrible smell of rancid cheese and sour milk hit me and caused me to withdraw my head quickly.

'What a smell,' I yelled. 'How can you stand it?'

'Y'get used to it after a while, sir,' said Tony Ackroyd.

'But what is it?' I asked. 'It smells like a sheep's died.'

Kenny crawled over to the tent flap and stepped out onto the wet grass.

'Mr Sheffield,' he whispered hoarsely, 'I'm reight sorry but it were me. Ah've been sick.'

'You've been sick?' I exclaimed. 'Where?'

Kenny glanced behind him furtively and then whispered again, 'Under t'groundsheet.'

'Under the groundsheet?' I repeated in alarm. 'Well, you had better take all your friends into the marquee.

Take your cards with you, then come back to me and we'll clean it up.'

The five boys, dressed in odd socks, odd wellington boots and muddy jerseys inside out, walked cheerfully over to the marquee, blissfully unaware of the wet grass, the pungent smell and sartorial elegance.

Moments later, Kenny was back beside me.

'Ah'm sorry, sir, ah didn't mean it,' said Kenny.

'Don't worry, Kenny,' I said, ruffling his damp hair. 'Now, show me where it is.'

'Well, sir,' explained Kenny. 'Ah were tekken short in t'night so ah pulled back groundsheet reight quick an' ah were sick.'

'I think we'll move the whole tent, Kenny. Let's put it on a clean piece of ground.'

Kenny proved a good worker and twenty minutes later the tent had been re-erected and the groundsheet was clean again. I disinfected the ground and buried the evidence and we walked to the stream to wash our hands.

'Thanks, Kenny, we've done a good job there.'

Kenny looked up a little nervously.

'Y'won't tell, will yer, sir?' said Kenny.

'Don't worry, Kenny. Just let me know in future if you feel sick,' I said.

A thought suddenly occurred to me.

'By the way, Kenny, when exactly were you sick?'

Kenny screwed up his face in concentration.

'Er, it were Wednesday, sir.'

I walked away, shaking my head in disbelief.

* * *

The campfire and barbecue proved to be one of the best nights of the year. The weather was perfect and everyone agreed that sausages cooked on an open fire and eaten outdoors tasted far better than those cooked indoors. Samuel and Rose came along and none of the children could resist their sheepdog as he begged for food. Sally had brought her guitar and we all sang countless verses of 'You'll Never Go To Heaven'. It was a tired but happy group of campers who spent their last night under the stars.

The next day the children left on the bus with Anne, Sally and Jo. Deke Ramsbottom arrived at the campsite in his Land Rover followed by his sons, Clint and Shane, who had brought Victor Pratt's empty wagon. We loaded up the equipment and set off home. Deke drove off with his sons in the Land Rover and John and I drove back in the wagon. Close to Skipton I pulled into the forecourt of the same garage that we had visited on our outward journey.

A portly man came out to serve us and I climbed down from the wagon.

'Fill her up please,' I said, 'with petrol.'

He nodded and unscrewed the petrol cap.

'Is the young man who served us last Saturday in?' I asked.

'That'd be young Paul,' he replied. 'He were a Saturday lad. We got shut of him after one day, he were reight dozy.'

John leaned out of the wagon and winked at me.

'Y'right there,' said John, 'definitely dozy!'

Chapter Seventeen

The Cricket Match

Reading Tests completed.

Previous HT, Mr J. Pruett, visited school and asked HT to continue the tradition of umpiring the annual Ragley and Morton cricket match.

The school nurse visited school and showed a film on 'Growing Up' to the girls who move on to secondary education next term.

Extract from the Ragley School Logbook:
Friday 2 June 1978

'Them cow claps'll 'ave t'be shifted,' said Big Dave as he cast an experienced eye over the village cricket field.

'Y'reight there, Dave, an' there's plenty of 'em an' all,' agreed Little Malcolm, nodding vigorously.

It was the first Saturday in June, the day of the annual cricket match between the rival villages of Ragley and Morton, and the warm sun and blue skies promised a perfect day. Big Dave had summoned the whole Ragley team to the cricket pavilion at nine o'clock on the morning of the match.

I had been asked to follow in the footsteps of the previous headmaster, John Pruett, and be one of the umpires. As I arrived, Big Dave was giving his usual motivational team talk.

'We're gonna stuff 'em this year,' said Big Dave. 'Ah can feel it in m'bones.'

'Y'reight there, Dave,' agreed Little Malcolm. 'Ah can feel it an' all.'

The team had assembled outside the cricket pavilion, a tired-looking wooden hut with a green corrugated roof and whitewashed, sun-blistered doors. It was erected on top of a short, steep grassy slope at the edge of the cricket field. Steps sawn from ancient railway sleepers led down the slope to a rickety gate attached to the white paling fence that surrounded the field. Wooden benches had been set into the grass on either side of the steps forming a tiered amphitheatre of seating.

We all sat there like students in a lecture theatre, an assorted collection of men and boys, ages ranging from sixteen to sixty-six. Everyone in the team appeared excited at the thought of the annual match against Ragley's oldest rivals. It was soon clear that, with the exception of England playing Australia in the Ashes series at Headingley, this was the most important fixture in the cricket calendar.

'This could be our year, Grandad,' said Tommy Piercy, the strapping sixteen-year-old butcher's boy, known by everyone as Young Tommy so as not to be confused with his grandad of the same name.

Old Tommy Piercy took off his flat cap and wiped his bald head with a large spotted handkerchief.

'Mebbe so, mebbe not,' said Old Tommy as he puffed slowly on his old briar pipe. Old Tommy had been a member of Ragley cricket team for fifty years. Although his fading eyesight had reduced his batting average to one point five, it was said in the village that what Old Tommy didn't know about cricket could be written on the back of a fag paper. He looked up at his favourite grandson.

'Ah'll tell thee summat,' he said. 'It's nigh on twenty year since we beat 'em.'

Everyone nodded in agreement. Only Old Tommy, Big Dave and Little Malcolm had ever played in a winning Ragley team against Morton. The enormity of the task weighed heavily on their shoulders as they stared at the overgrown cricket field.

'Grass'll need cutting, tha knows,' said Deke Ramsbottom, his beer belly straining the seams of his denim cowboy shirt. It was unbuttoned to reveal his hairy chest and a shiny gold medallion the size of a teapot stand. Deke was always selected as the team's wicket keeper because he could neither bat nor bowl, but his selection was secure so long as he brought with him his two hard-hitting sons, Shane and Clint.

'Y'reight there, Deke,' said Little Malcolm, still nodding in agreement, 'grass does need cutting.' Little Malcolm did a lot of nodding.

Deke looked up at his two sons.

'My lads'll sort it,' he said.

Shane ruffled his younger brother's long, permed locks.

'C'mon, Nancy, let's get it done,' he said cheerfully.

Clint flashed his brother a disapproving glance but, wisely, said nothing. His big brother's muscles bulged under his Status Quo T-shirt and the letters H-A-R-D were tattooed on the knuckles of his right hand. Whilst the long-haired Clint frequented Diane's Hair Salon every Friday night, Shane simply visited Trevor the gentleman's barber in Easington once every two months. Trevor liked to give value for money and was known locally as 'Chainsaw Trev' because of the severity of the short back and sides he gave to every customer.

Clint knew when to keep quiet. He caught up with his long-striding brother and they both set off to put some petrol in Stan Coe's gang mower.

The rest of us looked at the state of the cricket field. Around twenty cows munched contentedly at the long, lank grass in the bright morning sunlight. In the centre of the field, a rectangle of large metal spikes with a thick rope attached to each one protected the cricket square from Stan Coe's herd of Friesian cattle.

'Wicket looks good,' said Peter the Bank Manager. Peter Duddleston managed one of the two banks in Easington and lived in a pretty cottage next door to The Royal Oak. Peter's off-spin bowling was generally regarded as cannon-fodder by opposing batsmen but the fact that he contributed bats, pads, wickets and cricket balls every season meant his place in the team's middle order was guaranteed.

'It certainly does,' said Allan the Accountant. Allan Bickerstaff was the team's Treasurer and was famous for his sartorial elegance. His neatly creased white flannels and flawlessly ironed shirt contrasted sharply with the scruffy, dishevelled appearance of Big Dave when they walked out together to open the batting. Allan had modelled his style on his hero, Geoffrey Boycott, and would spend an hour mustering a dozen runs. He was proud to tell everyone that his batting average of sixteen point five was the best in the team.

'Looks a fast wicket t'me,' said Big Dave. 'What d'you think, Tommy?'

Whilst Big Dave was clearly the captain and led from the front, he acknowledged that Old Tommy knew every blade of grass on the cricket square.

'Aye, ah reckon it is,' said Old Tommy, his eyes watery behind a cloud of smoke.

I looked at the bumpy, sloping rectangle of close-cropped ryegrass that was Old Tommy's pride and joy. This was a long way from Lord's Cricket Ground.

'D'you reckon we should bat first if we win t'toss?' asked Big Dave.

The whole team turned to look at Old Tommy's wrinkled and weather-beaten face. This was a big decision. He puffed on his pipe and the sweet smell of Old Holborn tobacco mixed with the powerful odour of cow dung hung on the gentle breeze.

'Nay, lad,' said Old Tommy. 'Yon wicket'll be green 'n fast at t'outset. Let Young Tommy bowl from t'pavilion end and he'll nail yon buggers t'sightscreen.'

Everyone nodded in agreement at Old Tommy's wise

words. The team talk was over, tactics were clear and the other players went off to find wheelbarrows and shovels to clear the field of the flat pancakes of cow dung.

Old Tommy and I remained.

'So, have you had a good season, Tommy?' I asked, eager to show interest.

'We've got a lot of potential,' replied Old Tommy cautiously.

'What position are you in the York and District league?' I asked innocently. I was unaware that Ragley had not won a game so far in the season.

The wise old man put his hand on my shoulder.

'Put it this way, young Mr Sheffield,' he said with a twinkle in his eye, 'the only thing below us in t'*Easington 'erald and Pioneer* is t'Fishing News.'

He paused to let this sink in.

'An', by the way, when we're batting keep thy umpire's finger in thee pocket. D'you get me meaning?'

He winked, grinned, pulled down the neb of his flat cap to shield his eyes from the sun and set off to supervise the preparation of the wicket.

'I'll be back this afternoon,' I shouted after his stooped figure.

York was full of tourists. I avoided the crowds in the Shambles and walked down Parliament Street to do my shopping. At the end I turned into Coppergate to look at the archaeological excavations, destined to become a reconstruction of the Anglo-Danish settlement at Jorvik. These were exciting times in this wonderful city, the jewel in the crown of Yorkshire.

Not for the first time I thanked Petillius Cerialis who

in AD 71 decided to build his fortress on the banks of the River Ouse in the midst of the dense woodlands of the Vale of York. It became the military headquarters of the Roman Imperial Army and Eboracum was born.

I walked slowly up Lendal towards the City Library and then enjoyed the peace of the Museum Gardens. The carved stone towers of York Minster, the largest medieval cathedral in Britain, were etched against a cloudless sky. It was a perfect day for a leisurely boat trip down the river. It was also a perfect day for a game of cricket.

Back in Ragley village, all roads led to the cricket field. The whole population seemed to be on the move. Men carried deck-chairs, young women pushed prams, George Hardisty and his wife Mary carried a wicker-work picnic basket and Deke Ramsbottom roared by in his Land Rover to check that his two sons had erected the marquee borrowed from the Ragley Scout Troop.

Nora's Coffee Shop had done a roaring trade and was about to close for the afternoon so that Nora Pratt could join her brothers, Victor and Timothy, at the cricket field. Tidy Tim had arrived early and was carefully arranging his three folding chairs in a neat line directly behind the bowler's arm at the pavilion end. Word had got around that Young Tommy Piercy, Ragley's new Freddie Trueman, was to open the bowling with Big Dave, and Tidy Tim did not want to miss the fun.

When I arrived at the field, the whole team were gathered around the cricket square and Young Tommy had just completed the final trim of the wicket with an expensive Qualcast mower, purchased recently from the club funds, after long debate by the Committee, for £21.95.

Outside the marquee some plastic tables and chairs had been arranged and Vera the Secretary was sitting alongside Shirley the Cook and Ruby the Caretaker. Vera was wearing her new straw hat and showing a magazine article to Shirley and Ruby. It was about the announcement by Princess Margaret and the Earl of Snowdon of their divorce.

Vera shook her head sadly. 'If only she'd married that handsome RAF man,' she mused, and Shirley and Ruby nodded knowingly. Unknown to Vera, inside the marquee, her brother Joseph had just uncorked a second bottle of white wine to share with Albert Jenkins. Next to him, Victor Pratt was ordering two pints of real ale and a lime and lemonade. The bar was doing a roaring trade.

I took in the scene around me. With the sun shining on the white picket fence, the bunting fluttering on the marquee and the Ragley and District Brass Band playing 'Land of Hope and Glory', the whole cricket ground looked a picture. But as Vera used to often remind me, 'Appearances can be deceptive.'

In front of the pavilion, Ernie Morgetroyd, the Morton umpire, resplendent in his huge white coat, was deep in conversation with John Pruett who was carrying another white umpire's coat over his arm.

I walked over to meet them.

'Is that for me?' I asked John, pointing at the white coat.

'Y'don't know t'situation, then?' said Ernie ominously.

'Let me explain,' said John, taking me by the arm.

'Allan Bickerstaff's had a bad fall rushing to unpeg his wife's washing. He tripped over the clothes prop and he's twisted his ankle.'

'Oh dear,' I said. 'So who's playing instead?' I asked innocently.

'You are,' said John, 'and I'm umpiring.'

'Me!' I yelled. 'You're joking! I haven't played since I was at school.'

Ernie Morgetroyd grinned from ear to ear. This was music to his ears.

John was insistent. 'There's no one else, Jack. Don't worry. You probably won't have to bat. It's just to make up the numbers. Allan's sent his cricket flannels and shirt. You're about his size. I've asked Anne Grainger to call into school to pick up your trainers so you'll certainly look the part. Go on, you can do it.'

John Pruett could be very persuasive.

Twenty minutes later Geoff Pickersgill, the Morton captain, won the toss and elected to bowl. Big Dave shook his head in disappointment. This was a bad start.

Little Malcolm bravely volunteered to open the batting with his giant cousin and together they strode out to the crease, the little and large of Ragley village cricket. A murmuring of nervous conversation rippled round the ground as Big Dave took his guard to receive the first ball. Rodney Morgetroyd, the Morton opening fast bowler, ran in like an express train and hurled a lightning delivery at Ragley's favourite son. Big Dave didn't blink and promptly clubbed the ball to the far end of the ground for three runs.

This brought Little Malcolm to face the bowling. The

next ball was a bouncer. It leaped off the corrugated pitch and hit Little Malcolm just over the left eye. What Little Malcolm lacked in stature he made up for in courage. He was five feet four inches of pure Yorkshire grit and he didn't flinch. The third ball crashed into his rib cage with a sickening thud. Little Malcolm knew he mustn't rub the fiery pain as this was a sign of weakness and would encourage the bowler. This was also the era before body padding and helmets and, in any case, Little Malcolm would have refused them, as he didn't want to be called 'a big girl's blouse' by Big Dave.

The next ball was on a good length and Little Malcolm bravely put his left foot down the wicket and smacked the ball back over the bowler's head for the first four of the game.

'Stuff it!' exclaimed Handsome Rodney in frustration.

'Up yours, Goldilocks,' retorted Little Malcolm and walked down the wicket confidently to prod down a few of the bumps in the pitch.

The game was on; the crowd clapped appreciatively, the scorers rummaged to find the right numbers to hang on the rusty hooks of the wooden scoreboard and John Pruett put the fourth of his six old pennies into his pocket to remind him of the number of balls bowled.

The Ragley innings went well. Big Dave smashed a quick twenty-five; Little Malcolm cut and pulled his way to a lifetime-best fifty-six and Shane Ramsbottom followed the disappointment of his dad's first-ball duck with an exhibition of big hitting. He struck three sixes, including one that went into the marquee and caused the Revd Joseph Evans to spill a full glass of Muscadet. At the end of their forty overs, Ragley's total was 163 for 6 and, much to my relief, Old Tommy and I had not been called upon.

The Morton fielders sportingly clapped the unbeaten Ramsbottom brothers and followed them into the pavilion for tea and sandwiches.

With a ham and lettuce sandwich in one hand and a large mug of black tea in the other, I walked outside to find a shady spot. I found one under the drooping branches of a huge weeping willow tree and sat down to enjoy my lunch when I heard a familiar voice.

'Hello, Jack. I didn't know you were a cricketer.'

It was Beth Henderson in a light blue summer dress and open-toed sandals. Her fair hair looked even blonder than I remembered and her pale shoulders had begun to redden in the sun.

'I'm not,' I replied. 'I was press-ganged into playing. Come to that, I didn't know you were a cricket fan.'

She smiled and sat down lightly on the grass next to me.

'This match is always a good day out,' she said, 'even though Morton always win,' she added mischievously.

The Ragley Brass Band suddenly started up again with their rendition of 'The Dam Busters March' and I looked at the summer scene around me.

'Isn't this the most perfect day?' I said.

She stretched out and lay back on the grass, her hands behind her head.

'Perfect,' she said and closed her eyes.

Not for the first time I thought how pretty she was.

'I'm forgetting my manners,' I said hurriedly. 'Would you like a drink from the marquee?'

'That would be lovely,' said Beth, sitting up and rubbing the strands of grass from her shoulders.

As we arrived at the marquee, the two umpires suddenly appeared and walked purposefully towards the cricket square.

'You'll need to go in a minute, Jack,' said Beth urgently. 'Don't worry about the drink, you're fielding now.'

Big Dave was shouting into the marquee where Deke Ramsbottom, resplendent in his wicket keeper's pads, was sinking his second pint of Tetley's bitter.

'Perhaps I could buy you that drink after the game?' I asked. 'That's if you're still here,' I added hopefully.

'I'll definitely be here,' said Beth cheerfully. 'You never know, you might even win!'

'And if we do?' I asked expectantly.

'Then we'll utilize your tidy kitchen and I'll make you the best meal you've ever tasted,' said Beth.

There was a new enthusiasm in her voice that excited me. It was as if she had let go of a heavy burden and wanted to live life to the full again. As I joined the Ragley team and walked down the pavilion steps, I was determined to do my best to help win the game. I couldn't have had a greater incentive.

We trooped out onto the field behind Big Dave to enthusiastic applause and I was told to field on the boundary in front of the pavilion.

'Good luck, Mr Sheffield,' shouted Ruby as I took my place on the boundary rope and the game began.

John Pruett told the Morton opening batsman that Young Tommy would be bowling the first of the forty overs and that he was 'right arm fast'. This was the understatement of the year. The first ball almost took the batsman's cap off before he could blink. It soared over the head of Deke Ramsbottom behind the stumps and crashed into the fence for four byes. Tidy Tim wrote a neat number four on his scorecard in the 'extras' column and the crowd clapped politely. The Morton innings had begun.

I was kept busy running around the boundary. Old Tommy had been positioned to field forty yards from me beneath the shady branches of a tree that bordered the ground, so it was up to me to collect any balls that went in his direction as well. Slowly the Morton score climbed but Big Dave kept pegging them back. As each bowler could only bowl a maximum of ten overs, Big Dave had saved one over each for Young Tommy and himself to bowl the final two overs.

Morton's score of 156 for 7 meant they only required eight runs to win and still had three wickets in hand. They were clear favourites to win but in the thirty-ninth over, Young Tommy, bowling as if his life depended on it, took two wickets and only conceded three runs. The final over bowled by Big Dave would decide the match and a hush descended on the crowd.

Geoff Pickersgill had played a captain's innings, pushing and prodding his way to a gallant 46 not out. It was his job to win the match for his team and he made up his mind to attack Big Dave's first ball.

In lower league cricket it is unusual to hear the crisp

crack of willow striking a cricket ball with perfect timing. Whereas a Garfield Sobers or Don Bradman would always use the 'sweet spot' of the bat, the village cricketer is used to the sound of a dull thud as shot after shot is mistimed with a cross-batted swipe. Today was different. Geoff Pickersgill launched himself at the first ball of Big Dave's over. The sound of his bat striking the ball was like a gunshot and it echoed round the ground. All eyes looked skywards as the small red cricket ball hurtled high into the air and then began its descent in my direction.

'Yours, Jack,' screamed Big Dave.

'Yours, Jack,' echoed Little Malcolm.

I stared up into the bright sunshine and saw a tiny black dot growing gradually bigger like an earth-bound meteorite. I began to run around the boundary edge and in the split-second before the ball sailed over the boundary rope, I leaped in the air, stuck out my left hand and clasped the ball tight as it smacked into my palm. At the same moment I landed on something soft and slippery.

One solitary cowpat had been overlooked in the clean-up operation and as I landed flat on my back and slid like a runaway toboggan, I proceeded to reduce it to the consistency of lumpy gravy. When I came to a halt the ball was still in my hand and I held it aloft in triumph.

The Ragley team shouted, 'Howzat?' and John Pruett raised his umpire's finger. An explosion of cheers shook the corrugated roof of the pavilion. Ragley had won the cricket match.

Big Dave was the first to reach me.

'Great catch, Jack,' he said and held out his hand to help me up. When he saw what I had landed in he withdrew his hand quickly.

'Flippin' 'eck, Jack,' said Big Dave, 'ah'd wipe meself down with grass afore y'shek 'ands if I were you.'

We walked up the pavilion steps in triumph with cheers ringing in our ears. The single shower wasn't functioning so I changed out of the filthy flannels and shirt, stuffed them in a carrier bag, rinsed my hands in a bucket and headed for the marquee.

Beth was there, grinning hugely. At last it seemed I had made a good impression.

'Over here, Jack, and well done,' she said with a wave.

As I joined her at the bar, I saw her wrinkle her nose.

'Sorry,' I apologized, 'the showers weren't working.'

'Don't worry,' said Beth, trying hard not to laugh, 'it's supposed to be lucky.'

'Is it really?' I asked, finding it hard to believe.

'Yes, something about being lucky in love,' she explained.

I looked into her eyes and they were shining.

Before I could respond, the barman walked over to take our order and a roar went up as Big Dave and Little Malcolm arrived at the head of a triumphant group of Ragley cricketers.

Big Dave slapped me on the back.

'What a fantastic catch, Jack. Yurra 'ero,' shouted Big Dave above the din.

'Aye, yurra 'ero all reight,' confirmed Little Malcolm.

I looked up and then down at the two cousins. This was praise indeed. At last I had achieved something in front of Beth. The moment soon passed as Big Dave brought me back down to earth.

'By 'eck, Jack, y'stink like a bloody sewer!' he said.

'Sshh!' said Beth sternly to the giant captain.

Little Malcom nodded back politely in acknowledgement.

'Y'right there, luv, 'e smells like that an' all!'

Beth looked at me in wide-eyed amazement and then burst into peals of laughter.

We took our drinks outside and sat on the grass. I recalled Beth's words before the match.

'So, are you cooking me a meal tonight?' I asked eagerly.

Before Beth could reply, Ruby and Vera suddenly appeared.

'Congratulations, Mr Sheffield,' said Vera with a smile. 'We're all proud of you.'

'Thank you, Vera, that's kind of you,' I replied modestly.

'I bet y'young lady's proud as well,' said Ruby with a cheeky grin.

'Excuse us,' said Vera hastily and tugged Ruby's sleeve as they made off.

Beth looked thoughtful again.

'Is that what I am?' she asked quietly. 'Your young lady?'

'I couldn't wish for anything better,' I said and clinked her glass as if it was a toast.

'There's just one condition, Jack.'

I looked concerned, wondering what she was about to say.

'What is it, Beth? You must know I'd do anything for you.'

She appeared to be weighing up the words.

'It's important,' she said.

'Anything at all,' I replied. 'Just name it.'

'Before I make you my special pork chops in orange sauce there's something you must do for me.'

'Just tell me, Beth. I'll do anything.'

She held my hand and looked into my eyes.

'Please have a bath!'

Chapter Eighteen

Sports Day

School Sports Day 1.45 p.m. – 3.00 p.m.

Excellent event with good attendance.

Extract from the Ragley School Logbook:
Wednesday 14 June 1978

'You'll have to keep an eye on the egg and spoon race, Jack,' said Anne as she scanned the list of races. 'Mrs Brown cheats every year.'

'That's right,' agreed Sally indignantly. 'She holds the pottery egg on with her thumb. Mr Pruett never noticed.'

'Why not use long-handled wooden spoons with a paper collar halfway down the shaft?' said Jo. 'That's what they did at my school.'

Vera, Anne and Sally stared at Jo as if she had just discovered a slimming course that actually worked.

'Let's do it,' said Anne. 'Sounds revolutionary but worth a try.'

She ticked her list and went off with Jo to count bean-bags.

High summer was upon us. It was Wednesday morning, 14 June, and my first school sports day at Ragley beckoned. Sun streamed in the window and George Hardisty had borrowed Mr Dudley-Palmer's top-of-the-range mower to give the running track an extra short unofficial trim. Clint and Shane Ramsbottom had arrived early with string and a bucket of whitewash and they were marking out running lanes. Shirley had filled the school fridge with choc-ices and Ruby had dragged her husband Ronnie away from his racing pigeons to rake the sand pit and mark out a run-up for the long jump. The children were excited and little work was done during morning school.

When the bell rang for morning playtime the white lines on the field had a magnetic attraction for the children. Five-year-olds balanced on them as if they were tightrope walkers and ten-year-olds ran up and down the lanes practising relay races.

In the staff-room Anne had a look of disappointment on her face.

'That's a pity,' she said. 'Little Theresa Buttle is going to miss Sports Day. There's another classic letter here from her mother.'

She passed it over to Sally who read it out loud: 'Dear Miss, Pleese execute our Theresa as she has verookas. Betty Buttle.'

'Sounds a bit extreme,' said Vera.

The rattle of a galvanized mop bucket announced the arrival of Ruby just outside the room. There was a gentle tap on the door.

Vera went out into the corridor to talk to Ruby.

'I've just bought these, Miss Evans,' said Ruby proudly, pointing down to her new shoes. Ruby had purchased a pair of wide-fitting 'Diana' shoes from a cut-price shop in Micklegate for £3.00.

'They're really comfortable,' said Ruby, 'and I won't trip up in the egg and spoon race.'

'They look ideal,' said Vera generously, 'and we'll all be cheering you on this afternoon.' Vera was determined to do all she could to help Ruby. 'And is Ronnie running in the fathers' race this year?' asked Vera.

'I 'ope so,' said Ruby. 'Our 'azel's in the 'oop race, I'm in the Ladies' egg an' spoon race and our Ronnie is down for the Dads' race. It's the full set.'

'Well, good luck, Ruby,' said Vera, 'and the shoes are a really good choice.'

Ruby walked away, proud of her purchase and pleased that Vera had given them the seal of approval. Meanwhile, Vera looked at Ruby and felt a touch of sadness for this large lady with the generous heart for whom a £3 pair of shoes was the highlight of the month.

Back in the staff-room, Sally had made a list of the races, including the sprints for each age group, relay races, high jump and long jump for the older children, a sack race, obstacle race, hoop race, skipping race, three-legged race plus the races for mothers and fathers.

Sally filled the Roneo Spirit Duplicator with fluid,

took a metal-tipped stylus pen, selected a smooth white master sheet, put a blue sheet of carbon paper underneath and began to print neatly. When she had completed the list, she attached the master sheet to the cylindrical drum, loaded the tray with white paper and turned the handle one hundred times. As Sally turned the handle, she dreamed of having a photocopier in school like the one at her husband's office but, deep down, she knew they would always be too expensive for primary schools.

By half past one, Shirley the Cook was already doing a roaring trade selling choc-ices outside the back door of the kitchen. A large number of mothers and grandparents had turned up, along with a small number of fathers. The chairs from the school hall had been arranged in a straight line along the length of the track and many parents were settling themselves down for an enjoyable afternoon. Sheila Bradshaw, dressed in a bikini top and hot pants, was rubbing a liberal supply of sun cream over her bare tummy whilst Ruby's mother, Agnes, fastened a few more buttons on her mackintosh and tightened the knot on her headscarf.

At a quarter to two the Sports Day began. I had borrowed an electric loud hailer from the Ragley Scout Troop and my job was to announce each event and the results.

'Good afternoon, everybody,' I said and the echo of my voice bounced off the school wall and rebounded into my ears. I realized I would have to pause after every few words. 'Welcome to Sports Day.'

A ripple of applause ran along the line of parents

and was taken up by the children who were sitting in their class groups on the opposite side of the track.

'Races will be started by our official starter, the Revd Joseph Evans, and will be judged at the finish by Mrs Pringle and Miss Maddison.'

The vicar bowed a little self-consciously and Sally and Jo waved enthusiastically. More applause rang out as I announced the first race.

'The first race on your programme is the running race for five-year-olds.'

And so it went on. Everybody ran, skipped, jumped and hopped. Claire Phillips ran an astonishingly quick last leg of the boys versus girls relay race and, much to the delight of Ruby, little Hazel Smith upheld family tradition and won the hoop race for five-year-olds. A few impromptu races took place including a mothers and toddlers race with every competitor receiving a free choc-ice. The athletic Sue Phillips won the mothers' race narrowly from the scantily clad Sheila Bradshaw. Then there were only two races left: the egg and spoon race for ladies and the sprint for men.

The tension in the crowd suddenly increased as the fearsome sight of Mrs Winifred Brown appeared confidently on the start line. This was followed by a resounding cheer as Ruby lined up alongside her. They eyed each other like two Sumo wrestlers. A few other mothers tentatively gathered around the collection of wooden spoons and pottery eggs and looked curiously at the long-handled wooden spoons with the paper collars halfway down the handle.

'What's all this then?' shouted Mrs Brown. 'Where's proper spoons?'

'These are the ones we are using this year,' said Anne Grainger firmly, fixing Mrs Brown with a stare that brooked no argument.

'You start with your spoon and egg on the ground and one hand behind your back,' said Anne. 'If you drop the egg, you must pick it up with the spoon. If you use your other hand to pick up the egg or to stop the egg from dropping off your spoon, you will be immediately disqualified.'

Winifred Brown gave me a piercing stare.

'Trust 'im t'make changes,' she grumbled.

Anne walked jauntily away and as she passed me she whispered, 'I've waited years to put that woman in her place.'

The cheers of 'C'mon Mum,' reached a crescendo as Joseph blew his whistle.

I recalled telling a children's story during one assembly about a race between a tortoise and a hare. Deep down I never really believed in it. But before everyone's eyes a parody was being acted out. Most of the mothers struggled to pick up their eggs with the unwieldy spoons and, when they did, the pottery eggs quickly tumbled to the ground again. Mrs Brown, although she was the last person everybody wanted to win, at least did have some idea and she would run a few yards, drop the egg, kick it another yard and pick it up again with the spoon. In this way she gradually moved into first place with a series of sprints and stalls.

Ruby, on the other hand, picked up her egg on the

spoon, stood for a few moments like a tightrope walker getting her balance, and then set off with slow, steady, short strides. Years of carrying saucepans and boiling chip pans in her obstacle course of a kitchen had prepared her for this moment. The spoon was rock steady in her hand. It was as if her egg was glued to it. Perspiration ran down her bright red cheeks as she moved inexorably towards the finish line and the cheers were by far the loudest of the afternoon.

Sally and Jo on the finish line forgot all sense of teacher decorum and screamed, 'Come on, Ruby, you can do it!'

With two yards to go Winifred Brown's egg parted company with her spoon for the last time and Ruby sailed by to win the race.

It gave me the greatest pleasure to announce, 'Ladies and gentlemen, boys and girls, the winner of the Ladies' Egg and Spoon Race for 1978 is Ragley's own, Mrs Ruby Smith.'

Little Hazel could not restrain her joy and bounded over to her mother, jumped into her arms and gave her a big kiss. No prize could have been greater for Ruby as she lifted Hazel and beamed at Vera who walked over and gave her a hug. Ronnie Smith walked over to Ruby and gave her a self-conscious peck on the cheek.

'Well done, our lass,' he said graciously.

Ruby fixed Ronnie with a stare he knew only too well.

'It's your turn now, Ronnie, show us what y'can do.'

Ronnie went grey.

With cheers still ringing around me, I announced the

final race. After Ruby's triumph, the fathers' race looked as though it would be an anti-climax. Traditionally, very few men turned up for Sports Day because they were out at work. Today, when I announced the dads' race, only four men walked to the start line. In the long and noble history of human endeavour, it was hard to imagine a more diverse group of athletes. In order of height, tallest first, they were Geoffrey Dudley-Palmer, Peter Miles-Humphreys, Ronnie Smith and Eddie Brown.

Geoffrey Dudley-Palmer had called in at the request of his daughter on his way to a board meeting at the Rowntree factory. His pin-stripe shirt echoed his pin-stripe suit and his cuff links and matching tiepin sparkled in the bright sunshine. He surveyed the opposition and concluded he was the hot favourite as, in his mind, his privileged upbringing meant he was taller, slimmer and more confident than his competitors. He glanced down at his brand-new leather-soled black shoes and wished he had brought more suitable footwear but he knew that once he got into his stride he would leave these unfit members of the proletariat far behind. As a casual gesture that he was taking this seriously, he slipped off his jacket to reveal its silk lining and its hand-stitched ticket pocket. He took to his mark and stared down the track as if he was Harold Abrahams in the 1924 Olympics. For Geoffrey Dudley-Palmer, the track had become a tunnel and he was going to fly through it and burst out of the other end a winner. He mentally rehearsed the classic lean forward with arms outstretched behind him as he broke the finishing tape, which was, in fact, an unbreakable length of baling twine from Pratt's Hardware Emporium.

Peter Miles-Humphreys was having trouble with his new trousers. Mrs Miles-Humphreys had always wanted to marry a film star but had settled for a shy bank clerk with an unfortunate stutter. Even so, she was determined that, with a little prompting, he could look like a cross between Charlton Heston and David Soul. With this in mind, she had been to Mackinder's clothes shop in York to purchase a stylish pair of flared 'Evvaprest fashion trousers' at £8.95. Peter Miles-Humphreys was an analytical man and, as he stood on the starting line with a brisk breeze in his face, he had quickly concluded that flared trousers would produce more wind resistance and, in consequence, he had tucked his trouser bottoms into his long, green, diamond-patterned golfing socks. His wife looked on in horror as her husband committed fashion suicide and, looking like a 1920s American golfer, he took his mark behind the white line.

Ronnie Smith was sad. Fifteen years previously as a Ragley Rovers right-winger and with his whippet-like frame, he would have won this race easily. Unfortunately, the regular intake of Tetley's bitter had reduced his muscle tone and the delight he experienced, after the years of saving enough coupons to qualify for a garden swing and a dartboard from Kensitas cigarettes, was in inverse proportion to the damage done to his lungs by the cigarettes themselves. Ronnie was the oldest competitor in the race and his sharp, tactical, devious brain told him that his only chance of avoiding humiliation was to set off fractionally before the starter's whistle signalled the start of the race.

Eddie Brown had the misfortune to be married to Winifred. His workmates at the warehouse in York, who regularly described him as one sandwich short of a pack-up, looked at him with a mixture of admiration and sadness. No one could imagine what it must be like married to such a battleaxe as Winifred. Like a punch-drunk boxer, Eddie would boast, 'When she sez it's Thursday, it's Thursday.' That was probably his longest ever sentence, as Eddie was known as a man of few words. His usual responses were 'Y'what?', which provided him with much needed thinking time and 'Oh-kay, oh-kay', which meant he understood and there was no need to keep going on about it.

It was said in the village that if his belly got any bigger he would need a wheelbarrow to cart it around. From a distance, in his pink and silver Bay City Rollers track-suit with half-mast trouser legs, he looked like a giant candyfloss on a stick. Eddie wasn't bright enough to understand he had no chance. He vaguely remembered that he used to run for a bus to get home from work but now he was the proud owner of a three-wheeled, 1975 Reliant Robin complete with upgraded 850 cc engine with the remarkable acceleration of 0–60 mph in 16.1 seconds. As his son Dominic tied his father's shoelaces each morning, Eddie would sit at the kitchen table and imagine sinking into the comfort of his leopard-skin-covered seats and roaring off towards York with his fluffy dice bouncing madly in the front window. Eddie loved speed, and on the narrow country roads around

Ragley village, no one ever passed his Reliant Robin with its customized flame-red speed-stripe down the side. Today would be no different. When he looked at his fellow competitors he thought, 'Easy, two puffs an' clapped-out Ronnie,' but when Joseph Evans said, 'Take your marks,' Eddie could only retort, 'Y'what?'

'We're starting the race now, Mr Brown,' said Joseph patiently.

'Oh-kay, oh-kay,' said Eddie, not caring for the vicar's tone and flexing his arms. The tattoo on his right forearm that read 'SANDRA', the result of a pre-Winifred liaison with a barmaid at the Butlin's Holiday Camp in Filey, wobbled like jelly on a plate.

'Take your marks,' repeated Joseph.

'Get set!'

As he raised the whistle to his lips, Ronnie was off like a ferret down a hole.

A split second later Joseph blew the whistle by which time Geoffrey Dudley-Palmer had launched himself down the track. This caused his expensive leather shoes with the shiny soles to slip on the grass and he promptly fell flat on his face. Meanwhile, Peter Miles-Humphreys trotted off at a steady pace, as he wanted to make sure his designer flared trousers stayed firmly in his socks. Ernie was completely confused, first, by Ronnie setting off before the whistle and, second, by the sight of the posh guy next to him falling down as if he had been shot.

By now, Ronnie was ten yards in the clear and could taste glory but the sudden shock to his system was enormous. The oxygen in his blood stream was sufficient to carry a tray of five pints of Tetley's bitter across a smoky room but not to run with the speed of a racing pigeon across an open field. After twenty yards he coughed for the first time.

Peter was puzzled. The strange little man in the bobble hat was running as if his life depended on it, whereas running had never been an integral part of his own life. He knew for a fact that in the bank running was strictly forbidden. So he continued with his peculiar prancing motion with tiny strides as if he was running in an invisible sack: indeed, had he but known it, this action would have won him many sack races. In this way he progressed down the track and did not disturb the copious amount of trouser material stuffed down his socks.

Geoffrey Dudley-Palmer was in deep panic. Every time he attempted to stand up, his feet shot away from him like Bambi on ice. Five precious seconds had elapsed before he managed to take a few cautious paces and then he began to run. The lack of friction between his feet and the ground took him on a diagonal path across the course and he bumped into Eddie as he inadvertently changed lanes.

'Oh-kay, oh-kay!' shouted Eddie in disgust.

Eddie's prodigious belly bounced like a blancmange inside his Bay City Rollers tracksuit and his slow brain sent a message to his body to stop quickly, climb into his Reliant Robin and go home to watch *Coronation Street*.

At the side of the track the children cheered, Ruby shouted encouragement and Felicity Miles-Humphreys screamed as Ronnie's lead was gradually whittled away by the pitter-patter of Peter Miles-Humphreys and the late charge from Geoffrey Dudley-Palmer. The length of the track had been determined by the amount of white-wash in Clint Ramsbottom's bucket so fifty yards from the start line, Sally and Jo held the length of twine and waited in trepidation as, with five yards to go, Geoffrey Dudley-Palmer tried with all his might to catch the exhausted Ronnie, and Peter Miles-Humphreys drew level with Ronnie's shoulder. A split second before he was overtaken, Ronnie fell across the finishing line, wheezing badly. Geoffrey and Peter were declared equal second and Eddie was disqualified for coming to a shuddering halt after thirty yards and not completing the course.

'Teacher, teacher, my dad won, my dad won,' shouted little Hazel Smith to Anne Grainger.

Ruby ran with surprising speed to give Ronnie a hug that almost asphyxiated him.

'My 'ero!' she said.

'Ah'm knackered!' gasped Ronnie.

Peter Miles-Humphreys slumped into a chair next to his wife.

Nigel patted his father on the back.

'Well done, Dad,' said Nigel.

'Was I s-s-s?' stuttered Peter.

'Second, yes, Dad, you were,' added Nigel.

'Well run, darling,' said Felicity to Peter, dragging his trouser bottoms out of his socks. 'I didn't know you still had it in you.'

Eddie Brown was staggering back to his Reliant

Robin whilst receiving a tongue-lashing from his wife.

'You're a blooming disgrace t'family!' shouted Winifred to Eddie. 'If y'were a carthorse, they'd put y'down.'

'Y'what?' said Eddie.

Chapter Nineteen

Seaside Gladys and the Summer Fair

The Summer Fair raised over £500 and this will be used to buy resources for the new library area.

Extract from the Ragley School Logbook: Monday 26 June 1978

'Seaside Gladys tells fortunes,' said Ruby.

The Summer Fair Committee looked at her in surprise.

'Seaside Gladys?' said Anne Grainger, looking up from her list of stalls.

'She's my aunty in Skegness,' explained Ruby. 'She was born on the day Queen Victoria died in 1901 and she says it gave her special powers. She knows what's going to 'appen before it 'appens.'

'Well, it's different,' said Anne cautiously. 'What does everyone else think?'

Anne had always chaired these annual meetings and I was determined to stay in the background.

Conversations broke out everywhere. This was something new.

'Could be a real money spinner at fifty pence a time,' said Sally Pringle, 'and I've got a hippy friend with an authentic gypsy caravan.'

Vera looked less convinced.

'I'm not sure about fortune tellers,' said Vera and then saw the disappointment on Ruby's face, 'but I'll take Ruby's word for it.'

Ruby smiled, although she wasn't too clear why Vera should have a problem with her Aunty Gladys.

There were encouraging nods all around the table so Anne added to her list.

'Will you let her know please, Ruby?' asked Anne.

'Perhaps she knows already,' said Sally mischievously.

Anne read out her list.

'There's the usual mixture of parents, staff and villagers who like to help the school. We've got Jo's Prisoner in the Stocks, Tommy Piercy's Bowls Competition, Big Dave's Beat the Goalie, Vera and Ruby's Cross-Stitch Stall, Virginia's Pony Rides, Nora Pratt's Cake Stall, Val Flint's Win a Goldfish, Shirley's Refreshment Stall, Sue Phillips' Bash the Rat, the Dads' Cake Making Competition, half a dozen other stalls yet to be planned by the PTA, plus the Ragley and District Brass Band for the parade in the village and the Fancy Dress Competition.'

Anne ticked her list as she read them out.

'Finally, perhaps Sally would organize the gypsy caravan and take the money for Seaside Gladys? That's all, everybody, thanks for attending, all we need now is a fine day.'

Saturday 24 June dawned bright and clear and by nine o'clock the school field was a hive of activity. Stakes were being driven in the ground, signs were painted and nailed on, Young Tommy Piercy was mowing the bowls strip for his grandad and a brightly painted gypsy caravan was being unloaded from the back of a trailer. A few children peered in the windows thinking that Seaside Gladys was already inside but the blinds were down and no sounds could be heard.

In the school office, Vera was counting out piles of coins and filling twenty plastic bags so that each stall could begin with a float of five pounds, and Ruby was unpacking a beautiful collection of cross-stitch work.

'Miss Evans, will you be going in to see my Aunty Gladys?' asked Ruby.

Vera did not look up from her counting.

'I don't think so, Ruby,' said Vera. 'I don't believe in all that hocus-pocus.'

Ruby looked thoughtfully at Vera and decided that maybe it was something to do with being the sister of a vicar that prevented Vera from fully appreciating her Aunty Gladys. Many years before, Seaside Gladys had told the youthful Ruby that she would meet a handsome stranger and she would be blessed with children. Whilst her Ronnie was not exactly handsome in the generally accepted sense, back in the fifties in his purple drainpipe trousers and thick crêpe-soled shoes he once looked as though he could have been. In those pre-bobble-hat days, he had slick, black, Brylcreemed hair with a Bill Haley kiss curl that hung like an inverted question mark over his forehead. Ruby thought he was wonderful and she now had six children to prove it.

At one o'clock everyone gathered on the village green for the traditional fancy dress parade through the village, from where they would march to the school playground prior to the opening of the Summer Fair by Joseph Evans. Front doors opened and everyone in the village seemed to line the route. The lunchtime drinkers at The Royal Oak came to stand outside as the Ragley and District Brass Band marched by and played 'Yellow Submarine' whilst the children followed behind.

Deke Ramsbottom, pint glass in hand, particularly appreciated the two six-year-olds dressed as the Lone Ranger and Tonto and shouted 'Hi Yo Silver, Howay!' much to the confusion of the children concerned. Elisabeth Amelia Dudley-Palmer, dressed as Little Bo Peep, dragged a small wooden sheep behind her on squeaky wheels and Kenny Flanaghan and Tony Ackroyd, in Batman and Robin outfits, fought imaginary foes with fierce cries of 'Thwack', 'Biff' and 'Boom'.

It was a colourful and noisy crowd that walked up the school drive and noticed the strange sight of an authentic Romany caravan parked on the grass next to the school car park. The Revd Joseph Evans declared the Summer Fair open and promised that every penny raised would go towards a new school resource library to be sited in the corner of the hall and including shelving, books, visual aids and a slide projector. Everyone clapped politely, except for Stan Coe who muttered complaints that precious funds were being diverted from the Social Club.

This was followed by a mini stampede towards the gypsy caravan. Sally was right. This was a popular attraction. She had produced a large sign and propped it on an old wooden easel. It read, 'Fortune Telling with Seaside Gladys, only 50p, confidentiality guaranteed.'

A queue of mothers had already formed by the time Sally sat at her table alongside the wooden steps that had been propped against the caravan. Mrs Winifred Brown, at the front of the queue, didn't know what 'confidentiality' meant but, as long as she was told she would be rich one day, she didn't mind. No one had seen Seaside Gladys enter and I was tempted to spend fifty pence just to see what she looked like. A black curtain had been draped against the open doorway to add to the air of mystery.

I was the only member of staff not assigned to a stall. The intention was I could indulge in some public relations and also give each stallholder a ten-minute comfort break at some point during the afternoon. Val Flint was doing a roaring trade on her hoopla stall and was rapidly running out of goldfish. Little Bo Peep was announced as the winner of the Fancy Dress Competition and Jo Maddison was whipping up the crowd into a frenzy as they each paid ten pence for a wet sponge in order to throw it at some poor unfortunate, yet strangely willing, villager locked into the wooden stocks.

The Revd Joseph Evans saw the funny side of a brief conversation with two boys caught smoking behind the school cycle shed.

'Do you know where naughty boys who smoke go to?' demanded Joseph.

'Behind t'cricket pavilion, Mr Evans,' answered one of the boys, quick as a flash.

A delighted Mr Miles-Humphreys showed off his iced sponge cake topped with Smarties and hundreds and thousands, which won the Dads' Cake Making Competition. He spent the afternoon explaining how his elder son Rupert should get most of the credit for finding the perfect recipe in his grandma's Be-Ro recipe book.

Nora Pratt had supported this event for many years and was concerned at some of the detrimental comments directed towards her cake stall. She had resorted to hastily scribbling a notice and she had propped it up against a tired-looking Dundee fruitcake. It read, 'All ingredients in these cakes have been passed by the management'. After much giggling and a sudden drop in sales, her big brother, Tidy Tim, whispered something in her ear and the notice was removed forthwith. Tidy Tim paused to create a neat pattern of fairy cakes, with alternate white and pink icing, before he wandered off to try to win a goldfish.

Meanwhile, the shapely Virginia from the riding school had attracted most of the young men in the village. As she strolled around the makeshift paddock in her skin-tight jodhpurs, a group of adolescent men ogled in appreciation. Clint Ramsbottom wondered what he would look like with a riding hat perched on his long permed locks and whether it would ruin his cool image. He decided not to risk it and went to show his skill at Big Dave's Beat the Goalie. Sheila Bradshaw, who was having a short break from The Royal Oak, surprised all the men by achieving the top score in the target bowls competition. Most of the men stayed for an extra hour in order to beat her score but no one managed it and Old Tommy reluctantly delivered the prize of a crate of Guinness back to The Royal Oak from whence it came.

A familiar figure appeared on the driveway during the late afternoon. I recognized the summer dress and the honey-blond hair. Beth looked relaxed as she saw me and pointed to the gypsy caravan.

'That looks interesting,' she said.

'Good to see you, Beth, thanks for coming.'

Beth had just returned from an advisers' course at High Sutton Hall and I hadn't seen her for a few days.

'It's for a good cause today, Jack, so I'm going to work my way around the stalls, including the fortune telling. You never know, I might meet a tall, dark stranger one day who will sweep me off my feet.'

She looked up at the uncontrollable palm tree of brown hair that sprang from the crown of my head. Self-consciously I tried to flatten it but I knew it was a waste of time.

'Are you having your fortune told, Jack? It might be interesting.'

'I doubt it, I'm not sure I believe in that sort of thing.'

'Give it a try, Jack, you've nothing to lose,' said Beth in a determined voice.

'I'll see,' I said hesitantly. 'Anyway, I'm supposed to be giving people time off from their stalls, so I'll see you later.'

I wandered away reluctantly as Beth went off to queue for Seaside Gladys.

I took over from Val Flint and gave the last goldfish to a little boy who failed repeatedly to throw a hoop over any of the tin cans. Ruby left her cross-stitch stall and walked over to talk to me.

'Are you going to see my Aunty Gladys, Mr Sheffield?'

'I'm not sure, Ruby. Maybe at the very end, I'll pop my head in to say thank you.'

'Mr Sheffield, ah think y'should go, Aunty Gladys is very good at lookin' inside people.'

I sensed I would regret it but Ruby looked so keen for me to try.

'OK, Ruby, I'll do it.'

Beth saw me walking towards the caravan.

'I'm going to have a go,' I shouted to her.

'Good luck, Jack,' said Beth and then as an afterthought, 'it's really quite revealing.'

I paid my fifty pence to Sally and walked up the steps. It was surprisingly dark and humid inside the caravan. There were narrow bench seats on either side and I sat down beside a circular table covered with a lace tablecloth and on which a crystal ball reflected the flickering light from a strange, patterned candle with a pungent flame. As my eyes slowly adjusted I saw a pack of playing cards that appeared larger than normal placed face down on the table. Opposite me was an old lady with a red headscarf, huge dangly earrings and a face like ancient parchment.

'Hello, young man,' said Seaside Gladys. 'Now, tell me what's on your mind. You appear troubled.'

'No, I'm fine,' I said defensively, 'it's just a busy day.'

She stared at me intently. I felt as if she was looking right through me. Her long scarlet fingernails touched the pack of cards. 'Perhaps my Tarot cards can help you to find the path that you seek and the partner that waits for you.'

'I promised Ruby I would come to see you,' I said, eager to change the subject, 'and I've only got a few minutes.' Even so, I was intrigued by the comment about a partner waiting for me.

'It's Mr Sheffield, isn't it?' said Seaside Gladys with a knowing smile.

She handed me the pack of cards.

'Please shuffle the cards, Mr Sheffield, and don't worry, this won't take long.'

Misspent evenings as a student meant I was used to shuffling cards but this pack was larger and there were more cards than I expected. In my haste they scattered on the table before me.

'Sorry,' I said and gathered them up quickly.

'Don't worry, just shuffle them and, when you feel happy about it, pass them back to me.'

I took a deep breath, shuffled them slowly and deliberately and passed them back to her.

'I know there are many things on your mind, Mr Sheffield, but just relax for a few minutes. I've done this many times before and, you never know, it might just help.'

There was a hint of a warm smile from this strange old lady and I began to relax as she turned the cards over one by one. I noticed they had strange pictures on them and they were unlike any cards I had seen before. She put three in a pile in the centre of the table and then placed four around it like the points of a compass. After forming a cross shape, she then placed a column of four cards to the side from the bottom to the top. One or two of the cards were reversed so the picture was upside down and easier for me to read.

'This is a time for a fresh new beginning,' she said, lightly touching a card with a picture of a jester on it. I was concerned that it said the words 'The Fool' but Seaside Gladys looked content that it was there.

'You are at a crossroads but don't hesitate any longer or else you may be disappointed.'

She tapped the card entitled 'The World'. It was inverted.

'I see success but sometimes you fear it, you are unsure.'

Her eyes studied the bright yellow picture of a sun and the final card entitled 'Judgement'.

'I see a good, positive life for you, Mr Sheffield, but you must reach out and take it,' she paused and looked at me carefully, 'both in your work and in your personal life.'

The candle flickered, my heart slowed and in the far distance I could hear the faint sounds of children laughing and shouting. Here in the dim light of the caravan, rushing time paused, thoughts were cleansed and decisions became less difficult.

'Thank you, Gladys,' I said, getting up from the table. I sensed time was up, although I had not been asked to leave. 'You've given me a lot to think about.'

'You're a good man,' said Seaside Gladys, taking my right hand in her hands and squeezing it. 'I wish you a good life.'

As I left the caravan, bright, sharp reality rushed at me from all sides. Sally looked at me inquisitively as she collected her Tupperware box of coins and ethnic shoulder bag and popped her head around the curtain to tell Seaside Gladys that fortune telling was over for the day.

I guessed she already knew.

Back in school, Vera was collecting the takings.

'£463.28 so far, Mr Sheffield, and still counting. The best ever total for a Summer Fair,' she said as she stacked the silver and bronze coins in neat piles and rows.

'We can have our library now, Jack,' said Anne, looking distinctly sunburned as she put five pounds' worth of ten-pence pieces in a plastic bag.

'How did you get on with Gipsy Rosy Lee?' asked Jo who was filling the kettle at the sink. 'Did she see a pay rise for teachers in her crystal ball?'

'It was, how would you say, revealing,' I said quietly.

Vera gave me a sharp, curious look and then resumed her counting.

There was a tap on the door. It was Beth.

'Thanks for a lovely day, everybody, I'm sure it's been successful.'

Jo held up the teapot. 'Would you like a cup of tea before you go?'

Beth looked at her watch. 'Sorry, I must rush, I'm meeting a friend outside the Theatre Royal in York in half an hour, but thanks anyway.'

My heart sank and I remembered what Seaside Gladys had said about grasping the opportunity.

I shot an anxious look towards Beth but, as ever, she was in a hurry and busy with the immediacy of her life.

She looked at me and said, 'She's an old college friend, Jack. We shared a flat together many years ago and we've a lot to catch up on.'

I wondered if Beth noticed the instant of relief in my expression before she left. I resolved to ask her out to dinner when we met again. With only a few weeks to go before the end of term I really would have to get a move on. There were important decisions to be made. I had decided to book a holiday gite in Brittany during the school summer holiday and I was waiting for the right moment to ask Beth if she wanted to join me.

Through the window I noticed Sally helping Seaside Gladys out of the caravan. The power that seemed to exude from her when she was in the caravan appeared to have gone now and she just looked like a very old and frail lady casting long shadows in the late-afternoon sun. She stood by the wall of the car park and seemed to be searching for something in her large knitted bag.

Sally popped her head round the door and gave the plastic box of money to Vera.

'Jack, I'm taking Seaside Gladys round to Ruby's house now but she wondered if she could have a quick word with you and Vera.'

'Of course,' I said, 'I want to thank her.'

'With me as well?' said Vera in surprise. 'Why me?'

'I don't know, Vera,' said Sally, shaking her head, 'that's all she said.'

'Come on, Vera, let's see what she's got to say,' I said.

'I'll finish counting out the cash, Vera,' said Jo.

As we walked outside, Seaside Gladys walked slowly towards us and her carved walking stick tapped on the tarmac surface of the car park.

She stood patiently before Vera and gave her a small parcel, beautifully wrapped in lilac paper and tied with neat gold thread.

Vera looked both embarrassed and surprised.

'What's this?' asked Vera.

'A present for a true lady with a heart of gold,' said Seaside Gladys.

'I don't understand,' said Vera.

The old gipsy turned to grip the railings and lowered herself gently on to the coping stone of the school wall. It seemed to take a great deal of effort. When her breathing steadied she put her hand on Vera's arm.

'Ruby has told me all about you and I have always wanted her to find confidence. She's never had much of that. You've made her feel special and that's a great gift.'

Vera looked into her creased and weathered face, smiled and accepted the present.

She appeared to be trying to find the right words.

'I have an apology to make to you,' Vera said quietly but firmly. 'I called what you do hocus-pocus. I had no right to do that.'

'There are many things we don't understand and sometimes that makes us afraid,' said Seaside Gladys. 'Just have faith and follow your heart.'

With that, she struggled to her feet and climbed into Sally's car.

Everyone waved as the old lady disappeared down the drive.

Back in the office, Vera opened her parcel. It was a bottle of Old English Lavender Water made in Knaresborough, in the oldest chemist shop in England.

She held it up, unscrewed the top and offered it to Jo.

'It's beautiful,' said Jo, sniffing the scent of lavender, 'it's different, not too obvious but it could really grow on you.'

Vera looked for a long time at the bottle.

'Yes,' she said, almost to herself, 'just like Seaside Gladys.'

Chapter Twenty

The Accident

Miss Maddison's class visit to Brimham Rocks.

Mr Sheffield was involved in a Road Traffic Accident.

(A. Grainger, Acting Headmistress)

Extract from the Ragley School Logbook:
Tuesday 4 July 1978

I barely saw the car that hit me.

One minute everything was fine, the next my world was turned upside down in a tangle of metal and a screech of brakes.

It was Tuesday 4 July and I had driven over to Brimham Rocks to spend the morning with Jo Maddison and her class. The weather was perfect and the children were excited when they saw the weird and wonderful shapes of the huge rocks carved out during the Ice Age some three hundred million years ago.

Jo had asked Vera to go along and help her supervise

the children. Vera was thrilled to be asked and had donned her stylish wide-brimmed straw hat with a lavender ribbon and had taken charge of the packed lunches. Six parents had volunteered to help and when I left them to return to school, Vera was giving precise instructions to each of them about the disposal of plastic bags and glass bottles.

As it was such a beautiful day, I decided to take the quiet country lane from Brimham Rocks to the tiny village of Burnt Yates on the B6165 road. This took me on a scenic route home past Ripley Castle and on through Knaresborough. The road was narrow and winding and the hedgerows were so high it was impossible to see what might be round the next bend. I drove slowly and carefully and wound down my window to drink in the warm summer air. It was good to be alive in God's own country on a day such as this.

I meandered around a right-hand bend when suddenly I saw a white Lada 1200 four-door saloon hurtling towards me on the wrong side of the road. The young man behind the wheel hit his brakes and the back end of his car slewed sideways violently and hit the front offside of my car. It felt as though I was turning through a full circle in slow motion as my car mounted the nearside grassy bank and ploughed through the hedge. My head hit the side window and then there was an eerie silence before I lapsed into unconsciousness.

Eventually, in an endless tunnel of dark grey mist, I heard a voice calling to me. Through blurred vision I made out the shape of a young policeman and I realized I was lying on a bed in the back of an ambulance.

'What's your name?' he yelled in my face.

I tried to speak but I couldn't breathe. A stiff collar had been buckled securely around my neck by the ambulance team. I pointed feverishly to the inside pocket of my tweed jacket where my wallet contained all my personal details.

'Wall . . . et,' I mumbled.

'Wally?' said the eager young policeman, scribbling in his notebook. 'Wally what?' he yelled and stood up as if he intended to leave me to suffocate. I was desperate.

'No . . . oh, No . . . oh, don't,' I cried, trying to shake my head.

'Node, is that it?' he shouted. 'Wally Node? Don't worry, Mr Node, you're gonna be all right.' He wrote again in his little black notebook and stepped out of the back of the ambulance.

I fumbled with numb fingers at the neck support, knowing that I was about to pass out any moment. In the nick of time, the ambulance man came in and realized the cause of my distress.

'Calm down,' he said quietly and loosened the neck support. I sucked sweet oxygen into my lungs.

'What's his name?' he shouted to the policeman.

'Wally Node,' came the authoritative reply.

I shook my head vigorously.

'Just keep still, Wally,' said the kindly ambulance man. 'We're taking you to the hospital in Harrogate. Try to relax and we'll soon have you right.'

And so it was that on that beautiful sunny day in July 1978, a road traffic accident patient by the name of Wally

Node was admitted to the Accident and Emergency Department of Harrogate Hospital.

Back in school Anne Grainger was taking control.

Anne telephoned the ward sister at the hospital and asked for an update on my condition and checked on visiting times. Then she contacted my mother, reassured her that all would be well and dispatched her husband, John, to Leeds to collect her and her sister, May. The secretary at the Education Office in Northallerton was next and she promised Miss Barrington-Huntley would be informed and took Anne's home number.

The School Governors, Joseph Evans, Stan Coe and Albert Jenkins, were summoned to meet in school the following morning. Miss Flint's availability was confirmed to take over my class and a letter to parents was dictated to Vera the Secretary. Jo Maddison, Sally Pringle and Valerie Flint agreed to stay behind after school to discuss the implications for the following week's Centenary Day. All this was achieved with the calmness and professionalism of a deputy headmistress at the peak of her powers.

Someone was holding my hand. It was a nurse.

'We're just taking you for an X-ray, Jack. Just lie still,' said a voice.

I glanced down and wondered where my clothes were and why I was wearing a white smock.

Then it occurred to me. She had called me Jack. I was no longer Wally Node. Presumably, someone had the good sense to check my wallet.

'What happened?' I asked. 'What about the other driver? How is he?'

'Nothing to worry about, Jack. The doctor will explain everything to you soon.'

As we swept along the never-ending corridor, above my head the bright fluorescent lights flickered by with the metronome regularity of telegraph poles outside the window of a train.

There were too many questions and not enough answers so I closed my eyes and slept.

I knew I was dreaming. The sky was turning, fields swept by, the hedgerow was upside down and two people were staring down at me. They both looked like my mother.

'Jack, it's me. How are you?'

One of the two women was gently pushing my hair out of my eyes.

Margaret sat down on the bed whilst her sister stood alongside, holding her hand.

Slowly my eyes focused.

'Mam, it's you.'

The emotion was too much for me and I felt a tear running down my cheek.

I remembered my mother's old adage.

'Sorry, Mam,' I mumbled, 'boys don't cry.'

She squeezed my hand.

'But men do,' she whispered and wiped the tear from my eye. 'Now just rest and everything will be fine.'

The next morning bright sunlight lanced across my eyelids and I awoke. My headache had gone and, apart from a bandage wrapped around my forehead, I seemed to be in good shape. There were no broken bones, only stiffness in some of my joints.

A nurse arrived at the side of my bed.

'So, how are you feeling now, Jack?' she asked.

'Fine,' I replied, 'just a little confused.'

'You've had a bang on your head, Jack,' she explained, 'so we needed to keep an eye on you overnight and probably tonight as well. The doctor will call in to see you later.'

'I remember my mother being here,' I said. 'I spoke to her.'

'She's coming back with her sister this afternoon. You've had lots of people ringing up to see how you are. Some of them will be coming during visiting hours.'

I managed to sit up in bed to eat a little porridge and drink some tea. After that, I felt much better and it was a relief to see the young policeman again. I half expected him to address me as 'Wally' but he seemed to be well briefed. He took a statement and told me that the driver of the other car had just overtaken another vehicle on the bend. The driver and passenger of that vehicle had confirmed he was driving recklessly and that, in spite of my evasive action, he had caused the crash. The prints of my tyre tracks on the nearside grass verge were added proof of this.

'Your car's been taken to Pratt's Garage in Ragley, Mr Sheffield,' said the constable. 'The mechanic said he'd make it good as new.'

Reassured that my pride and joy was in safe hands, I sank back on the pillow.

When the policeman had gone, I noticed the routine

of hospital life going on around me. Cleaners came in and mopped the floors. Nurses took my temperature and blood pressure and then recorded their results on a clipboard hung over the metal rail at the foot of my bed. Opposite me a patient by the name of Harry Bartholomew was staring forlornly at the sign above his bed that said 'Nil by Mouth'.

'What are you in for?' I asked.

'Hernia,' came the despondent reply.

'You OK?' I added cheerfully.

'No,' said Harry, 'I'm not allowed to laugh.'

'Why not?' I asked.

'Stitches,' mumbled Harry.

A long pause ensued. This was to be the pattern of our conversations for the next twenty-four hours.

'What do you do for a living?' I asked, eager to establish support.

'I'm a professional comedian,' said Harry.

Only by stuffing the corner of the pillow into my mouth did I avoid laughing.

'So you won't be practising your act on this lot then?' I added.

Around us the other members of the 'Nil by Mouth' club groaned, coughed and mumbled, and doctors with serious faces examined them, shook their heads and walked slowly away.

'Too bloody right, mate,' he grumbled.

Suddenly a doctor appeared and pulled the curtain around the curved rail above my bed. His white coat looked as new as the stethoscope hanging around his neck. He looked so young, barely old enough to take his driving test, but he spoke with wisdom beyond his apparent years.

'We intend to keep you in for observation for one more night, Mr Sheffield. You took quite a blow to the side of your head. We'll give you something for the pain, change the dressings and make sure everything has settled down before you go back home. I'll be back to check on you tomorrow.'

Time passed slowly as the afternoon dragged on. I stared through the open doors of the ward at the posters on the notice board in the corridor. The two largest posters had been placed side by side. One was a health education poster and the other was advertising fund raising for the new scanner appeal. It stated where tickets could be purchased. If you read only the bold print at the top of each poster from left to right, it said, 'Venereal Disease – We Got Ours At The Co-op'. I pointed this out to Harry who laughed out loud and then groaned in pain.

Visiting time was 3.00 p.m. to 8.00 p.m. and I wondered who might visit. John Grainger was the first to arrive. He had brought Margaret and May with him and they fussed around, plumping my pillows and force-feeding me with grapes while John unpacked a carrier bag of Get Well cards.

Aunt May was her usual tactful self. She pointed at my surgical smock.

'Y'look a wee sissy, Jack, in that skirt,' said May.

John stepped in quickly with his news.

'Jack, Anne sends her love and said every child in the school has made a card for you.' He looked down at a note written in Anne's flowing handwriting. 'She says be sure to read the ones in Miss Maddison's class, particularly, Sarah and Jimmy.'

He tipped the cards out. The one on top was from Anita in my class. It read predictably, 'Your the best teecher in the wurld.'

Sarah's card had a beautiful drawing on the front of a skinny man with huge glasses and big feet. He was standing next to a bright green car that had been squashed flat. Six-year-old Sarah Louise Tait was one of our very best storytellers and she had a wonderful vocabulary for one so young. Sarah had written, 'This morning Miss Maddison and our class took assembly. It was about the creation of the world. It took a long time, nearly ten minutes. Adam and Eve were supposed to hold hands. Eve wanted to but Adam didn't. At the end Mrs Grainger said "onbe-half". She always says "onbe-half". I don't know why she says "onbe-half". I miss you because if you are on the front row the little ones can play with your laces and you pretend not to notice. You have a tall smile. On Saturday I saw you in Asda next to the cornflakes in shorts. My mummy says you are older than you look.'

As I displayed the card on my bedside unit, I remembered why teaching young children is the best job in the world.

Jimmy Poole had drawn a picture of himself giving me a large green object the size of a saucepan. Next to it was an arrow with the word 'sweet'. I recalled the gift of a fruit pastille many months ago.

Jimmy was another good writer and Jo Maddison

was outstanding at encouraging the children to write long and descriptive sentences. Any word that they couldn't spell they wrote in their 'Word Books' and either checked in their dictionary or put up their hand to ask Miss Maddison to check for them. Jimmy had written, 'Hello, Mr Sheffield, how is your car? We are saving up for a present for you. If you could have anything in the world what would it be? We have 52p.'

Eventually, reassured that I was looking fine if a little tired, they got up to leave.

May looked at me wistfully as she said goodbye. She had a wonderful habit of saying the wrong words but still making sense.

'Dinna worry, Jack, ye will be all right soon,' said May. 'It's just a phrase ye are going through.'

My mother gave me a kiss, took her sister's arm and they walked out in step, chattering away with John following close behind.

John had brought a morning newspaper with him and I settled down to read what was happening in the world outside. A photograph of Arthur Scargill, the left-wing Yorkshire Miners' leader, dominated the front page. Britain's 280,000 miners wanted a 41 per cent pay rise, which would give face workers £110 for a thirty-hour week. This was bad news for Jim Callaghan who wanted to keep pay increases down to 5 per cent. I flicked through the sports news and then rested again.

At five o'clock, Jo and Sally arrived with another huge bag of grapes.

'We're the first shift,' said Sally.

'You're only allowed two visitors at a time,' explained Jo.

Suddenly, Jo's attention wavered.

'Dishy doctor,' said Jo appreciatively as another teenage clone in a white coat walked by, his flared trousers flapping around his ankles.

Sally nodded.

'Bit young for me,' she said, staring after the young doctor whose wavy ringlets hung down over his collar.

'Excuse me,' I said, feigning disappointment, 'weren't you supposed to be coming to see me?'

'Sorry, Jack,' said Jo, tearing herself away from the many distractions around her. 'Did you like the cards, by the way?'

The nurses had strung up the cards from the curtain rail so my bed was gradually taking on the appearance of a carnival float.

'They're wonderful, Jo, thanks so much. They really cheered me up.'

Sally looked at the bags of grapes.

'Are you sure you can eat all these grapes, Jack?' she asked.

'Please help me out,' I said, thrusting them in their direction. 'I'm getting sick of grapes.'

Sally and Jo had just about finished the whole bag by the time Anne and Vera arrived for the next shift. Anne was her usual reassuring self.

'Don't worry, Jack, everything is fine at school and we're all set for next week's Centenary. If you feel well enough by then, just call in, but you mustn't overdo it. Don't come back too soon.'

'I've got Joseph to lead the assembly on that day instead of you, Mr Sheffield,' said Vera firmly, 'so don't think you have that to prepare.'

I quickly realized I was faced with two very determined women.

'Here's a bag of grapes for you,' said Vera. 'Eat them up, they'll do you good.'

I tentatively bit into yet another grape.

'And don't worry about that precious car of yours,' said Anne. 'I called into Pratt's Garage this morning. Victor was his usual grumbling self but he'll do a good job for you.'

The conversation rattled on until at around seven o'clock Vera saw that I looked tired again.

'Come on, let's leave him in peace,' said Vera.

'I've asked John to come and collect you if they let you out tomorrow,' said Anne. 'Is that OK with you, Jack?'

I nodded and thanked her. Within minutes I was dozing again.

Working with females for most of my professional life had given me an insight into the mysteries of perfume. Vera always wore her traditional and elegant Chanel No. 5, whereas the youthful Jo Maddison had begun to wear Charlie by Revlon, aimed at the under-twenty-five market. Even with my back turned, I could recognize who had entered the school office. The staff thought I had got eyes in the back of my head and I didn't enlighten them. But there was one perfume that I would never forget, and the scent of it was with me now, softening the antiseptic air of the hospital ward. It was Yves Saint Laurent's Rive Gauche and it was the perfume that I had come to associate with Beth Henderson.

I opened my eyes and she was standing next to my bed holding a small bunch of summer flowers and her brown leather briefcase. She looked a little tired and her blond hair was windswept.

'Jack, I had to come and I'm sorry I'm late but I was so worried about you,' said Beth anxiously. 'I had to work late at the office and then I came straight here.'

She held my hand and gently touched my bruised forehead. It was only for a moment in time and I stared into her soft green eyes. I didn't want to let her go. I felt she sensed my vulnerability and she stood up to collect a vase from a trolley next to the washbasin at the entrance to the ward. She filled the vase with water, arranged the flowers skilfully and placed them on top of the cupboard next to my bed. Then she displayed a few of the cards around the base of the vase.

'What a lovely collection of cards, Jack,' she said appreciatively. 'Aren't children's drawings so wonderful?'

She picked one up and smiled as she read the message.

'Look at this one, Jack, from a little girl called Amanda.'

She read out the spidery infant printing.

'Miss Maddison says me and Jane are going to sing a duel when you come back.'

We both laughed and she sat down at the foot of the bed and looked thoughtfully at me.

'I'm so glad you came,' I said and reached for her hand again.

'You gave us such a shock, Jack, when the news came through to the Education Office. Miss B-H can be an absolute tyrant at times but she's definitely got a soft spot for you. She's sent a card and made sure everyone in the office signed it.'

Beth handed over a large envelope addressed in Miss Barrington-Huntley's distinctive, expansive cursive handwriting. As usual with everything she wrote, the writing began at the bottom left and raced to the top right with the final flourish of a severe black line to underline the words. The card was full of signatures and messages and included Beth's signature. But there was no written message from her and I felt a momentary pang of disappointment.

'Jack, Miss B-H has heard about your Victorian Day to celebrate the centenary of the school and thinks it's a brilliant idea. She wondered if you might like us both to come along, in costume, of course. Secretly, I think she likes the idea of dressing up. She was also hoping you might like to invite the photographer from the *Yorkshire Evening Press*. It would be good publicity for the school.'

'That's fine with me, Beth,' I said. 'Just check it out with Anne Grainger, she's Acting Head during my absence.'

A warning bell rang. Visiting time was over. Beth got up to leave and, as an afterthought, she began to rummage in her voluminous briefcase and produced a large paper bag and a small envelope.

'For you,' she said simply and leaned forward. She stared at me and then slowly and deliberately she kissed me tenderly on the lips. It was a surprise and I felt a thrill pass through me. I closed my eyes and wished the moment would last for ever.

'Get well soon, Jack,' she whispered softly.

Moments later I opened my eyes but Beth had gone, leaving only a trace of perfume and the memory of a loving kiss.

I opened the envelope. Inside was a small card with a picture of yellow lilies on the front. I looked inside and in small, neat writing she had written 'Thinking of you, with love Beth', and in that moment I felt my life was complete.

Harry the Comedian, who had obviously unashamedly listened to the whole conversation, shouted from his bed.

'What's in the bag, Jack?'

I opened it and pulled out the biggest bunch of grapes I had ever seen.

Harry was literally in stitches. He didn't know whether to laugh or cry.

As for myself, I read Beth's card again and made up my mind that even if I had to crawl into school for the Victorian Day, I was going to make it.

Chapter Twenty-one

The Victorian Day and Albert

School Centenary Day. All children, teachers and governors were in costume. Miss Barrington-Huntley and Miss Henderson (Education Office) visited school (in costume). A photograph of children and staff appeared in the Yorkshire Evening Press. *Many people from the village supported the wide range of events. Mr Sheffield returned to school following his road traffic accident to support the event and will return to full-time duty next Monday.*

(A. Grainger, Acting Headmistress)

Extract from the Ragley School Logbook:
Friday 14 July 1978

Albert Jenkins looked like a character from a Charles Dickens' novel. It was the school Centenary Day and his Victorian costume was perfect in every detail. He took the heavy brass pocket watch from his waistcoat, wound it up, listened for the ticking and nodded to me. 'Time for the school bell, Jack.'

It was Friday 14 July and I had returned to school for the first time since my accident. During my absence, Anne Grainger had done a wonderful job and it seemed as though she had mobilized the whole village to celebrate one hundred years of education in Ragley School. Lofts had been searched for Victorian artefacts; old photographs appeared on the school notice boards and the memories of senior citizens were suddenly in demand. As well as the teachers, many parents had arrived in costume to support the children's activities, including an imposing Sue Phillips in an authentic Victorian nurse's uniform and armed with a large metal nit comb.

All the School Governors had been persuaded by Anne to come 'in character'. Albert Jenkins was to be a Victorian School Inspector, the Revd Joseph Evans was the Parish Vicar and Stan Coe was secretly very pleased to act the part of local Squire and Landowner. Albert had loaned me an old, charcoal-grey, three-piece suit, complete with watch-chain, in order to 'blend in' as a Victorian gentleman and I had been told very firmly by Anne to enjoy the day and not do anything too demanding. Apart from a little bruising around my right eye I was almost back to my old self.

Albert pointed towards a huge poster with his brass-topped walking cane. 'I'll be enforcing every one of these, Jack,' said Albert with a twinkle in his eye.

The Victorian School Rules had been written in beautiful cursive handwriting at an angle of sixty degrees on a large sheet of white paper.

Children must call teachers Sir or Ma'am.
Children must stand when an adult enters the room.
Children must use their right hand at all times for handwriting.
Children must not ask questions.
Children with fleas or nits must not attend school.
Children who are late will be caned.
Children who do poor work will be caned.
Children who behave badly will be caned.

It occurred to me that left-handed latecomers with learning difficulties must have had a tough time in Victorian England.

Albert and I walked on to the school playground where a remarkable sight met our eyes. In the bright morning sunshine, Anne Grainger, Sally Pringle, Jo Maddison and Valerie Flint were standing in line, side by side, and looking very severe. They wore ankle-length black skirts, black shiny boots and frilly white blouses buttoned up to the neck. Valerie Flint, who was in charge of my class, was also wearing a beautiful Victorian brooch that was a family heirloom.

The children had been transformed, thanks to Anne's regular practices during the week. Instead of strolling up the drive in their lightweight summer T-shirts, the children had lined up in perfect silence, boys in one line and girls in another. The boys wore collarless shirts, waistcoats, flat caps, baggy shorts cut below the knee, long grey socks and old boots. The girls wore long dresses, white pinafores and bows in their hair and brought sighs of admiration from the large group of mothers at the school gate, many of whom were taking photographs.

Anne raised a whistle to her lips and blew two short sharp blasts. As if by magic, the children marched into school like clockwork soldiers.

Anita Cuthbertson giggled as she stepped into the school entrance and Miss Flint boomed, 'Children should be seen and not heard, Anita Cuthbertson.' It appeared Miss Flint was taking this very seriously.

Inside the school hall, all the children had lined up again with their hands outstretched, palms upwards. The teachers walked up and down the lines of children, inspecting the cleanliness of their hands, like officers inspecting the troops.

Albert and I followed Miss Flint into my classroom. The tables were no longer arranged in groups but in straight lines. The children stood alongside them whilst Miss Flint read out their names in the register and they sat down quietly when their name was called.

'Now, hands together, eyes closed,' said Miss Flint.

The children recited the Lord's Prayer and then Miss Flint asked a monitor to give out a map of the British Empire to each child. In complete silence, the children used a pink colouring pencil to colour in the countries of the Empire. Next door, in Sally Pringle's classroom, we could hear the children chanting their tables whilst Sally beat out the rhythm on her desk with a wooden cane.

At a quarter past nine, the whole school assembled in the school hall and Joseph Evans, with a slightly whimsical air, told the children the purpose of the school.

'You come to school,' said Joseph, 'to prepare yourself for future work. Always remember your place in life. You must show respect to the important people in the village. They include the Squire, the landowners, the factory owners and the vicar.'

Joseph smiled sheepishly at this whilst Stan Coe, sitting at the side of the hall, beamed from ear to ear.

Then Claire Phillips read out a simple prayer.

'Lord teach a little child to pray,
And fill my heart with love,
And make me fitter every day,
To go to heaven above.'

Anne stood up, thanked the vicar, and the children filed quietly back to their classrooms.

'That's what they should be like every day, seen and not heard,' said Stan Coe to the Revd Evans.

Joseph looked embarrassed by the remark.

'That's a little harsh, I think, Stanley,' said Joseph. 'We need to listen to children to know how to help them.'

'Rubbish!' grunted Stan. 'Anyway, what time is this photographer coming? Ah've got things t'do.'

Joseph looked at his watch. 'The *Yorkshire Evening Press* reporter said ten thirty. Mrs Grainger has arranged for all the children and staff to assemble on the playground, so you will have to wait until then.'

I had never seen Joseph angry before and he walked briskly out of the hall and into the staff-room where Vera had just welcomed Miss Barrington-Huntley and Beth Henderson.

It was like suddenly arriving on the set of a BBC costume drama. All three ladies looked magnificent. It was immediately obvious that they had all hired specialist costumes. They stood admiring each other's attire.

'You look stunning, Miss Evans,' said Miss Barrington-Huntley. 'I love the jewellery and the elegant shawl.'

Vera smiled graciously.

'Thank you,' she said, 'and both of you look absolutely perfect. Deep purple and lilac go so well together.'

Albert and I followed Joseph into the staff room and stood in admiration.

'Thank you for coming,' I said. 'You all look wonderful.'

I could barely take my eyes away from the sheer elegance of Beth's outfit.

'I've got Miss Barrington-Huntley to thank,' said Beth modestly. 'She knew the perfect costume shop in Northallerton. According to the owner these dresses are copies of those worn by Emmeline Pankhurst and her daughter, Dame Christabel Pankhurst, the famous suffragettes.'

'Ah, we must remember to be polite, ladies,' said Miss Barrington-Huntley mischievously, 'here're three eligible men who have the vote and make all the decisions in Victorian times.' She beckoned me to sit in a chair. 'Now, how are you, Jack? You gave us all quite a scare. I do hope you're not overdoing it.'

I was surprised to be called by my first name. Miss Barrington-Huntley looked genuinely concerned and her fearsome reputation seemed distant as she pulled a chair alongside and looked at me enquiringly.

'I'm much better now, thank you,' I said, 'and it's good to be back in school on such a special day. Anne has done a wonderful job in my absence.'

'I know, Jack, word does get back to me, you know.' Miss Barrington-Huntley glanced across at Beth. 'Miss Henderson never seems to stop telling us what wonderful things go on here in Ragley.'

The piercing look that I remembered from my interview was there again but this time it was softer and her eyes were creased with a hint of a smile. I wondered if there was more to the remark.

'You're welcome to tour the school if you wish before the photographer comes.'

'Excellent idea,' said Miss Barrington-Huntley. 'May I start in Mrs Grainger's class? I would like to see how that little boy from Barnsley has progressed,' and she walked off with Beth towards Anne's classroom.

A few minutes later I was in the hall talking to Jimmy Poole, now a stocky six-year-old.

'Hello, Mithter Theffield,' said Jimmy. 'Do boyth 'ave to wear capth in thchool?'

Jimmy was wearing his grandad's flat cap. It was pulled down over his eyebrows and perspiration was running down his face.

'Mithith Grainger didn't thay take it off, tho I 'aven't,' said Jimmy mournfully.

I took the cap off his head, told him to put it somewhere safe and sent him for a drink of water. He wandered off, looking relieved.

A large shadow appeared on the floor beside me. I turned and saw the bull-like frame of Stan Coe.

'Ah'd like a private word, Mr Sheffield,' said Stan Coe, tapping the side of his bulbous nose with a chubby forefinger as a sign of secrecy.

I was intrigued. 'Let's walk on the playground,' I said and ushered him towards the door. We looked an incongruous pair walking around the playground on a beautiful summer's day: me in my severe three-piece suit and Stan Coe dressed as if he was about to refuse Oliver Twist another bowl of gruel.

'It's like this,' said Stan with a smile that revealed his brown and broken teeth. 'I've got a chance to be nominated for the local Council and, if I did, it would be good for you. Ah'd be able to support things like this 'ere library y'want. So, ah was jus' checking ah'd got y'support.'

'Sorry, Mr Coe, I couldn't on those conditions. If I supported you it would be for the right reasons,' I responded quickly and firmly.

'Now, don't be too 'asty,' he said with a voice like syrup. 'Jus' think about it. Outsiders like y'self certainly don't want powerful enemies in a small village like this, you 'aving jus' arrived 'ere.'

I stopped in my tracks and looked him squarely in the eyes.

'I'll take my chances, Mr Coe. Now if you'll excuse me.'

With that, I walked quickly back into school, teeth clenched and inwardly seething.

At ten thirty the *Yorkshire Evening Press* photographer arrived accompanied by a young female reporter. Stan Coe was soon deep in conversation with her and kept pointing his finger at the spiral-bound notepad as if he was insisting on what was being written. The young woman looked slightly overawed by the heavyweight farmer.

Fortunately, the experienced photographer knew exactly what he wanted and he took a series of photographs, including one of all the children, another of the teaching staff and one of everyone lined up on the playground.

After a short break for the children, a series of 'workshops' had been set up in the school hall and children of all ages could choose which one to attend. Jo and Sally had invited some of the senior citizens of the village into school for a coffee and a talk with the children. I listened in on the first discussion group, which included four generations of the Cade family.

Ada Cade was the oldest inhabitant of the village at the age of ninety-one. Her granddaughter, Emily, helped the frail old lady when she needed prompting. Ada told the children that she was one year old when Queen Victoria celebrated her Golden Jubilee in 1887. Her memory was remarkable and she told the children many stories of a world without television, aeroplanes and cars. She had attended Ragley School when it was relatively new and recalled the days off for blackberry and potato picking (which appealed to the children) and the harsh punishments and regular canings (which didn't). As a teenager in 1904 she remembered meeting her first boyfriend in Lord Mayor's Walk in York, alongside the city walls. Then, instead of busy traffic, there were only flocks of sheep grazing contentedly. The children were spellbound throughout and later wrote letters of thanks to Ada.

Jo Maddison was working with another group of children who were interviewing Albert Jenkins. Jo was tape-recording the question-and-answer session to use as a teaching resource during follow-up work. Albert told of a time fifty years ago when he was thirteen years old. He had been taken out of Ragley School to become a Fire Tender Worker for the railway in York.

'I was a chimney sweep for the railways,' said Albert. 'I used to climb inside the firebox and use a brush and my bare hands to clean it out. All the time I was surrounded by dangerous asbestos. My ambition was to become a train driver and twenty-six years later I fulfilled my ambition.'

Albert produced lots of old photographs of the giant steam engines that he had driven and the children bombarded him with questions.

When it was over I shook his hand.

'Albert, that was wonderful, the children loved it. Thank you so much, I had no idea you had worked on the railways.'

'Seeing their faces made it all worthwhile,' said Albert.

He looked at me intently.

'Are you all right, Jack? If you're feeling tired we can get you home.'

'No, I'm fine, thanks, and I wouldn't want to miss today,' I said.

Albert was a perceptive man.

'Something's troubling you, I can tell,' he said. 'I saw

you with Stanley just before the photograph. Is that it? Has he been putting pressure on you?'

I said nothing and stared at the ground.

'The old fox,' exclaimed Albert. 'It's the Council election, isn't it? He's been canvassing everybody who is anybody in the village. Don't let him get to you, Jack.'

'I just want to do my job well,' I said cautiously.

'I understand, Jack,' said Albert, looking at me carefully. 'Words without thoughts never to heaven go.'

'Shakespeare,' I said.

He nodded but still looked thoughtful as we walked over to John Pruett's workshop. John had taken the old school logbooks out of the safe in the vicarage and displayed them on a table in the middle of the hall. He had a captive audience and held up a large, leather-bound tome.

'This is one of the collection of school logbooks,' said John. 'Since 1878 every headteacher has recorded the life of Ragley School.'

He turned the gold leaf pages with quiet reverence and held up the first volume.

'Here's one of the earliest entries from the first volume,' said John. 'First February 1878, the outside toilets are frozen and the rooms have been fumigated with sulphur candles.'

John selected another volume, pointed to the date, 1901, and read another entry.

'Today lice were observed crawling in the children's hair.'

The children groaned and began to scratch their

heads. John called Sue Phillips over to show everyone her fierce-looking nit comb.

'And this is one of my first entries,' continued John. '17 September, 1946, electric lights were installed today and the children cheered.'

John lined up the volumes neatly so that the children and visitors could look through them.

'So please have a look. Every teacher's name, every holiday, every special event, even every punishment is in here.'

Albert suddenly put his hand on my shoulder and said, 'I've had a thought, Jack. I'll catch you later.'

With that, he picked up one of John Pruett's logbooks and began to flick through the pages.

Beth was suddenly at my elbow.

'Come and look at this, Jack.'

She tugged my sleeve and we walked into my classroom. It was like stepping back one hundred years. Miss Flint was leading a writing lesson and the children were dipping their scratchy, metal-nib pens into inkpots and copying the sentence, 'Good handwriting is essential if you wish to become a clerk.'

'Upward strokes are light,' said Miss Flint, 'downward strokes are heavy.'

The efforts of the children were extraordinary and even the voluble Anita Cuthbertson had barely spoken a word all morning.

'They've really entered into the spirit of the day,' whispered Beth. 'You must be proud of them all.'

I looked down into her green eyes and decided it was time to take the plunge.

'Could I have a brief, private word with you before you leave?'

'Of course, Jack. Miss Barrington-Huntley and I have to attend meetings this afternoon at County Hall so we're leaving at twelve o'clock. I'll see you then,' said Beth.

Then she smiled and went to sit next to Miss Barrington-Huntley who was working with Vera and Ruby. They were teaching children to sew intricate patterns around the edge of small white handkerchiefs.

'Jack, I need a word.'

It was Albert and he looked triumphant. He had a school logbook under his arm with a sheet of paper marking a page.

I followed him into the staff-room where he opened the book.

'It was when John mentioned punishments, Jack. After that it was just a matter of working out when and then finding the record.'

'Sorry, Albert, but I don't know what you are talking about,' I said.

'Just listen to this,' said Albert and he began to read from the logbook.

'Tenth November 1932, Stanley Coe (age ten years) was caned and excluded from school for three days for persistent bullying of girls.'

'Albert!' I cried. 'How on earth did you find that piece of news?'

'Stanley has always been a bully, Jack, particularly at school. I knew he had been punished when he was about ten years old and I also knew he was born in 1922. The rest was simple detective work.'

'So what do we do now?' I asked.

'I think we should take him down a peg or two, don't you? But first, let's show this to Joseph.'

The vicar was thrilled when he read the extract.

'I'm not sure that revenge is a particularly Christian thing to do,' said Joseph, 'but somehow, with that infuriating man, it doesn't seem to matter.'

'Let's invite him in,' said Albert, 'and strike while the iron is hot. Jack, will you do the honours?'

It wasn't difficult to find Stan Coe who was loud in every sense of the word.

'Mr Coe, could you come into the staff-room for a quick meeting with the other governors?'

Stan looked puzzled as he walked in.

'What's all this then?' he asked gruffly.

'Stanley, we've heard that you don't support the idea of a new school library, is that so?' asked Albert.

Stan glowered at me. 'Money would be better spent in the village. He's raising so much through that bloody PTA that there's none left for t'Social Club.'

'Even so,' said Joseph, 'after careful consideration we have decided to support your application to be a County Councillor.'

Stan wasn't expecting this. Suddenly a smile creased his face.

'Well, ah'm glad you've come t'your senses,' said Stan.

'There's just one proviso,' said Albert.

Stan looked vacant.

'One what?' asked Stan.

'You have to print this at the bottom of your election leaflets.'

Albert lifted the logbook, pointed to the extract and shoved it under his nose.

Stan looked as though he was going to internally combust. He writhed in confusion and his anger left him speechless. An oath left his lips as he stormed out of school.

'About time he was excluded again,' said Joseph with a saintly smile.

I glanced at the clock. It was twelve o'clock.

'Please excuse me for a moment,' I said.

Beth was waiting for me in the entrance hall.

'Can we talk outside?' I asked.

She gave me a curious look and we walked towards the car park.

'Beth, I've been meaning to ask you something for quite some time now.'

Beth stood quietly. Her green eyes looked thoughtful.

'This may be inappropriate,' I continued, trying to find the right words. 'But it's crossed my mind a few times now.'

Beth stood patiently.

'Would you say we've got on quite well?' I asked.

'Yes, Jack, we've become good professional colleagues,' Beth teased.

The words 'professional colleagues' seemed to hang in the air.

'Oh,' I said, feeling a little deflated.

'What exactly is it, Jack, that you want to say?'

I took a deep breath. Miss Barrington-Huntley had emerged from school and had begun to walk towards the car park. It was now or never.

'Well, I was wondering if you would be interested in a holiday in France?'

She shook her head.

'I understand,' I said hurriedly.

'No you don't, Jack. I just thought I would have to wait another hundred years before you asked. So I was thinking of asking you to come to Cornwall with me.'

'Why not do both?' I blurted out before I had time to think.

Beth smiled and squeezed my hand.

At that moment, Miss Barrington-Huntley arrived, hitched up her voluminous skirt and squeezed into the passenger seat of the Beetle.

'And what are you two plotting, votes for women?'

'No,' said Beth quietly, 'I've already voted.'

Chapter Twenty-two

Teacher, Teacher

83 Children on roll. Ten 4th-year junior children left the school today and will commence secondary education at Easington in September. The under-fives who will join the Reception class in September visited school with their parents. The cycle shed and bell tower will be re-pointed during the school summer holiday.

Extract from the Ragley School Logbook:
Friday 21 July 1978

'Teacher, teacher, can I 'ave some more beef 'n' sewage pudding, please?'

Hazel Smith's vocabulary was clearly taking after her mother's and it was impossible to refuse her eager request. Even after three terms in school, Hazel still began all her sentences in the same excited way.

I spooned some more beef stew and an extra suet dumpling onto her plate. It was Friday lunchtime, 21 July, the last day of the school year, and Shirley the Cook had made an extra effort to provide a really good school dinner.

For half of the children in my class, the fourth-year juniors, it was their final day at Ragley and in September they would all go into the first year at Easington Comprehensive School. It was a daunting prospect for them, even though they had enjoyed a few preliminary visits. After lunch they had all wandered back into the classroom to talk to me, reflecting on their favourite memories.

'School Camp was great, Mr Sheffield,' said freckle-faced Kenny Flanaghan. 'I 'ope we do things like that at the big school.'

'Last week was good when we dressed up as Victorians,' said chatterbox Anita Cuthbertson. 'Mind you, pretending to be good was hard work,' she added thoughtfully.

'Sports Day was brilliant,' said the tall and leggy Claire Phillips, 'especially when Mrs Smith won the egg and spoon race.'

'I'd like to come back next Bonfire Night, Mr Sheffield,' said the budding artist and musician, Jenifer Jayne Tait, 'and help to make the guy. I bet we won't do anything like that at Easington.'

'Ah'll miss my tuck shop,' said the plump and practical Claire Bradshaw sadly. 'What a time to have to leave, just when ah'd introduced different flavoured crisps.'

'Food up there'll be different,' said Claire Malarky. 'Don't get me wrong, Mr Sheffield, ah like Mrs Mapplebeck, an' she's a great cook an' all, but at t'big school y'can go into Easington an' buy chips wi' loads o' ketchup.'

The group pondered on this culinary delight until the silence was broken by one of Wayne Ramsbottom's rare sentences.

'Ah'll miss spam fritters,' said a forlorn Wayne. He sounded positively suicidal and everyone considered this catastrophic announcement. Fortunately, Wayne was rarely downbeat for long. With a father who wore spurs and a cowboy hat, you needed a sense of humour.

'Mind you,' said Wayne, 'chips in Easington might be OK.'

There were a few nods of optimism and slowly they meandered out together for what remained of their last lunch-break at Ragley. I followed them out of the main entrance to get some fresh air and I watched them as they walked onto the school field. They sat down in a circle, boys and girls together, bonded at last by their imminent departure from this stage of their lives.

Briefly, they were a united group. The carefree days of primary school were over and they were sad to see them go. Having the same person teaching them each day for a whole year was now a thing of the past. They would meet specialist Mathematics and English teachers and a whole host more. Some they would love and some they would hate. Forty minutes would become the length of a lesson whether they were enjoying it or not and they wouldn't question why. Adolescence was just around the corner just as sure as long trousers, make-up and teenage acne. This was the tenth group of fourth-year juniors who had left me in my career and it occurred to me that I was on a strange treadmill where I got older each year but the children stayed the same, only their faces were different. I also knew it was a treadmill I had chosen and one I enjoyed.

The hot sun was on my neck as I walked around the edge of the playground. A group of carefree five-year-olds were playing ring-a-ring-o'-roses and Mrs Critchley, the dinner lady, had joined in. I leaned against the wrought-iron railings under the welcome shade of the horse chestnut trees that were now heavy in leaf and dipped their branches over the warm tarmac beneath my feet. In a shady corner, four ten-year-old girls were deep in conversation. They were negotiating who would run the school tuck shop next year. In six weeks' time they would become the oldest pupils in the school and they relished the responsibilities that came with their newly acquired status.

On the village green, tiny toddlers collected daisies and their mothers helped them to make daisy chains. In front of The Royal Oak, Old Tommy was sitting on a bench by the village pond, smoking his pipe and feeding the ducks. Down the High Street, outside Pratt's Hardware Emporium, Tidy Tim was arranging a neat line of inverted besom brooms so they looked like guardsmen on duty outside Buckingham Palace. Next door, Nora Pratt was receiving a cut-price delivery of two-day-old jam doughnuts from the Bakery in Easington. The door of Piercy's Butcher's Shop jingled as Young Tommy carried out Emily Cade's carrier bag, containing a leg of local lamb and two pounds of pork and beef sausages, to the boot of her white Ford Escort. Sleepy summer was upon us and life beyond the school walls was progressing at a gentle pace. My first year at Ragley was almost over and I felt I was beginning to know and understand this beautiful little Yorkshire village.

In his Little Giddings 'Four Quartets', T. S. Eliot had written,

We never cease from exploration
And the end of our exploring
Is to arrive where we started
And know the place for the first time.

It had taken a year but I realized that I had become a member of a community in which the school played a vital part. This really was a special place to live and work.

I had also had dinner with Beth twice in the last week, once in York and once at Bilbo Cottage where the *Good Housekeeping* recipe book guided me through the onerous preparation of a chicken casserole. We had planned our holiday together and I knew it was the start of something very special. Beth's secondment was almost over and she was due to return to her deputy headship in Thirkby after the holiday in September.

Anne brought a cup of tea for me from the staff-room.

'Penny for them, Jack,' she said with a tired smile. 'We're nearly there, the finishing line is in sight.'

I realized how lucky I had been to have such an outstanding deputy headmistress as a trusted colleague.

'Thanks for everything, Anne,' I said. 'I couldn't have managed without you, particularly during the last few weeks. No wonder you're tired, teaching a Reception class and running the school.'

We sat down on the low wall that bordered the cobbled driveway where we could overlook both the playground and the field.

'Well, I must say, I've enjoyed working with you, Jack. We were all a little scared when John Pruett left and you arrived but it's worked out well.'

Anne appeared to be thinking out loud. I glanced across at her. There were a few grey hairs I had not noticed before. Then she pointed to the group of leavers relaxing together on the school field.

'And there's the proof of it. That's what we're turning out: confident, literate, numerate young people who love learning, regardless of their abilities. Some will be doctors and some will dig ditches but all of them will look back fondly on Ragley School and the start in life we've tried to give them. Let's hope the government doesn't introduce that central curriculum they're talking about and mess it all up for the next generation. If they do, then I think I'll look for early retirement.'

'I'll drink to that,' I said and we supped our tea together until the bell summoned us for the final afternoon of the school year.

It was a tradition for children to play games on their last afternoon. In the carpeted book corner, Kenny Flanaghan was playing tiddlywinks with Claire Bradshaw and Wayne Ramsbottom. It wasn't until I saw the pack of cards and heard Claire Bradshaw say, 'My flush beats your two pairs,' that I realized the plastic counters were being used as currency in a poker school.

I turned a blind eye and went to join in a game of Scrabble with Anita Cuthbertson. Losing to the worst speller in the class did my self-confidence no good at all and it was almost a relief when the bell went for afternoon playtime.

Jo and Sally volunteered to do playground duty together whilst Vera and Anne were in the staff-room discussing arrangements for an informal get-together immediately after school. They had organized tea and cakes in the school hall and all the staff were invited plus a few friends and colleagues. George and Mary Hardisty were the principal guests and Mrs Hardisty had offered to bring along one of her strawberry tarts. Albert Jenkins and Roy Davidson said they would call in and Beth had told me she would come straight from County Hall where a small presentation was to be made to her at half past two.

At a quarter past three, the infant children went home and Ruby came into the hall with a large broom and a collection of dusters. Little Hazel had stayed with her to help. I left my class to enjoy their games and walked into the school hall. Ruby was quietly singing 'My Favourite Things' to herself whilst she swept the hall floor. Alongside her, Hazel was dusting the piano with the flourish of an expert. They made a happy pair, with Ruby singing the words and Hazel humming the tune as they worked side by side.

'Hmm hmm hmm hmm hmm, my fa-vor-wit fings,' sang Hazel.

Ruby jumped when I came into her line of vision.

'Oh, I 'ope y'don't mind, Mr Sheffield,' said Ruby,

nodding towards Hazel. 'Only, there's no one at 'ome to look after 'er.'

'That's not a problem, Ruby. I just came to see if you would like some tea and cake in the hall at the end of school. We're all gathering together before the holiday begins.'

'That'll be lovely, Mr Sheffield. Shall I bring some buns?'

'Just see Vera and Anne, if you don't mind, Ruby. They're organizing it.'

Vera suddenly appeared in the doorway from the entrance hall.

'Mr Sheffield, two parents have called in,' said Vera, 'they've got something for you.'

Sue Phillips and Sheila Bradshaw were in the entrance hall. Sue passed over a neatly wrapped parcel to me. Sheila pointed to the large label that said 'Thank you'.

'The parents of the leavers have signed it, Mr Sheffield,' said Sheila.

'It's just a small token of our appreciation for all you've done this year,' said Sue.

Vera was hovering and Ruby, never one to miss anything, was leaning on her broom and waiting for me to open it.

I unwrapped the heavy parcel and found three hardback books inside.

'*The Lord of the Rings* trilogy,' I said out loud in delight, 'by J. R. R. Tolkien. That's a wonderful gift. It's my favourite book by my favourite author. How on earth did you know?'

'We asked your young lady,' said Ruby in a matter-of-fact voice.

Vera gave her a stern look and Sue and Sheila looked amused.

'I presume you mean Miss Henderson, Ruby,' I said.

'I think that Ruby didn't quite mean it the way it came out,' said Vera quickly, in a vain attempt to paper over the cracks.

Sue Phillips regained the sense of decorum, opened *The Fellowship of the Ring* and showed me the list of signatures. 'We couldn't track down Mrs Brown,' said Sue, ever the diplomat, 'otherwise, every parent has signed it.'

'I'll always treasure it,' I said and I meant it.

At a quarter to four the bell rang again and all the junior children left, many cheering at the thought of the long holiday, some sad because it was their last day. I shook hands with all the leavers and they went off to say goodbye to Val Flint who had just arrived in the hall and was helping Anne and Vera to put doilies on plates and arrange a selection of home-made cakes and biscuits.

Joseph Evans and Albert Jenkins met George and Mary Hardisty on the school drive and walked into school together. The three men began to collect the comfortable chairs from the staff-room and carry them into the hall. Mary Hardisty displayed her magnificent strawberry tart and Ruby went with Hazel to her store-room to hang up her overall. Sally and Jo helped Shirley to wheel in a large metal trolley from the kitchen on which a collection of cups and saucers were arranged alongside a large jug of milk and a Baby Burco boiler that steamed with boiling water. Two cars arrived in convoy in the school car park and Beth Henderson and Roy Davidson walked in together.

Vera served them both with tea and directed them towards plates, serviettes, forks and cakes. John Grainger wandered in from work with the dust of wood shavings still on his eyebrows and Anne put her David Soul record on the turntable of the music centre to provide background music. Gradually, everyone relaxed, drank tea, had an extra serving of Mary Hardisty's strawberry creation and chatted about the highs and lows of the academic year that was now indelibly written into the school logbook.

Roy Davidson had attended Beth's leaving presentation at County Hall.

'Biggest bunch of flowers I've ever seen,' said Roy, 'and Miss Barrington-Huntley made a lovely speech.' He walked away with his refilled cup and left Beth and I by the tea trolley.

'She also sent her best wishes for the holiday,' said Beth. 'She definitely thinks a lot of you, Jack. It must be that shy unassuming manner of yours. It's certainly not your cooking.'

'I followed the instructions for that casserole to the letter,' I said indignantly. 'Anyway, you didn't complain.'

'How about me doing the cooking in Cornwall and you buy the croissants in France?' said Beth with a grin.

'I'll bring my cookery book for you.'

She gave me a friendly dig in the ribs and went off to talk to Sally and Jo.

I watched her step lightly across the hall floor and thought of Ruby's description of her as 'your young lady'. I hoped it would always be so.

Joseph Evans was standing with Vera and Ruby and he beckoned me over. 'In a few minutes I would like to say a few words, Jack, if you don't mind, just to say thank you to the staff.'

'Thanks, Joseph, and I'll respond if I may.'

Suddenly, a look of alarm crossed Ruby's face.

'Just look at that,' said Ruby, pointing out of the window. 'Mark my words, no good will come of that.'

'Do you mean him?' I asked in surprise.

Stan Coe was walking purposefully up the drive.

'No,' said Ruby, 'look at the magpie on the school field, there's only one of 'em.'

Ruby could see from our blank expressions that we didn't know what she was talking about.

'Don't you remember the old saying?' said Ruby. 'One for sorrow, two for mirth, three for a wedding, four for a birth.'

'Ruby's right,' said Vera, 'it's well known that a solitary magpie is a sure sign of misfortune.'

Stan Coe disappeared from sight and the magpie flew away in fright. The front door banged and we could hear his heavy footsteps in the school entrance hall. Joseph and I sensed trouble and walked to the double swing doors to meet him. In his customary manner, he walked straight in and thrust a brown envelope into Joseph's hand.

'What's this, Stanley?' asked Joseph.

'That's my resignation, Vicar,' he said bluntly. 'Ah've got other strings t'my bow.'

Joseph belied his gentle, retiring nature and fixed the florid-faced farmer with a steely gaze.

'Well, we won't keep you, Stanley, you're obviously a busy man,' said Joseph with an unfamiliar hint of sarcasm.

Stan Coe blinked in surprise. He wasn't used to the mild-mannered cleric standing his ground. Every face in the hall turned towards him and no one spoke. With that, Stanley Coe, full-time bully, part-time farmer and one-time school governor, turned on his heel and walked out. His corpulent figure bounced down the cobbled drive and the solitary magpie hopped behind him as if it was saying, 'Good riddance!'

Vera looked with pride at her brother.

'More tea, Joseph, and perhaps a piece of Mrs Hardisty's excellent strawberry tart?' she said theatrically in a voice suited to a stage in the West End.

'With pleasure, Vera,' said Joseph, looking a little ashen-faced. He went to stand beside her and gently squeezed her hand.

'Teacher, teacher!' It was Hazel Smith. She had been playing on the school field and had run into the hall holding a small bouquet of tiny daisies.

'I'm sorry, Mr Sheffield,' said Ruby. 'Off you go, 'azel, can't you see Mr Sheffield is busy? And you shouldn't run in school.'

Little Hazel stopped in her tracks.

'That's all right, Ruby, no harm done,' I said.

I knelt down on one knee to face the little girl and she thrust a pretty little posy of newly picked daisies into my hand and gave me a big smile that only lacked her two front teeth.

'Thank you, Hazel, they're lovely,' I said.

Beth leaned over and sniffed them appreciatively.

'What beautiful flowers,' she said.

I extracted one tiny daisy and held it up to her.

Beth took it and held it delicately between finger and thumb and gave it a thoughtful stare. Her mind seemed elsewhere.

Little Hazel looked up at me and then to Beth holding the flower.

'Mr Sheffield,' said Hazel.

Everyone stopped talking and stared at the little girl with the cheerful round face, bright pink cheeks and tangled hair. It was the first time she had spoken to me and not started with the words 'Teacher, teacher'.

'Yes, Hazel, what is it?' I asked.

She took a deep breath.

'Mr Sheffield?' she repeated.

There was a long pause.

'Go on then, 'azel,' said Ruby, 'tell Mr Sheffield what it is you want to say.'

'Mr Sheffield,' said Hazel slowly and clearly, 'can I ask you a question?'

Everyone smiled at Ruby's little pride and joy.

'I'm listening, Hazel. Now what is it you want to ask me?'

Her little brow was furrowed. She took another deep breath and pointed at Beth.

'Are you going to marry this lady?'

For once I was speechless.

I looked at Ruby who had gone bright red.

I looked at Anne who gave me an encouraging nod.

I looked at Vera who was smiling at Beth.

Finally, I looked at Beth and her green eyes were shining.

The moment was suddenly shattered as Ruby pointed out of the window.

'Well ah never,' she cried, 'just look at that.'

Three magpies had just landed on the school field.

And in a heartbeat I knew what I wanted.

THE END